Close To The Bone

Close To The Bone

Mark Morris

PIATKUS

First published in Great Britain in 1995 by
Judy Piatkus (Publishers) Ltd of
5 Windmill Street, London W1

**The moral right of the author
has been asserted**

*A catalogue record for this book is available
from the British Library*

ISBN 0 7499 0277 9

Phototypeset in 11/12pt Compugraphic Times by
Action Typesetting Limited, Gloucester
Printed and bound in Great Britain by
Bookcraft (Bath) Ltd.

Acknowledgements

Green: originally published in *Narrow Houses 3*, edited by Peter Crowther (Little, Brown), 1994
The Fertilizer Man: originally published in *Darklands*, edited by Nicholas Royle (Egerton Press), 1991
Progeny: originally published in *Invasion of the Sad Maneating Mushrooms*, issue 3, 1992
Homeward Bound: originally published in *Dark Dreams*, issue 6, 1988
Birthday: originally published as *BFS* Booklet number 18, 1992
Warts and All: originally published in *Fear*, issue 23, 1990
Playing God: originally published in *Skeleton Crew*, issue 1, 1990
Down To Earth: original to this collection
A New Man: originally published in *ME*, 1989
The Other One: originally published in *Darklands 2*, edited by Nicholas Royle (Egerton Press), 1992
The Chisellers' Reunion: original to this collection

This one's for the chisellers –
Nick Royle, Conrad Williams, Mike Marshall Smith,
Graham Joyce and Chris Kenworthy.
'That top is gorgeous!'

Contents

Foreword

Let me tell you in a roundabout way – my detractors will say I have no other – how I encountered Mark Morris. Back in 1986, in a moment of dishonesty which I was later to admit to myself, I agreed to teach a writers' workshop in Suffolk. I didn't really believe in such workshops, though more than I do now. Better writers than I are happy to participate in them – Lisa Tuttle comes immediately to mind – but I must speak for myself. While I'm happy to address writers' groups and share all the tips I know, I feel uncomfortable about criticising their work, not least because the only honest comment in too many cases would be that it is unpublishably bad. Nevertheless, in 1986, as so often, the apathy inherent in accepting an invitation months distant led me to commit myself to the Suffolk weekend.

The months passed, and the organiser at Eastern Arts rang me. Only four people had signed up, not least, he felt, because the local radio station had refused to publicise a course in writing horror fiction. Did I still want to go ahead? I vowed I did, and thought for a few minutes about a day's journey in each direction, and rang back to change my mind. Not wishing to disappoint anyone, though, I undertook to read and criticise anything which the quartet would have brought to the workshop.

Four packages duly arrived on my doorstep. One, you will be unsurprised to learn, came from Mark Morris, but I'll come to him in due time, while he waits with, I trust, suitable apprehension. Some of the others destined for the weekend I don't remember. One I do, and the comments I

1

wrote to him. Let me leave him unnamed; may he not have seen publication by now, twenty-eight years old as he will be? This is part of my response to the synopsis he sent me of a novel:

I think it presents me with a problem, insofar as I'm not sure how qualified I may be to comment on what you tell me is a novel intended for teenagers, since my fiction is written very much for adults. Still, as long as you keep in mind that I may be mistaken in some of my comments, I'll do what I can ...

To be honest, you've made it sound somewhat incoherent, with several contrived plots crowding in. I wonder if you need to take a closer look at what you most want to do in the book, and concentrate on that. For instance, do you want it to be a supernatural or not? You've a ghost (real), a werewolf (fake), a small trained animal. The animal will, I suspect, come as something of an anticlimax when it is revealed as the cause of all the havoc ... You've put in all the ideas that occurred to you, rather than use the process of writing as a means of weeding out the bad ideas from the good, throwing out those aspects of the book that don't feel convincing when compared with those that do. Part of the process of writing − and this is as true of fantasy as of any other kind − is to ask yourself constantly if people would really act this way in the circumstances. In fact, one of the most basic aspects of the craft of writing is to develop a sense of whether what you're writing rings true ...

So much for the synopsis. I invited him to send me his choice of sample chapters. Of my many comments on them, these are representative:

"'It really is no life for a camera monitor,' remarked one beautiful young girl named Manuela Schultz. 'I find it a tremendous difficulty to keep these wonderful big blue eyes of mine in a perfect condition!'" Well, I suppose someone called Manuela Schultz might talk like that, but I wonder, and you might.

As for the business of the villain's helping kidnap the

2

daughter of a shareholder in a computer firm so as to force him to sell his shares to a rival, only for the villain to be infected with rabies by a raccoon she had hidden in her blouse and then to dress up as a werewolf 'throttling to death with his teeth' anyone who looks 'even remotely like' her, I find this a bit strained; so too the development in which his adversary, finding that there are no more girls who resemble the original, has to bait a trap using her. I mean, that's a lot of girls.

'At least she thought they were footsteps. She'd never heard such silent, muffled footsteps before in her life. They were clearly coming from some considerable distance away.' If they are silent, she can't be hearing them now, nor can they also be muffled. If they are only muffled and at some considerable distance, they would hardly be audible either.

'Hassler was humming to himself in German.' A difficult feat, I should think.

As to the finale, I would question whether two Gurkhas, an SAS officer and an SAS private, not to mention Sergeant Thomas Mahon of the Blue Berets (together with others, I gather) would all be involved in hunting down a wolverine, even a trained one. You might also ask yourself whether, once it had been shot through both legs and one shoulder as well as having one foreleg almost blown off by two bullets, even an unusual wolverine would be capable of killing 'two Gurkhas, two police marksmen, a luckless observer from the Ministry of Agriculture, and a bounty hunter'. Or perhaps you're gently pulling our legs, are you?

Good luck with whatever work you may find in the future.

Was that and the rest of it helpful? Difficult to know, since I never heard from this person again. With Mark Morris, who has been waiting nervously in the wings of this introduction long enough, it was a different matter. He sent me five stories, on the subject of which I waxed avuncular, suggesting structural improvements to one tale not in this book and counselling succinctness in another, and wagging a stern finger at usages such as 'alright' (which I certainly hope Denis Norden intends as a joke on his television show)

3

and American invaders such as 'anymore'. But I also praised his work as 'strikingly written, at times better than that' and found some of the scenes of terror 'very effective, helped by your sense of timing and your ability to slow down at these points − writers often rush them and spoil them'. While writing to Mark I felt eerily like the ghost of August Derleth, my old mentor, who had written me a rather more critical letter in response to some of my mid-teenage tales. I felt Mark had the real stuff and should be encouraged, and *Close to the Bone* − a title which, having used it for my autobiography on television, I gladly pass on to him − proves me right.

It isn't just that his heart is in his genre, though I'm sure that when the hacks dash off in pursuit of the next success to imitate, Mark will be continuing to explore, which means expand, the limits of his field. This book shows his commitment to imaginings as bizarre as he can make them; I don't sense the demon of whether they will sell (which, happily, they do) whispering in his ear. In one case − *The Chisellers' Reunion* − he reinvents the bad dream which we all have and which most of us in the field have tried to write, that we are the children we always were and our traumas are as alive as us. In *Birthday* he inflicts an endless sweaty nightmare worthy of Whitley Strieber at his most alienated on a victim no more able to understand than the rest of us. Some of his tales trick the reader into expecting the predictable, and indeed we could expect nothing else of the narrator of *Playing God*, which reads all too like the kind of unsolicited manuscript Mark may expect to receive in due course from an admirer or several; perhaps he already has. (None to me, please − I've had my turn, and plenty of them.) *Down to Earth* undertakes to be a gentle ghost story before digging into darker, more primeval areas, and *The Fertilizer Man* has altogether odder developments in store than its opening might suggest. The dreamlike and surreal are seldom far from Mark's work. *Warts and All*, like many of the tales, demonstrates his willingness to embrace the inexplicable; some − *A New Man, Homeward Bound, The Other One* − are just that. The last in particular owes something to a European tradition of the fantastic, and

4

like *The Chisellers' Reunion* and others, seems to conceal a secret to which the reader is at liberty to apply different keys. Let me not daunt the gorehound readers: one tale boasts a knife-wielding maniac, the product of a family which any of us might have as neighbours or as ourselves, and Mark isn't averse to ladling on the fluids when he feels the need. In a genre whose perceived business is the breaking of taboos, however, he knows when to show some reticence and taste, qualities which render *Progeny* especially affecting. I sense, and am heartened by it, that he is reaching for more than horror.

What more can I say about him? Not everything his publishers have quoted me as saying. In America I was shown as having hailed his novel *Stitch* as 'an awesome and terribly moving tale of madness and the supernatural, one of the most remarkable novels the field has produced for a considerable time, a masterpiece', a comment which was actually my response to Jessica Amanda Salmonson's *Anthony Shriek*, on which it also appeared, with the last word spelled 'masterpeice'. His British publishers managed to attribute a quote from *Science Fiction Chronicle* to me, or rather to someone spelled almost like me, on the jacket of *The Secret of Anatomy*. I hope I've provided enough useful quotes in the present introduction that publishers need look no further.

But readers should: they should look both to Mark's previously published books and for surprises in the future. Meanwhile, Mark and Stephens Gallagher and Laws and I comprise the Horror Roadshow, often to be seen reading and otherwise disporting ourselves in bookshops around the country. Come and see us.

Ramsey Campbell
Wallasey, Merseyside
20 July 1994

Introduction

When I was eight or nine years old, long before I started reading 'grown-up' novels, I was reading collections of short horror stories aimed at the adult market. At that time, the early seventies, there were a lot of them around. Each year Pan would bring out two collections – one of horror stories, one of ghost stories – as would Fontana, and these collections would contain a mixture of genre classics by writers such as Algernon Blackwood, M.R. James, Edgar Allan Poe, Sheridan Le Fanu and Guy de Maupassant, and stories by more modern writers, among the most notable of which were people like Robert Bloch, Ray Bradbury, David Case, Robert Aickman, Rosemary Timperley and the incomparable Martin Waddell.

I well remember one New Year's Eve spent at a friend's house. I was sleeping on a sofa bed in a ground-floor study-cum-storeroom at the front of the house. For bedtime reading I had taken along my newly purchased copy of *The Eleventh Pan Book of Horror Stories*. I have the very copy of the book in front of me as I write this. The cover, depicting a wedding cake on top of which are a skeletal bride and groom, still gives me a *frisson* of fearful delight whenever I look at it, as does a quick glance down the contents page. There's a wonderful, long werewolf story called *The Cell* by David Case, there's Nigel Kneale's story *Minuke* taken from his collection, *Tomato Cain* (a book I have long coveted), and there's a story called *Fried Man* by Martin Waddell, which I seem to remember is about a man who is killed and his body dumped in a deep-fat fryer in a fish and chip shop.

However, despite this *The Eleventh Pan Book of Horror Stories* isn't a particularly brilliant or influential or seminal collection; it's not lauded in horror circles as a classic of its kind. What makes this collection important to me is that due to a particular set of circumstances it was the first fiction I ever read which terrified me enough to give me a sleepless night. The room helped, of course – the strange, unfamiliar shadows, the fact that anyone (or anything) could have stepped off the street and tapped on the window. Even now I recall the joy and relief I felt when dawn finally started to break and crouching, twisted shapes in corners were revealed to be no more than bags, chairs, boxes.

But what's so good about being terrified? I hear you cry. How can you possibly derive any pleasure from a sleepless night spent in a state of barely restrained panic? It's my belief that everyone needs to be taken to the edge – of excitement, of fear – every now and again. It enriches us, puts things into perspective, makes us appreciate our lives all the more. Although reading horror stories on that particular night twenty-odd years ago did not seem a good idea once I'd turned the lights out and crawled down beneath the bedclothes, I can't deny that it stimulated my imagination. Ultimately the experience was a positive one. To be taken to the edge and to survive is, and continues to be, exhilarating.

I think if you asked most professional writers working within the horror/fantasy field how they became involved in the genre, they would tell you that they started off by reading and writing short stories. But trying to sell a collection of short stories these days is difficult. Publishers will tell you that they don't sell, that people don't read them. If this is true, then it's a tragedy. Short stories are wonderful things. Reading an anthology (as opposed to a collection, which I've always thought of as a book of short stories by a single writer) enables you to read widely within a particular genre, to sample the different styles and themes and approaches that each individual writer has to offer. Similarly, reading a collection probably gives you a better idea of a single writer than reading one of his or her novels. In these days of increasing competitiveness within the market place, one has to be sales-orientated to survive. Publishers, therefore, are forever on the lookout for the biggest, the most exciting, the most commercial, and whilst they can hardly be blamed for this, it doesn't leave much room for the writer who tries to be experimental, daring, *different*.

Which is where short story collections come in. In an anthology or a collection, there is always room for an oddball story or two. There are a few oddball stories in this collection – *Playing God*, which is told from the perspective of a disturbed individual, complete with spelling and grammatical errors (you'd be hard-pressed to sell a novel told in such a style), *The Other One*, which is a surreal story about madness and paranoia, and which, perhaps alarmingly, I found extremely easy to write, and *Progeny*, a story about betrayal which was based on a newspaper report I read.

Perhaps the most out-and-out horror story here is *Green*, which is primarily a story about a little known but very real superstition, but which is also my attempt to embrace that much maligned subculture of horror fiction known as 'Stalk-'n-Slash'.

Warts and All and *Birthday* are both horror stories with science-fiction elements. *Warts and All* was written soon after my dad and then my granddad died in 1988, and is about how life sometimes *doesn't* even out, about how sometimes it just gets worse and worse. It's also an example of how a number of wildly disparate ideas can often blend to create a story. Apart from the unfairness of life theme, I also wanted to write about warts; this because a couple of years previously I had had warts on my hands which spread to my nose and which seemed impervious to Compound W (I eventually had them frozen off). Plus I wanted to write a story which recaptured the science-fiction 1950s B-movie feel of a small rural town threatened by a seemingly unstoppable alien menace. All these elements came together in *Warts and All*, though whether successfully or not, I leave you to judge.

As for *Birthday*, it's a kind of dark Narnia story. I've always loved stories about secret doorways that lead to other worlds, and this is something of a downside to that. It's also about that agonising limbo time for parents between kids going missing and then being discovered, whether dead or alive.

The earliest stories in this collection are *The Fertilizer Man* and *Homeward Bound*. I'm very fond of *The Fertilizer Man*, which was inspired by the hedge-enclosed allotments across the road from the rented house I shared with five others as a student.

Homeward Bound was written for a competition, and together with *A New Man*, which I wrote as a specific commission for the women's magazine, *Me*, should be seen as a palate-cleanser, a tasty little bite between more substantial courses.

Which just leaves my two most recent stories, *Down to Earth* and *The Chisellers' Reunion*, both of which are appearing here for the first time. In a way they are both ghost stories, albeit very different from one another. In the summer of '92, my wife, Nel, and I moved into our second house, a terraced cottage in a village about fifteen miles outside Leeds. This story is set in the house, or at least in a replica of it. Some of the events in the story are true — the clearing out of the shed, the spectacularly large spiders — but most of it, thankfully, is pure fiction. *The Chisellers' Reunion*, on the other hand, in about ninety per cent true. I'll leave you to decide where the fact ends and the fiction begins.

Okay, that's it. The only thing left for me to say is that I hope you enjoy the stories so much that in years to come you'll take this book down from the shelf and open it with a little thrill of delight, remembering how it kept you awake one dark winter's evening towards the turn of the century.

And who knows? Maybe some of these tales will inspire you to pick up a pen and start writing your own. For me, that would be the ultimate accolade.

Mark Morris
14th June, 1994

Green

'It's a lovely dress, Claire, but I can't possibly accept it.'

'Course you can. Think of it as an incentive, something to slim into once the baby's born.'

Hilary Sterland gave her sister a rueful smile. 'It's not that. It's the colour. Bob would do his nut.'

Claire rolled her eyes in exasperation and lowered the backless, strapless, emerald-green evening gown she'd been flourishing like a toreador's cape. 'Oh God, you're joking. Can't you tell him to stuff it just this once? It's his daft superstition, not yours.'

Hilary merely shrugged, apologetic but resigned. Claire bit back her vitriol; she wouldn't have another go at Bob, however much he grated on her, however much she thought he pushed her sister around. She knew that Hilary doted on him. Horses for courses, as their grandmother was wont to say. Claire loved her sister dearly, though it bugged her that she had inherited their mother's blind spot when it came to men.

To put it bluntly, their father had been – and probably still was – a bastard. None of the family had seen hide nor hair of him for twelve years, not since he had run off with that whore from the bakery, who had merely been the latest in a long line of whores. Not that Bob was like that; his disrespect for women took a different form. He saw them as pretty objects – amusing, desirable, but ultimately trivial. Claire was not the first woman he had laughingly referred to as "one of those feminist lesbo-types" because she actually had the temerity to stand up to him, to *dare*

13

to pick holes in his woolly, bigoted world-view. In Claire's opinion, men like Bob needed to dominate women for the simple fact that they were scared of them. His was the classic inferiority complex.

She folded the dress carefully and replaced it in the box, thinking that the next time she and Dave were invited round to her sister's for dinner, she'd wear it herself purely to spite Bob. To cool down she made more coffee, and then she and Hilary discussed the topic that had dominated their conversation for the past seven months: the imminent arrival of Hilary's second child.

Claire knew that Hilary was worried because of her age — she was thirty-four — and because she did not know what kind of reaction to expect from Bob and her eleven-year-old son, Kim. The three of them had a comfortable, if somewhat staid, lifestyle; a kind of balance had been established over the years that Hilary was afraid the new baby would comprehensively disrupt. If that happened, the odds were that Hilary would get the blame. When she had first revealed to Bob that she was six weeks pregnant despite her coil, he had tutted and shaken his head in exasperation and told her she was 'a silly girl' for allowing it to happen. In the seven months since then his attitude did not seem to have changed. He appeared to regard her pregnancy as some minor, typically female misdemeanour, like putting one of his white shirts into the washing machine with the red duvet and turning it pink, or forgetting to buy cereal at the supermarket. Of the two of them — father and son — it was Kim who had shown Hilary the greater support. However he was going through a sullen, secretive stage. When he was in the house he spent most of his time in his room playing with his computer games, or stuck in front of the TV, face blank.

'Maybe I should have had an abortion,' Hilary sighed, not for the first time.

'Don't you dare say that!' Claire responded. 'When you got married you told me you wanted a boy and a girl.'

'Yeah, but ...' Hilary's voice tailed off. She sighed and linked her hands over her swollen belly as though protecting it from disapproval.

The front door opened and Kim walked into the lounge,

14

school tie awry, Puma sportsbag over his shoulder. 'Oh ...
hi,' he said, as if surprised to see the two of them there.

'Hello, Kim,' said Claire. 'How are you?'

'Fine, thanks.'

Claire noticed that the boy's hands were stained blue and
that he had an orange smudge on his cheek. 'Been painting?'
she asked.

'What? Uh ... yeah.' Kim looked guiltily at his hands.
'At school.' He turned to Hilary. 'What's for tea, Mum?'

Despite her pregnancy, Hilary was still expected to run
the house and cook all the meals. Suppressing a sigh she
said, 'How does beefburgers, chips and beans sound?'

Kim shrugged, pulling a face. 'Okay, I guess. I'm ...
er ... going upstairs.'

'Have you got much homework?'

'Nah ... a bit.' He left the room.

Hilary sighed as though communicating with her son was
an ordeal. 'I think my being pregnant embarrasses him,' she
said, and tried (and failed) to smile.

Claire crossed to her sister, put her arms around her
shoulders and gave her a hug. 'Hey, come on,' she said.
'He'll be thrilled when the baby comes and so will Bob,
you'll see. This baby will be the best thing ever.'

A weak smile filtered across Hilary's face. 'Yeah, I know,'
she said, but she sounded unconvinced.

Bob Sterland rolled back the sleeve of his shirt and looked
at his watch. He did it with a flourish, as a magician might
do to show he had nothing to hide. Though he did not know
it, this was one of the many things that his sister-in-law,
Claire Adams, despised him for. Bob, of course, was
completely unaware of this habit he had of transforming
his most insignificant gesture into an exaggerated, somehow
arrogant statement. He looked across the open-plan office
that housed the entire workforce — some sixteen in all — of
the Starmouth Leisure Services, and he loudly announced, as
he did most days, 'Soon be hometime boys and girls.'

There were a few mutters of acknowledgement, one or
two nodding heads. Most people, however, ignored Bob
completely. Mike Travis, whose cluttered desk was directly

15

opposite Bob's, looked up and glared at him. The unspoken statement conveyed by Mike's expression was clear and bright as neon: I knew you were going to say that. I just *knew* it. Why, just this once, couldn't you keep your irritating gob *shut!*

Bob grinned at Mike, naturally oblivious. Then he did something else that never failed to drive Mike silently wild. He inclined his head, made a clicking noise out of the side of his mouth and gave a conspiratorial wink. 'Got anything lined up for tonight, Michael?'

Bob was the only person who called him 'Michael'. He somehow managed to make it sound both pally and belittling. Mike bared his teeth in a snarl that purported to be a grin. 'Lined up, Robert?' he said tightly. 'I don't know what you mean.'

'Oh, I think you do,' said Bob heartily. He jerked his elbow, nudging air. 'How's that new totty of yours?'

'Barbara's fine.' Each syllable was a bullet that Mike wished would penetrate Bob Sterland's crocodile-thick skin.

'I bet she is,' agreed Bob. 'Nothing like a bit of what you fancy to put some colour in your cheeks. Am I right or am I right?'

Mike raised his eyebrows and grunted, wishing as always that he could pluck up whatever it took to vent the anger that seethed beneath his veneer of equanimity. He knew under ordinary circumstances that he never would. But the Christmas office party on December 16th was only a week away, and Mike was already harbouring vague plans of getting blind drunk and telling Bob exactly what he thought of him. Ideally, he'd love to smash the creep's nose all over his leering face, put him in traction for the festive season, but he doubted that things would go that far. To be truthful he even had doubts as to whether consuming copious amounts of alcohol would finally enable him to speak his mind. It was likely to loosen his stomach before his inhibitions. He stood up abruptly, scooping his bomber jacket from the back of his chair.

'Right, I'm off,' he said.

Bob tutted in playful disapproval. 'Naughty, naughty. It's only ten to.'

16

'I don't care. I've done my bit for today.'

'What's the situation with Ken Dodd?'

Mike was responsible for booking the acts for the summer season. He knew that Bob had asked him the question purely in an attempt to prevent him leaving early. 'A bit iffy,' he said. 'I don't think we'll get him.'

Bob contrived an expression of interested concern. 'What's the problem?' he asked earnestly.

'Well, would you do Starmouth when you've been offered Blackpool?'

'Starmouth's more refined,' Bob said almost sulkily.

'Exactly. Smaller crowds, less money.'

Bob sighed, as if Mike had disappointed him in some way. 'So what has his manager said exactly?'

'That he'll ring me tomorrow, but I shouldn't start making any plans.'

Bob shook his head, tutting like a schoolteacher. 'That won't do at all, will it? Would you like me to have a word with him?'

Mike clenched his teeth, felt the band of anger around his temple tighten a further notch. 'There's no point,' he said tersely, 'because *I've* already spoken to him. At great length. All that could have been done has been.'

'That's as may be, Michael, but let's face it, there's no substitute for experience. I think if I could just – '

'Please,' Mike blurted, raising his hand. His voice was louder then he had intended. He became aware of faces turning towards him, and immediately felt embarrassed.

'Please,' he said again, lowering his voice. 'Just trust me on this one will you, Bob. I'm quite capable, you know.'

Bob spread his palms exaggeratedly, fingers pointing towards the ceiling like a mime artist encountering an invisible wall. 'Oh, I don't doubt that, Michael, not for a minute. No, no, I wouldn't dream of casting aspersions. I simply felt a different approach, a separate voice . . .' He smiled expansively, the good Samaritan ever prepared to aid a struggling colleague.

Mike managed to contort his facial muscles into a fair approximation of a smile. 'Thanks, Bob,' he said. 'That's

17

very kind of you, but if you don't mind I'll handle it myself.'

Bob shrugged like a cartoon Italian. 'Okay, okay. It's your funeral. But if Ken slips through the net you're going to have to find an alternative pretty pronto.'

'It so happens I've already got one lined up,' Mike said smugly.

'Oh, really. Who?'

'Hinge and Bracket.'

'Not the nancy-boys?' exclaimed Bob. 'Oh, come on, Michael, you can't be serious!'

'They're very popular.'

'They're woolly woofters.'

'What's that got to do with anything?'

Bob smote his brow. Mike wondered how he could make that crack sound without knocking himself senseless.

'I can't believe you asked me that. Don't get me wrong, I've got nothing against them personally. But ... well ... it's their following, isn't it?'

'I'm sorry, Bob, I'm not with you.'

'Their *fannns*,' Bob emphasised. 'Before we know it, the place'll be crawling with arse bandits.'

Mike simply stared at him, unsure whether to laugh or cry, though in truth it was not an unexpected reaction from Bob. He was not exactly a man renowned for his tolerance. Of course, Bob always insisted that he had nothing against *them* personally, he was sure most of *them* simply didn't know any better. *Them*, of course, was an all-embracing term which included racial minorities, homosexuals, feminists, vegetarians, lefties, AIDS sufferers, punks, hippies, men with earrings (who were, by definition, either homosexuals, lefties or punks anyway), Southerners and a fair proportion of women.

Finally Mike managed to squeeze out a laugh. 'Don't be daft,' he said. 'They've had a series on the BBC.'

'Ah, but why do you think they're not on the BBC any more? Answer me that one, eh?'

'Oh come off it, Bob. Anyway, I couldn't give a monkey's who their fans are. At least they've got fans. Which means bums on seats.'

18

Bob shook his head. He looked mortified. 'Have you no sense of responsibility? Think of the citizens of Starmouth. Think of the children.'

'The *children*? Don't you think you're over-reacting slightly?'

'You don't know what these people are *like*, Michael. You don't know what they get up to.'

Mike yanked up the zip of his jacket. 'I'm going home.' He stomped out before Bob could reply.

Bob stared after him for a few moments, shaking his head. Michael was a pleasant enough lad, but misguided, and altogether unsuited to the responsibility of his position. In Bob's opinion the boy had been promoted too early. He was bound to make mistakes, impetuous decisions he would regret later. It was up to his elders and betters to put him right, to keep him on the straight and narrow.

Bob looked around, and was satisfied to see that none of his colleagues were paying him the slightest attention. The majority of them were in the process of finishing up for the day; some had already left.

Casually he stood up and sauntered across to Mike's desk. He tutted at the disorder – papers strewn about, a half-finished mug of cold tea sitting in a pattern of white rings on the wooden surface, biscuit crumbs, a spidery pot plant trailing green fronds among the debris. Really, this was just a reflection of Michael's inability to cope. For goodness sake, the boy still wore jeans to the office! If that wasn't an indication of his attitude, Bob didn't know what was.

He allowed his gaze to wander across the jumble of letters, official memos, scribbled notes. Despite his bluster, Bob was sure that the boy would be grateful for a surreptitious push in the right direction. Ah, there was what he was looking for. Typically, the letter from Ken Dodd's agent was crumpled beneath Michael's pot plant and speckled with soil.

Shaking his head, Bob reached for it. As he did so his hand brushed against the hanging fronds of the plant. Suddenly and shockingly, a searing pain, like a cross between a bee sting and the touch of a red-hot poker, sizzled across his skin where the plant had touched it. Bob let out a high-pitched howl and snatched his hand away. As if he'd been infected with a toxin whose effect was deadly and instantaneous, his gorge rose, sweat broke out on his brow, he felt faint. Just before the world swam away from him he looked at his hand and saw deep grooves carved in the flesh, grooves filled not with blood but with a viscous luminous-green liquid which actually seemed to be *bubbling*. As his knees buckled and the darkness rushed in, Bob thought of his mother's antipathy to the *bad* colour, the *unlucky* colour, and his own unquestioned inheritance of it. He had never really thought about *why* it was bad until now. But suddenly he knew, he *really* knew. Such a pity he'd found out too late ...

Frankly he was surprised to wake up. He came to, feeling sick and dizzy, faces hovering above him like balloons. The muzz of sound sloshing against his eardrums slowly clarified, fragmenting into separate voices. 'Is he all right?' 'Do you think he had a heart attack?' 'Look, he's coming round.' 'Get back everybody. Give him some air.'

Bob struggled to sit up and was aware of hands fluttering down like birds to aid him. Hands, he thought fuzzily, and then with sudden panic remembered his own hands, the green poison that had sizzled like acid in his wounds. He cried out, was aware of the crowd jerking back in unison, like a single entity. He brought his hands up to his face, turned them over and over, but his eyes refused to focus.

'Are you all right, Bob?' asked a tentative voice. A lined, heavily jowled face drifted down to him, came to rest on the tips of his fingers like the sun poised on the horizon.

'My hands,' Bob tried to explain. 'I must see. I *need* to see.'

The flabby features creased in puzzlement. 'Your hands? Your hands are fine, dear boy. Nothing wrong there.'

Bob closed his eyes, blew air from his mouth, fought to control his senses. He felt hands touching him again, presumably in comfort, but he found them intrusive, unwelcome. 'Leave me,' he said, shrugging them off. 'I'm fine. I'll ... I'll ... just don't touch me.'

The hands fluttered away. After a few moments, Bob felt ready to open his eyes and examine his own hands again. He did so. He turned his hands over and over, but there was not a mark on them. Not a scratch, not a scar, nothing.

He was still the centre of attention, still surrounded by alarmed, expectant, concerned faces. A modicum of his old pride began to seep back, and he said brusquely, 'Help me up. I need to get up.'

Eager volunteers rushed forward and hauled him into a chair. He tried to smile but it was a shaky effort, not his usual wide, almost savage, grin.

'Thank you,' he said. 'Thank you very much. I'll be perfectly all right now.'

'That was quite a fall you took there, son,' said the balding, heavily jowled man.

'What ... what happened, Mr Sterland?' asked a young girl with a blonde corkscrew perm and wide eyes. 'Did you faint?'

Bob bridled. 'Of course I didn't faint,' he snapped. 'I'm not a swooning schoolgirl. No ... I ... I slipped and hit my head. Must have knocked myself out for a minute or two.'

'Hit your head?' said Trevor Dicks, the Parks and Gardens Co-ordinator. 'Are you sure? You haven't got a lump or a bruise or anything.'

Bob glared at him. 'Of course I'm sure. It was *my* head, wasn't it?'

Dicks shrugged and turned away. To Bob's relief the crowd was dispersing a little now. However some remained, like Bernard Hoyle, the heavily jowled man who always smelled of pipe tobacco and called everyone 'My boy' or 'My girl'.

'Nevertheless,' Hoyle was saying, 'I think it might be an idea to pop you down the infirmary, get you checked out.'

'Oh no,' Bob said, 'no need for that.' He hated hospitals because he hated the idea that anything might be wrong with him.

Bob didn't notice the blonde-haired girl – Shirley – had left until she reappeared holding something out to him. 'Here, Mr Sterland, drink this.'

Ordinarily Bob would have welcomed Shirley's attentions.

The number of times he'd fantasised about sinking his face between those gorgeous tits ... But right now all he could do was look with horror at the object she was holding out to him. It was a glass filled with water. A *green* glass filled with water.

'No!' Bob yelled, jumping up and making the chair he'd been sitting in rock backwards. Shirley flinched, slopping water onto the floor. A second later she screamed as Bob's arm swept round and dashed the glass from her hand.

The glass sailed across the room and smashed against the wall, causing a spray of water and glass fragments to rain down on Bernard Hoyle's desk. 'What the hell ...?' Hoyle cried, then he too was staggering backwards as Bob barged past him.

'Just leave me alone!' Bob shouted. 'I've told you I'm fine, I'm bloody fine. Are you all too stupid to understand that?'

He turned and fled from the room, eyes wild, back hunched, panting like an injured animal.

'Bob,' asked Hilary tentatively, 'are you sure you're all right?'

Immediately she'd asked the question she wished she hadn't. She quailed at the thunder in Bob's eyes. He drew back his lips and snarled, 'Of *course* I'm all right. I've *told* you, haven't I? Now stop fucking going on at me. Leave me alone.'

Hilary looked down at her meal, cowed. She opened her mouth, wanting to tell him she was sorry, she was only concerned, but she knew that the sound of her voice would only exacerbate his anger, and so in the end she said nothing.

Very few people saw this side of Bob. To everyone else he was the life and soul, always laughing, always joking. Oh, she knew he could be narrow-minded, opinionated, of course, and she knew that some people found this irksome. But he was generally regarded as harmless, uncomplicated — even her sister, Claire, thought of him in this way and Claire was closer to Hilary than anyone. It was only Hilary who saw the anger in Bob, the way he brooded sometimes. It was only

Hilary who had felt the sharp edge of Bob's tongue, had heard him spew invective like poison. Thankfully his anger never lasted for long, and never spilled over into physical violence. And yet Hilary couldn't help thinking that the propensity was there. The best thing to do, as always, was simply not to antagonise him, not to give the anger a target. With nothing to feed on it would retreat back into its hole until the next time. And so they sat silently, eating their meal, Hilary stealing no more than the occasional glance at her husband. She wondered what he was brooding about – something at work maybe; he had a very responsible job. She wondered too why he was not eating his peas. But she didn't dare ask.

After the meal, Bob stomped out of the kitchen without a word of thanks, without bothering to offer to wash up. Hilary sighed and eased herself slowly from her seat, her back aching intolerably, the baby like an anvil in her belly. If anything, she should be the angry one. Eight and a half months pregnant, and not once had her husband asked her how she had been today. He had not kissed her, had not even asked where Kim was. She collected up the crockery, scraping his uneaten peas into the flip-top bin.

She was putting the last of the pots away when the doorbell rang. She listened for a moment, wondering if Bob would answer it, but there was no sound from the lounge. 'I'll go,' she called, and waddled into the hall. When she opened the door and saw the uniformed policeman her immediate thought was: *Bob's done something. That's why he's so preoccupied. My God, what's he done?*

Then she saw Kim. His face was clenched and pale as if he were readying himself for some ordeal. He was standing behind and to one side of the policeman. A policewoman, almost concealed from view by the policeman's bulk, was lightly holding Kim's left forearm.

'Mrs Sterland?' the policeman said. He was younger than she had at first thought.

'Yes.' She looked at the policeman's face and then at Kim's. 'What's happened? What's going on?'

'Mrs Sterland, your son was caught with three other boys defacing council property earlier this evening.'

23

'Defacing ... You mean vandalism?'

'In a sense. He was spray-painting graffiti onto the walls of the Public Conveniences building in Beachside Park.'

'Oh, Kim,' said Hilary sadly. She looked at her son, but his head was bowed, his gaze fixed firmly on his shoes. 'Will he have to go to court?' she asked the policeman.

'That's not for me to say, Mrs Sterland. We'll let you know of any developments.'

The policewoman let go of Kim's arm and he shuffled into the house, still refusing to meet his mother's gaze.

'Well ... thanks for bringing him home,' Hilary said.

'That's all right, Mrs Sterland, no problem. Goodnight.'

'Goodnight,' said Hilary. She closed the door.

As soon as she had done so, Kim bolted up the stairs and into his room, slamming the door behind him.

'Well, young man, what have you got to say for yourself?'

Hilary stood, hands on hips, glaring down at the top of her son's head.

Kim was sitting on his bed, hands clasped between his knees. He looked small, huddled and pathetic. Hilary fought down an urge to feel sorry for him, an urge to sit beside him and gather him into her arms. She *wanted* to sit down – the weight in her belly made it feel as though a screw was being slowly tightened at the base of her spine – but she felt that doing so would somehow undermine her authority. In a way she felt more angry at Bob for being in one of his moods than she did at Kim. Bob should be handling stuff like this at this stage in her pregnancy. She could do without all the upset.

'Well?' she said. 'I'm waiting.'

Kim flinched, his shoulders hunching as though her words were sticks she was using to beat him with. He glanced quickly up at her, his untidy fringe curling darkly over his eyebrows.

He needs a haircut, she thought, and immediately felt guilty for not noticing before now. His hunched shoulders twitched in a shrug and he murmured something.

'What? I didn't hear you.'

'I said I'm sorry.'

24

His voice fractured on the apology. When he next looked up tears sparkled in his eyes.

That did it. Her resolve melted at once, an ice cube before the raging fire of his misery. She crossed to him, sat beside him, draped an arm across his thin shoulders.

She couldn't remember the last time she had seen him cry. It made him look so childlike, so vulnerable.

'Oh, Kim,' she sighed, 'why did you do it?'

He answered her question with one of his own. 'Are you going to tell Dad?'

She said nothing for a moment. She *ought* to tell Bob but the thought of doing so just now made her shudder. 'I don't know,' she said. 'Not yet. He's got a lot on his mind at the moment.'

A little of the tension seeped from him and he rested his cheek against her swollen breast. She noticed the hands in his lap smeared with paint, orange and blue and black. Gently she prised his hands apart and turned them over, confronting him with the evidence.

'You know you shouldn't do this sort of thing, don't you? Defacing property . . . it's as bad as breaking things up. It's senseless. You should know better than this, Kim.'

She felt him tense again at her words. 'It's not,' he muttered.

'Not what?'

'It's not like breaking things up. It's making things better, more colourful. It's art.'

'Spraying paint on walls is art?' she said scornfully.

'Yes!' The tears had gone now. He stood up abruptly, moved away from her, turned and faced her so that their positions of a few moments before were reversed. She could see him struggling to express himself, and despite everything, she wanted him to succeed, to convince her. Finally he shook his head and muttered, 'You don't understand.'

'No I don't. But I want to. I can't condone these things, but I want to know why you did them.'

The look he gave her was part suspicion, part eagerness. He stood, apparently undecided for a moment, then seemed to come to a decision and nodded abruptly. 'All right,' he said, 'I'll show you.'

25

He walked back across the room, got down on his hands and knees and rooted under the bed. He dragged out two large books, brushed fluff from their covers, and placed them beside her. Hilary picked up the first book, *Subway Art*, the cover of which showed people standing on the platform of an underground station in New York, about to board a train smothered in breathtakingly psychedelic graffiti. The other book, entitled *Inner-city Dreams*, depicted two boys, one black, one white, wearing baseball caps and shell suits, leaning proudly against a wall that had been transformed into a stunningly colourful space battle.

She began leafing through the books. On each page colours leaped out at her, a kaleidoscope of images demanding her attention. Kim hovered beside her, watching her face closely, as nervous for her reaction as if the work were his own.

'Where did you get these?' Hilary said, putting down the first book and opening the second.

'I bought them,' Kim said. 'I saved up my pocket money.' When Hilary looked at him he shrugged and looked embarrassed. 'And my dinner money,' he admitted.

She decided not to comment on that. She began looking through the second book. After a minute or two, unable to contain himself, Kim said, 'Well, what do you think of them?'

'They're ... amazing,' Hilary admitted. 'Are you as good as this?'

'Nah. But I'm not bad. With a bit more practice—'

'Kim,' Hilary said warningly.

Kim looked sheepish, knowing he had overstepped the mark. 'Sorry, Mum, but you've got to admit a lot of places do need livening up, don't they? I mean, like that toilet wall in Beachside Park. It's just all covered with names and stuff at the moment, it looks a real mess. We were going to do something really good on it, something that people could look at and .. and ...'

'Admire?'

'Yeah, admire. Like a real work of art.'

Kim looked appealingly at his mother, willing her to understand. Hilary sighed and shook her head.

'I can see what you're getting at, Kim,' she said, 'but don't

26

you see it's not up to you to make that sort of decision? That wall is not your property.'

'Yeah, but where can I practise then? I haven't got any property.'

'What about if I got you some boards of wood? Like old doors or something?'

'Where from?'

'I don't know. The tip maybe.'

Kim pulled a face. 'Nah, I need something really big. Hey, what about if I had a wall of the house? I could do some really good pictures. And I could keep painting over them, doing better and better ones.'

Hilary almost smiled at the idea of this but managed to suppress it. 'I don't think so, Kim,' she said. 'Your dad would do his nut.'

Kim tutted disgustedly. 'Well, what about the garage then?'

Hilary raised her eyebrows. 'What do *you* think?'

'Aw, it's not fair,' Kim said. 'I never get to do anything I want.'

Hilary was silent for a moment. She felt she ought to be nipping this in the bud right now — it had already got him into trouble with the police, for God's sake! And yet she admired Kim for wanting to brighten up the world, felt almost proud of his need to express himself in this way. He had always liked drawing and painting, and it had been something she had always sought to encourage in him. She would feel a hypocrite if she now condemned him for what he had done.

'Look,' she said, 'I'll have a think about it. Just promise me you won't spray graffiti on any more public property in the meantime.'

Kim set his mouth in a stubborn line, his only response a petulant shrug of the shoulders.

'Promise me, Kim,' Hilary said firmly. 'I'm trying to be fair with you. I could always tell your dad about this and take away these books.'

Kim puffed out his cheeks, expelling air through his pursed lips. 'Okay,' he acceded, though his voice was low and reluctant. 'Okay, I promise.'

27

Bob stared at himself in the bathroom mirror, half-expecting to see some evidence of the truth in his face. He had been struggling to grasp the exact nature of that truth since he had woken up on the office floor with his colleagues leaning over him. But it remained veiled in his mind, a bright moon of knowledge wrapped in dark stifling cloud. All that Bob could be sure of was that his superstition, which he had borne unquestioningly since childhood, had finally been revealed as possessing an authentic and terrible significance. Though exactly what that significance was, what form it would take, Bob did not know.

He stared deep into his own eyes and willed the clouds to shred, for the light of his moon to come blazing through. It was no good. He would have to be patient. But waiting was hard, for he sensed that something was coming, something awful and relentless. All night he had stared unseeingly at the TV screen, trying to recapture that split second just before he had passed out, when his moon had shone bright and clear. But there were too many distractions; his mind felt dulled by them. Absently he reached for the soap, then glanced down and froze, realising he had almost fallen straight into a trap.

The soap was green. A pale milky green, it supposedly exuded the scent of fresh pine. Bob's mouth went dry, his stomach clenched and his heart began to pound uncomfortably. Glancing behind him to ensure he was not stepping into any more traps, he edged slowly backwards until he felt the cold shock of the metal towel-rail touch his spine. He stood for a moment, staring at the soap, and slowly an idea, an urge almost, formed in his mind. He would try a little experiment, see if he could rip the clouds apart through force. He took three steps forward until he was standing before the sink again. His face in the mirror was pale, jaw muscles clenched into knots of bone. Squeezing his right hand into a fist, he extended his little finger, reached out and touched the soap with its tip.

Instantly his flesh shrivelled and peeled back like cellophane exposed to heat. Raging pain hissed up his finger and into his hand, engulfed his wrist and then surged towards his elbow. Bob wrenched his hand away, the pain so bad he could not even cry out. His knees buckled and he collapsed to the floor, his shoulder colliding with the edge of the bath.

Gritting his teeth, blinking furiously, he fought against the emerald darkness that flowed through him, struggled to stop himself losing consciousness. At the same time he prepared himself to receive the truth that he hoped the pain would bring, to capture it before it could slip away. He won his battle against unconsciousness but the truth eluded him. His thoughts raged bitterly: All this for nothing! His vocal cords were beginning to release involuntary sounds of pain now. He grabbed a damp towel from the edge of the bath and stuffed it into his mouth, biting down hard so that Hilary wouldn't hear.

Green pus was leaking from his finger, bubbling like acid. Fighting against nausea, Bob dragged himself over the edge of the bath and twisted the cold tap. Water spattered on enamel. Bob thrust his hand into it and held it there. A minute or so later the pain eased enough for him to spit the towel from his mouth. He pulled his hand from the water and examined it.

It was completely healed.

The moon was green, bloated, like rotting fruit. It filled the sky, casting its Halloween light onto slate roofs and tarmacked roads.

Bob stood at his bedroom window staring out, like a child watching the skies for Santa Claus. But it was no benign presence he was waiting for. It was evil . . . and he was afraid.

As he watched, something fell from the moon − a drool of light, pulsing in the centre like a heart. The moon convulsed as it gave birth. The green skin of its light shivered on the earth, cold and reptilian. The speck of light which had fallen from the moon, tumbled towards the horizon, a falling star, destined surely to become a cinder in the earth's atmosphere or to shatter like glass on the planet's surface. But no. The light fell slowly, sedately, and though he was far away and couldn't possibly have known, Bob *did* know that the light

29

was in control and aware not only of the world towards which it fell but of *him*, Bob Sterland, and of his knowledge of its coming.

With a final flash it disappeared behind the horizon, burning the sky with green fire. As the glow faded, darkness seemed to rise and swallow the moon, plunging the earth into the blackest midnight. Bob knew it would not be long now. He could feel the threat of it, the promise of its evil, crawling on his skin like electricity.

Sure enough, moments later, the green light reappeared, a thin line of it which expanded along the horizon. Then, slowly and relentlessly, it began to sweep across the earth, moving towards him, devouring as it came.

Bob had never known such terror, yet he did not vacate his place by the window, he did not run, he did not cry out. The light came closer. Now it was three streets away ... now two ... now one ...

And suddenly here it was, sidling around the chimneys, across the roofs, filling the gaps between houses on the other side of the street.

And still Bob did not move. He felt paralysed, bound to the spot. The light seeped across the road, turning cars to lumps of corroded metal, felling street lamps. It edged onto the pavement on his side of the street, just a yard from his garden gate. Now Bob could see it sizzling at the edges like an egg in hot fat. The flagstones of the pavement became porridge at its touch. It extended tendrils, touched his garden gate, which instantly began to smoulder and within seconds was a charred ruin. The tendrils reformed, became one fat tentacle of light which surged up his garden path. Just a few feet away from the house itself, directly beneath his window, it halted, quivered for a moment, then reared up like an angry cobra.

As Bob watched, the light transformed into the shape of a man. Limbs sprouted from the central column; above that a neck and head flowed from the shimmering flux like clay moulding itself. The form was basic but powerful. An umbilicus of light trailed from the centre of its back, linking it with its greater mass. The light-man took two strides forward and placed its palms flat on the walls of the house. The brick

30

began to hiss like escaping gas; smoke curled between the man's blazing green fingers.

Like a mountaineer without support, the green man began to scale the wall. Bob watched as it climbed towards him, leaving smoking, blackened brick in its wake. When its head was just a few feet beneath the window it stopped, trembling on its perch like a spider. Slowly, with a sound like fire, it raised its head so that Bob could see its face ...

He was torn from the dream so violently that he felt he'd left bits of himself behind, shreds of flesh and cloth clinging to the barbed-wire fence of sleep. He was bleeding inside, could taste it at the back of his throat, feel the pain of his wounds in his heart. 'It's coming!' he was shouting at the darkness. 'It's coming! It's coming! It's coming!'

Beside him Hilary, belly huge, jerked awake. 'What?' she blurted in a voice thick with sleep. 'What's the matter? Bob, what's wrong?'

Bob was hunched up, pressed against the headboard, knees drawn up to his chin, arms wrapped protectively around himself. 'It's coming,' he repeated in a voice that was hoarse and afraid.

'What is?' snapped Hilary. She was in no mood for vagaries. 'Bob, what is?'

Bob turned to her and his eyes were wide, the pupils almost lost in the gleaming whites. 'Something,' he hissed.

Over the course of the next two weeks, Bob Sterland's work colleagues noticed a marked change in him. Gone were the expansive gestures, the domineering manner of the old Bob, and in their stead came a man who was subdued, covert, nervous, watchful.

Some people welcomed this sudden change of character, and hence failed to question it, whereas others found that this new Bob, for entirely different reasons, unsettled them more than ever. Mike Travis, for instance, had been merely irritated, and occasionally infuriated, with the old Bob – but this new one was even worse. Though he kept himself to himself much of the time, Mike felt constantly on edge.

Office rumours as to what had precipitated this change grew rife. Bernard Hoyle believed it was caused by Bob's hitting his head on the desk when he'd fallen recently; others whispered of marital problems. A few propounded with fearful relish the notion that Bob had some terminal illness — cancer or a brain tumour or perhaps even AIDS; the least melodramatic wondered whether someone 'high up' had had 'a quiet word' with Bob about 'his attitude', because 'let's face it, he gets up enough people's noses'.

What unsettled Mike Travis most of all was not so much the fact that Bob was always looking around as if afraid someone was out to get him, nor even the way he flinched when the telephone rang or someone called his name. No, the thing that *really* made Mike's flesh creep was the fact that Bob Sterland had taken to wearing gloves.

They were grey gloves, very tight-fitting, and made of some soft material like felt. And since that day when Bob had fainted or knocked himself out or whatever he had done (Mike had not been there so could rely only on hearsay), he had worn them constantly.

On a number of occasions Mike had almost asked Bob about his gloves but had always chickened out at the last minute. Though they seemed sinister (connotations of criminals not wishing to leave fingerprints), there was probably some perfectly innocent explanation for them. Perhaps Bob had something wrong with his hands — eczema, for example — and needed to keep them covered. That would kind of fit in with his personality change too, wouldn't it? Wasn't eczema often a result of stress? Mike tried hard to convince himself that Bob's undoubted problems were home-based and ordinary, either financial or marital, but it didn't quite ring true. Bob's reactions were *too* extreme. He acted more like a man who'd been threatened by the Mafia than one who fought with his wife.

At least Bob's behaviour rescued Mike from having to speak his mind at the Christmas party, because for the first time in the four years since Mike had been with the Leisure Services, Bob simply didn't turn up. Normally he was there, quaffing the free alcohol and chatting up anything in a skirt, but this year he slunk out of the office at five o'clock and failed to reappear.

Another advantage from Mike's point of view was that

he was able to work without interference. He finally booked Hinge and Brackett with not even so much as a disapproving glance from Bob.

Nevertheless, however much he tried, he could not relish this new-found impunity.

Despite all this general unease, however, there was really only one *truly* disturbing and significant event throughout these two weeks leading up to Christmas, and that was right at the end, when Shirley brought some mistletoe into the office. It was December 23rd, and Shirley was tipsy. Unlike some of the office staff – Mike, for instance, who had to oversee the start of this year's panto on Boxing Day – she was about to start a ten-day holiday and had begun celebrating already.

There was a festive mood in the office that afternoon, not least because a light snow had started to fall outside. The office was bright with cards and decorations, someone had brought in a tape of Christmas carols which was playing softly in the background, and Elsie Marsden, who was responsible for The Evergreen Club (Entertainment for the Over 60s), had been handing out her legendary mince pies which Mike proclaimed quite truthfully to be the best he'd ever tasted.

Shirley's boisterous and meandering return from an extended lunch break was, therefore, received in the right spirit. No one objected as she tumbled into laps, brandishing her mistletoe, and greasily smothered the men-folk with lipstick. When Mike's turn came he laughed along with the others and hoped that he wasn't blushing *too* strongly. As Shirley clambered unsteadily off him he caught a glimpse of Bob sitting rigidly behind his desk, watching Shirley's antics with an expression of wariness and hostility. Bob's teeth were showing in a near-snarl, his grey-gloved hands were gripping the edge of his desk as if the room had begun to tip and he was trying to stop himself from falling. Mike felt a thrill strong enough to be termed fear, and he thought, Surely not. Surely even Shirl's not *that* drunk?

But she was. Apparently oblivious to the way Bob was uncoiling in his seat like a panther preparing to spring,

33

Shirley advanced upon him, giggling. 'Come on, Bobby, your turn,' she said. She held up the mistletoe as though to lash him with it.

Mike saw Bob's face turn bestial, saw him pounce across the desk, arms outstretched, and he tried to yell a warning, but was too late. '*Getawayfromme!*' Bob screeched at the same instant as his gloved fists slammed into Shirley just above her breasts.

An expression of almost comic surprise appeared on her face, then her legs shot from under her and she fell backwards, landing heavily and unceremoniously on her bottom. Mike felt his desk vibrate as her blonde head made sickening contact with it. Horror and fury rose within him. He leaped up, knocking his chair backwards, and advanced on Bob, hands curling into fists.

'What the bloody hell did you do that for?' he shouted, and then added with feeling, 'You bloody nutcase!'

Bob was backing away, crouched over like an animal. When he screamed, 'Leave me alone!' spit flew out of his mouth.

Other people were shouting at Bob, but Mike was so enraged that he barely heard them. He glanced down at Shirley. She looked dazed but not unconscious, and thankfully there appeared to be no blood.

'What's wrong with you?' Mike yelled. 'You're bloody unhinged! You should be put in a looney bin!'

Bob was still backing away, hands clenching and unclenching. He glanced behind him, and then with an abrupt change of direction, leaped forward, screaming.

Mike was so surprised that he didn't even have time to defend himself. He thought afterwards that Bob must have done what he did to catch him off guard, but at the time he'd seemed genuinely terrified. But there was nothing behind Bob to frighten him as far as Mike could see: just a low filing cabinet with the two-foot high office Christmas tree sitting atop it. He hardly saw Bob's gloved fist lash out before it impacted with his nose. More shocked than anything, Mike fell onto one knee like a suitor about to propose. The pain was clean and sharp.

As his blood began to patter on the floor and Shirley sat

up, rubbing her head, Bob whirled and made his exit.

I'll get you next time, Mike thought dazedly, just see if I don't.

But he never saw Bob Sterland again.

'Come on, Hilary, I'm your sister. I can *tell* when something's wrong.'

Hilary gazed down into her teacup as if she'd found something interesting among the tea leaves. 'No,' she mumbled, 'it's nothing really. I'm okay.'

Claire sighed. 'Is it the baby?' she persisted. 'Is that what's worrying you?'

Hilary's hand crept to the dome of her stomach and caressed it absently. 'No, no,' she said a little irritably, 'the baby's fine.'

'Well, what then?' said Claire.

Hilary scowled. 'I've told you, it's nothing.'

'Yes it is, and I'm not leaving until you tell me. For God's sake, Hil, the baby's due any day. You can do without any sort of upset at a time like this.'

'What would you know about it?' Hilary snapped, and then immediately regretted her words. She saw Claire's face fall. An ectopic pregnancy at the age of eighteen meant that Claire could never have children.

'Oh God, Clarry, I'm sorry. I didn't mean it like that.'

Claire's voice was small, hurt. 'I know I'm bossy, but it's only because I'm concerned about you.'

'I know, Clarry, I know. I'm so sorry.' Hilary picked up her teacup, swirled the dregs around and put it down again. As if to herself she said, 'It's Bob.'

'Bob,' repeated Claire, and immediately felt her hackles rise. She fought to keep her anger under control. 'He hasn't been hassling you over this again, has he?'

'Oh no,' said Hilary, 'nothing like that. It's just that ... well ... he's been acting very strange lately.'

So what's new? thought Claire but didn't say so. Instead she asked, 'How do you mean — strange?'

'Well, you know how he usually is? Quite sort of ...'

(A pain in the arse, thought Claire.)

' ... outgoing?'

35

Claire nodded.

'Well, these last couple of weeks he's been very ... quiet. Moody. Sort of introverted. I daren't ask him what's wrong because he just gets annoyed. And he's been ... doing strange things as well.'

'Oh yeah?' said Claire wearily.

'Mmm. Like for instance – ' Hilary swept a hand around the room. 'Do you notice anything different in here?'

Claire looked around. She *had* noticed something as soon as she'd come in, but had been unable to put her finger on it. 'Yes,' she said suddenly. 'It looks ... sort of bare. Like there's something missing.'

'My plants,' said Hilary. 'Bob burnt them all.'

'*He did what?*'

'He said they were all infected with something. He took them out into the back yard and put them in a pile and burnt them.'

'Didn't you try to stop him?'

'I ... I protested, but he went mad. You don't know what he's been like to live with these past couple of weeks, Claire. It's not been easy.'

Claire shook her head. 'The bastard. And just when you need support too. You should have given me a ring.'

Hilary shrugged. 'There's been other things too.'

'Like what?'

'I don't know. Strange things. *Really* strange things.' She paused for a moment as if struggling to find words to describe complex ideas. At last she said, 'He refuses to step on the lawn. He says that the grass is infected too and will have to come up. And the other night, when Kim asked him when he was going to fetch the Christmas tree, Bob looked absolutely horrified and said, 'We're not having one this year.' When Kim and I both started to protest he absolutely flew off the handle and made Kim cry. He won't have holly or mistletoe in the house, and he even refused to let me get the Christmas decorations out.

'Also there are some foods he won't eat any more, like salad and vegetables and apples. He says they make him sick. What else? ... Oh, yes. He's started wearing gloves when he goes out. It's as if ... I don't know ... as if he thinks the whole world's infected with some disease that he's going to catch.'

Claire shook her head worriedly. 'He sounds like he's going off his trolley, Hil. I think you ought to tell someone.'

'I'm telling you.'

'No, I mean a doctor or something. Bob sounds like he needs help.'

Now it was Hilary's turn to look worried. 'Oh no,' she said, 'I'm sure it's not as bad as that. He's just under a lot of strain at the moment.'

'*He's* under a lot of strain? You're the pregnant one.'

'All the same ... It'll probably just blow over. Bob *can* get a bit obsessive sometimes.'

Claire sighed. 'Has he said anything about how he's feeling? Have you tried talking to him about it?'

'Not really,' admitted Hilary. 'He just loses his temper all the time. He's not sleeping very well. He keeps having bad dreams.'

'What kinds of dreams? Does he talk about them?'

'Not really. He shouts out sometimes, though. He seems to think that something is coming to get him.'

'Bloody hell,' said Claire, shaking her head. 'Sounds like serious paranoia. Something's got to be done, sis. You can't be dealing with this now.'

'No,' Hilary admitted, and then abruptly she burst into tears.

Claire moved across and comforted her as best she could. She felt worried for her sister and the baby, and angry at Bob. Though mental illness was nobody's fault, she couldn't help thinking that this was just bloody typical of the man.

'Look,' she said, 'why don't you bring Kim and come and spend Christmas with me and Dave? We'll look after you.'

Hilary shook her head firmly, then blew her nose. 'No,' she said. 'Bob needs me. He's going through a difficult patch, that's all. I can't abandon him.'

'I'm not suggesting you abandon him, I'm just talking about the next few days until the baby's born. You really need to relax, Hil, to be pampered a little bit.'

'All the same,' said Hilary. She shrugged, sighed. 'I'll stay here. I'll be okay.'

37

'God, you're bloody stubborn,' Claire said, not without affection. Often she felt like the elder sister. 'You will call me, though, won't you, if you need anything? Anything at all?'

'Yes,' sighed Hilary.

'Promise?'

'Yes.'

'You'd better mean that,' Claire warned, 'or there'll be trouble.'

Hilary smiled tiredly, then looked up as they both heard the front door open and close. 'Kim?' Hilary called. 'Is that you?'

'Yeah, Mum.'

'Come here a minute, will you? Say hello to your Aunt Claire.'

There was silence for a moment, then they both heard Kim's dragging footsteps. He appeared in the doorway wearing a grey and turquoise sweatshirt, hands stuffed into his jeans pockets.

'Hi, Aunty Claire,' he said dutifully.

Claire felt a little hurt but tried not to show it. There was a time when Kim would have been excited to see her, would have demanded her constant attention. When he'd been six, Kim had said, 'When I grow up, I'm going to marry you, Aunty Claire.' Now, though, he seemed to regard her visits as an intrusion. On the occasions when she'd broached the subject with Hilary, her sister had assured her, 'It's just a phase. He's like that with everybody nowadays.'

Smiling brightly, Claire said, 'Hi, Kim, how's it going?'

'Okay,' Kim said. He had stopped just inside the door and was rocking back and forth on his heels as though readying himself for a quick getaway.

'I've got something for you,' Claire said.

'Oh, yeah?'

'Yes. But you're not to open it until Christmas, okay?'

Kim glanced at his mother with an expression that seemed to say, "Christmas? What Christmas?" He shrugged as if he couldn't care less. 'Okay.'

Claire reached into the plastic Sainsbury's bag she'd brought with her and lifted out a box wrapped in silver

38

and red-striped paper. 'Ta da!' she proclaimed and held it out to him.

Kim simply stood where he was, making no move to enter the room and take the box from her. He looked decidedly uncomfortable.

'Well?' Hilary said. 'What do you say?'

'Uh, yeah. Thanks,' said Kim, and started to edge backwards out of the room.

'Kim!' exclaimed Hilary. 'Don't be so rude. Aren't you going to accept Aunty Claire's present?'

Kim seemed actually to consider the question – Claire felt sure he was about to say 'No' – then his shoulders slumped and he seemed to brace himself for some ordeal. He slunk into the room, hands still stuffed in his pockets, and positioned himself very deliberately with his back to Hilary. Only then did he remove his right hand from his pocket and reach out to take the brightly wrapped package. Claire saw that his hand was stained with green and yellow paint. She glanced up at Kim and saw an appeal in his eyes.

'Kim.' Hilary's stern voice spoke from behind him. Claire saw Kim flinch, his face scrunching up in anticipation of trouble.

'Yeah, Mum,' Kim said.

'Show me your hands.'

'What for?'

'I'm not stupid, Kim. Show me your hands.'

Kim closed his eyes briefly, then opened them again. He turned, dragged his hands reluctantly from his pockets and held them out to his mother.

Hilary stared at them for a long moment, glancing from one to the other, face cemented with anger. 'You've been at it again, haven't you?' she said. 'And after you promised me you wouldn't.'

'It's not what you think, Mum,' Kim said.

'Isn't it?' she snapped.

'No.' Kim frowned. His voice became whiny but defiant. 'Phil Wallace's granddad has got a big wall that we practise on.'

'Oh, really?' said Hilary in clear disbelief.

39

'Yes. You can ring him if you don't believe me. I'll give you his number.'

'If it's all so innocent, why were you being so secretive?'

'Because I knew you'd be like this. You don't really like me spray-painting at all.'

'That's not true.'

'Yes it is. You said you'd sort something out for me, but you haven't done anything.'

'I've had a lot to think about, Kim.'

'Yeah, same as always. What do you have to have a stupid baby for anyway?'

He stormed out of the room, slamming the door behind him.

Claire looked at Hilary's stricken face and asked gently, 'What was all that about?'

Bob pulled up at the traffic lights and sat there, staring straight ahead, gloved hands fidgeting on the steering wheel. He knew they wouldn't be following him – they didn't have to, they were already everywhere – but he kept glancing in his rear-view mirror nonetheless.

They'd almost got him back there in the office. For a while now he knew they'd been planning something, surrounding him with all those awful things. With Christmas almost here the world had become a minefield. He'd never realised before quite how pervasive the influence of that evil colour was. Glancing to his right he shuddered at the shop window displays – there were lurid imitation fir trees, cut-out representations of holly and bells with green bows, green lettering spelling out the words MERRY CHRISTMAS.

The sight of it all, all that green, was beginning to hurt his eyes and he looked away, concentrating on the snow-dusted road ahead. That was another way in which they were out to get him. Over the past couple of days, the colour had actually started to make his eyes prickle like hay fever; if he stared at it for too long he got a headache. This meant that he couldn't be as watchful as he would have liked. Slowly but surely the colour was building up its power, undermining his own defences. Bob felt sure that soon it would launch

40

its final, most devastating attack. It was a nightmare. Only he knew of the threat, the terrible build-up of evil, and yet alone he was helpless.

As he sat, waiting for the lights to change – to green, of course (a further example of how deeply the roots of the evil had embedded themselves) – Bob heard the roar of an engine approaching from behind. He was waiting to turn right on a dual carriageway. He glanced to his left as a car pulled up alongside him. Immediately he went rigid, his hands tightening on the steering wheel, puppyish whimpering slipping from between his whitened lips. The faint squeaking of his windscreen wipers as they swept the snow aside was like the sound of his own mind as its hinges strained and buckled.

The car beside him was big and American, with a bonnet you could play football on and fenders like barricades. It had shark-like fins curving above the trail-light clusters, and a soft-topped roof which had been rolled back like a giant concertina. What terrified Bob Sterland was the car's colour – its bodywork was a bright lime-green, its interior well-padded olive-green leather – and its occupants. Driving the car was a female chauffeur in green shades and green livery, whilst standing up in the back was a green Father Christmas, complete with green suit, green skin and a green beard.

Father Christmas leaned towards him, grinning wolfishly, and Bob saw that he had green teeth. 'Hello, Bobby,' he said. 'Merry Christmas. Ho Ho Ho.' Saliva like snake venom drooled into his beard; Bob saw the hair sizzle and char, saw little spirals of green smoke rise and disperse in the cold air. Snow did not settle on this apparition, nor on the chauffeur, nor even on the car itself.

Father Christmas blinked, and when his eyes opened a split-second later they were no longer human. They were grape-green, with black vertical slits for pupils.

Though Bob had his car windows rolled up he could hear Father Christmas' voice clearly, as if the creature was speaking inside his head. 'It's coming, Bobby. It's near,' Father Christmas hissed.

Bob felt his paralysis snap like a frayed rope. He screamed,

41

released the handbrake, slammed the car into gear and floored the accelerator. Horns blared, cars swerved, the screams of Christmas shoppers tore the seasonal atmosphere apart.

Bob saw a wall of screeching metal rearing up to meet him.

Then all became confusion, pain . . . and darkness.

Later, after she, Hilary and Kim had visited Bob in hospital, Claire found herself wondering whether her sister's husband had tried to commit suicide. It would be just like him to choose a method whereby other people could get hurt too. Thankfully, no one had been killed, or even seriously injured. Even Bob's injuries, though ugly, were superficial − cuts and bruises, whiplash and a cracked rib. He was to be kept in overnight for observation and then discharged the next day, Christmas Eve. Claire was aware she knew too little of the situation to seriously contemplate whether Bob had been trying to end his life, and yet the thought nagged her nevertheless.

Not that she would ever share it with Hilary. Her sister had been shaken enough by what had happened. And if anything, their visit to the hospital had made things even worse. Not only was Bob's face a mess but his mind was too.

Hilary, of course, had told her all about Bob's peculiar behaviour these past few weeks, and yet Claire was shocked by the extent to which he had changed. When they had first entered the ward, he had been hunched up like an old man, hands squeezed tightly into fists and drawn up under his chin, eyes darting everywhere. The moment he saw them he had grown agitated. As soon as they got close enough to hear, he leaned over as far as his injuries and the white surgical collar encircling his neck would allow. 'Please,' he had croaked, 'you've got to get me out of here.'

Their reassurances had fallen on deaf ears. Gazing into space, seeming at times oblivious to their presence, Bob had kept moaning about 'needing my gloves', and 'that thing in the corner', which he claimed was 'out to get me'.

Only Kim had seemed unfazed by Bob's behaviour. He had squinted at 'that thing in the corner' and then back at his father. In a matter-of-fact voice he had said, 'Don't be silly, Dad. It's just a Christmas tree.'

When they left, Bob was frowning and muttering to himself, and Hilary was more upset than ever. Claire wondered whether the accident was to blame for Bob's scrambled thoughts, or whether this was simply the extent to which his mind had now deteriorated.

It was one-fifteen on Christmas Eve morning. Claire was lying on Hilary's narrow camp-bed in the half-finished nursery, staring at the darkness writhing on the ceiling like bacteria. She knew this wasn't really her problem, that Hilary had to make her own decisions, and yet she felt nervous tension chewing at her stomach, felt her mind turning the situation over and over in its search for answers.

Her instinct was to advise Hilary to jettison Bob, to get him out of her life, but as a solution it was neither practical nor compassionate. God knew why but her sister loved the man. And right now Bob needed all the love and help and support he could get. He couldn't simply be discarded, thrown away like a faulty toy.

And yet ... Hilary had the baby to consider. That, surely, had to be her first priority. It was a pity Bob couldn't simply be put on hold for a while, thrust into deep-freeze and thawed out when a more opportune moment arose.

That was the trouble with life, she thought. Like a bad comedy the timing was always lousy and the laughter was tinged with despair. No amount of strategy or planning could ever change that. The thing to do was simply to muddle through, to rely on instinct and fate, and to salvage what you could.

She drifted to sleep with the matter still unresolved, with questions, problems circling around and around in her head. She dreamed of planets orbiting the heavens. It was her task to keep them grinding slowly, remorselessly on. She moaned, tossing and turning. The duvet slid to the floor like a melting bank of snow. When she awoke it was with a start, her eyes popping open. Though her limbs ached, she felt alert, wide awake. It was quiet, yet she knew that *something* had woken her.

'Claaiiirrre.' The supplication was feeble, racked with

43

tiredness and pain. Immediately Claire's heart began to thump so loudly that she could hear the blood roaring in her ears. Barefoot, dressed in one of her sister's billowing nightshirts, she jumped up and ran across the landing into Hilary's room. Hilary was a heaving mound in the darkness. When Claire switched the light on, the first thing she saw was her sister's open mouth trying to draw breath.

'Hil, what's wrong?'

'Where've you been? I've been calling for ages.' Before Claire could even say 'asleep', Hilary jabbered, 'Phone for an ambulance. I need an ambulance.'

Claire wanted to ask questions but all she said was, 'Right,' and ran out of the room. Halfway down the stairs she almost slipped; her reflexes and the strength of her grip on the banister prevented her falling headlong. As she dialled 999 she drew two long breaths and muttered, 'Calm . . . calm . . .' over and over. With the ambulance on the way she felt better, her head clearer. She switched the hall and landing lights on and ran nimbly up the stairs.

Ten minutes later, when the ambulance arrived, Hilary was downstairs on the settee with her dressing gown on and her overnight bag, which had been packed and re-packed over the course of the past ten days, by her side. The ambulance men were kind and calm; one of them smelled of coffee and peppermints. Claire saw Hilary into the ambulance, deposited Kim with Hilary's sleepy but accommodating next-door neighbour, hastily dragged on some clothes and followed in the car.

'Mr Sterland? Mr Sterland?'

The voice, booming and distorted, slipped like a razor into the sac of Bob's dreams and slit it open. Bob clawed his way out, shaking and whimpering. Behind him formless horrors lurched and stirred sluggishly, forerunners of the greater horror from which there would be no escape. Bob rubbed the afterbirth of sleep from his eyes and goggled up at his rescuer. A round-faced nurse with scraped-back hair and a pimply forehead was smiling down at him. Bob reached out, his hand inadvertently clutching her breast. 'It's almost here' he said. 'It's so close.'

Her smile faltering only slightly, the nurse gently disengaged his hand and helped him sit up. 'Don't you worry, Mr Sterland,' she said, 'you're safe now. You've been dreaming is all.'

Her voice, a soothing Irish brogue, reassured most patients but Bob was suffering from more than post-accident trauma.

'No,' he urged, 'you don't understand. Nobody understands but me.'

The nurse sat by his side, enclosed his clenched left fist between the cool softness of both her hands. 'Now then, Mr Sterland,' she said, a trace of firmness creeping into her voice, 'would you just hush up a minute. Don't you want to hear the good news I've brought you?'

Bob looked at her as if she were mad. 'Good news?' he repeated.

'That's right.' She paused a moment, a smile playing on her lips. Then she told him, 'Your wife gave birth to a healthy baby girl at seven o'clock this morning.'

Bob didn't say anything. He just stared at the nurse, a look of incredulity on his face. At last, as if it were a word he'd never heard before, he muttered, 'A baby?'

'That's right,' the nurse said, disappointed by his reaction. 'You have a baby daughter, Mr Sterland. Aren't you pleased?'

'Pleased,' repeated Bob bleakly. How could anyone, ever again, be *pleased* about anything? Maybe once, in another life, he might have been pleased ... But now ... He shook his head. The idea was almost obscene.

'Come on,' the nurse said briskly, strong arms wrapping themselves around his back, shoulder supporting his injured neck. 'Maybe *seeing* your little girl will clear your head a bit.'

She got him into a wheelchair and began to push him from the ward. As they neared the double doors, Bob pointed at the Christmas tree standing to one side of them and said in a panicked voice, 'Don't take me near that. Keep it away from me.'

The nurse shook her head but obliged. Anything to keep the peace. She knew from experience that a whack on the head could do the queerest things to a person's reason. On

45

the short journey to Maternity, Bob flinched from the most innocuous objects – plants, a trolley draped with a green cloth, a poster with a crocodile on it. Once he screamed when a chubby black lady wearing a green overcoat walked by, scaring the poor woman half to death. The nurse, whose name was Maeve Fenton, wondered if this was such a good idea. But she knew Mrs Sterland had been asking for her husband. And besides, you couldn't keep a father away from his own child when the sight of her might help bring him to his senses.

In Maternity they were directed down a corridor to a row of blue doors. Hilary was in room number 6. They halted outside and Maeve helped Bob to his feet. The room would be poky and cluttered enough, she knew, without Bob's wheelchair taking up more space. 'Now then, Mr Sterland, lean on me.' Maeve pushed the door open and the two of them awkwardly entered the room.

It was a drab room, almost colourless, the half-drawn curtains adding to the gloom. It was a far cry from the idealised images of frothy fiction: a radiant mother cuddling a rosy baby, everywhere sunny and spotless and riotous with flowers. Hilary was in bed, her belly still large. She looked pale and exhausted, her fringe a limp, sweaty curtain. Whenever she moved, her face creased in pain. On the side of the bed nearest the door, Claire and Kim sat on tatty metal-framed chairs with blue plastic seats.

'Hello,' said Maeve shyly as the three of them looked up. 'I've brought a visitor to see you.'

'Bob!' Hilary's voice was a half-sob of relief and joy. 'Oh, Bob, it's so good to see you.'

Bob said nothing, simply looked at Hilary as if bemused by the whole situation. He glanced back at Maeve, seeking guidance. She applied pressure to the small of his back, the merest suggestion of a push. Pointing to what looked like a plastic fish tank on the other side of the bed, she said, 'Don't you want to see your daughter, Mr Sterland? You'll be able to make it okay if you hold onto the bed.'

Bob glanced quickly round the room as though searching for booby traps and then dutifully obeyed. As he edged his way round the bed, using it to steady his bruised legs, his family watched him. Hilary was nodding in unconscious approval, Claire was scowling slightly and Kim's expression was unreadable. Kim it was, however, who spoke first. 'She's brill, Dad,' he said. 'You'll really like her.'

Bob reached the fish tank and peered into it. A tiny red thing in a nappy lay there, a scrap of humanity, its fists clenched and its mouth clamped in a grimace. Its eyes seemed to bulge behind closed eyelids as though too big for its head. The hair on its head was black and spiky. It looked, thought Bob, like a skinned chimpanzee.

He looked up to see his wife smiling blissfully at him. 'Well, what do you think?' she said softly. 'Isn't she beautiful?'

Beautiful. The word was an arrow in Bob's heart. What was the point of beauty any more? 'Yes,' he mumbled and looked back down at the crib. The baby moaned and wriggled, then opened its eyes and looked at him.

The attack took Bob so by surprise that he couldn't even scream. As the paralysis set in, he cursed himself for not realising. This was why he had been chosen. He had *known* it was coming and yet he had been blind to its methods, its true nature. He stared down with abhorrence at this ... *thing* that purported to be his daughter. To think, that he could possibly have fathered this! He felt the green light that shone from its eyes driving him to his knees. 'Bob,' he heard someone calling from far away. 'Bob! Bob! Bob!' He wanted to scream at them, to warn them that this was the vessel, the gateway, through which the evil would be unleashed. But the green light swamped his brain and bludgeoned him into unconsciousness.

If it had been any other time of year, Hilary might have stayed in hospital for a couple of days. However she couldn't face the thought of spending Christmas in that dire little room, and so, just twelve hours after giving birth, she was being helped through her own front door by Claire. Kim brought up the rear, holding his new sister as if she were bone china. Hilary thought it wonderful the way he had taken to the baby, especially in light of his previous comments.

'Ow,' she complained. Whenever she moved too suddenly, her stitched-up flesh informed her of the fact in a loud and piercing voice.

'Are you okay, Mum?' Kim asked anxiously.

Hilary managed a tired smile. 'Yes, darling, I'm fine. Just a bit sore, that's all.'

The house was cold, though not unwelcoming. Whilst Kim fetched the carry cot from upstairs, Claire made tea. They installed the baby in the front room, then the three of them sat around the fire, quietly talking.

'I still think you should come and spend Christmas with me and Dave,' said Claire. 'Honestly, we'd love to have you. It wouldn't be any trouble.'

'Yes it would,' said Hilary. 'Sleepless nights, nappy-changing, constant feeds. Your place is too small for that not to be intrusive.'

Claire wafted a hand dismissively. The emerald-green evening gown, which she had offered to Hilary a few weeks before, and which she was now wearing in readiness for a meal out with Dave, shimmered like lizard-skin. 'None of that matters,' she said.

'I'm sure that's not what Dave thinks.'

'Is that why you won't come? You think Dave wouldn't like it?'

Hilary sipped her tea and shook her head. 'No, no, not really. I just ... I want to be here, at home. I'll be fine. I've got Kim to look after me.'

Kim nodded. He looked honoured and a little surprised to be thought capable of such a responsibility. 'Yeah,' he said, 'I'll look after Mum.'

'I know you will,' said Claire. She raised her hands palm upwards in defeat. 'All right. I can see I'm not going to persuade you.'

'No,' said Hilary, smiling, 'you're not.'

'But at least allow me a compromise?'

Hilary sighed, good-humouredly and exaggeratedly. 'Go on.'

'Let me and Dave come round here tomorrow, say about noon, and cook you Christmas dinner?'

Hilary looked at Kim. He was nodding eagerly, eyes wide

and bright. It was as if the birth of the baby had somehow changed him back to the boy he had once been, sapped his sullen rebelliousness. She was realistic enough to know that it probably wouldn't last. Best to enjoy it while she could.

'Okay, okay,' she said. 'You've twisted my arm.'

'Great,' said Claire. 'This is going to be an excellent Christmas.'

'Mm,' said Hilary. She looked at her new daughter and smiled wistfully.

Kim was sitting by the carry cot, fascinated by the way the baby's tiny hand gripped his index finger. He glanced up and noticed his mother's expression.

'You okay, Mum?'

'What? Oh yes. I was just thinking . . . I wish your Dad could be here, sharing all this.'

Claire took a large gulp of tea and turned to look out of the window. Neither she nor Kim said anything.

If she had been a split second earlier, Claire would have seen a bruised, blank-eyed face on the other side of the glass, staring back at her. As soon as her head began to turn, however, the figure stepped back from the window, concealing itself in the shadows.

'Gone? Well, where's he gone *to*?'

Nurse Fenton squirmed under Sister Leach's accusatory glare. 'I don't know, Sister. I've had a look round for him, but I can't find him anywhere.'

The two of them looked down at Bob Sterland's empty bed. The cupboard beside the bed, which had contained a neatly folded change of clothes brought to the hospital by his wife, was now yawning emptily.

'Perhaps he's gone home,' Nurse Fenton suggested. 'His wife's just had a baby. Maybe he wants to spend Christmas with the family.'

'But he was in no state to go home, was he?'

Nurse Fenton shrugged. 'It was more his mental state than his physical state that Dr Singh was worried about. I think he just wanted to keep him in for observation for another day or two.'

Sister Leach puffed out her cheeks in exasperation. 'Well, I don't suppose there's a great deal we can do about it now. This is not a prison, after all, and with the Christmas Eve revellers due in at any minute we haven't got time to hunt for wayward patients.'

'Shall I give his wife a ring, see if he's arrived home?'

'Only if you've got a minute. I know I won't have.'

She waddled off, puffing, having made that last comment sound admonishing. Nurse Fenton stuck her tongue out at Sister's back. If she was quick she could call the Sterlands now ... but just then Mrs Laverton in Bed 4 began feebly to request her assistance. Maybe later, she thought, but she was still thinking the same thing at three o'clock in the morning when the demands for her attention finally began to abate. She felt guilty, but not as guilty as she would feel in three days' time when she read about Bob Sterland in the *Starmouth Gazette*. Despite telling herself it was not her fault, she would be unable to help feeling at least partly responsible for the terrible things he had done.

When the knock came on the front door, Kim was sprawled on the settee, watching *The Terminator* on BBC 2. It was now ten o'clock. At nine-thirty, Aunty Claire's boyfriend, Dave, had rung, and Kim had heard his tinny voice over the telephone demanding, 'Are we going for this meal or what?' Though Aunty Claire had assured Dave she would be home in ten minutes, she had stuck around for at least another twenty, fussing over Mum and the baby, making sure they were all right and had everything they needed. Kim thought that Mum was quite relieved when Aunty Claire finally left. She told Kim she was tired, and that she was going to take the baby upstairs and lie down for a while.

Kim was quite disappointed to have his new sister taken away from him, but he just nodded and said, 'Okay.' Though *The Terminator* was a film he had been wanting to see for ages (Phil Wallace had seen it on video and had described it as 'totally excellent'), Kim found he was having trouble concentrating on the action. He kept thinking how momentous this day had been, how amazing it was to have a little sister. The spectacle of Arnold Schwarzenegger slaughtering the entire clientele of a nightclub with a machine gun seemed petty and unreal.

He did not mind, therefore, dragging himself off the settee to answer the front door. He wondered who'd be calling at this time of night. He was reaching out for the handle before he realised it might be the police. He'd lied to his mum about Phil's granddad's garage wall; what in fact had resulted in him having green and yellow hands had been the painting of a dragon that he, Phil and Rod had been doing on the back wall of the primary school. He rubbed his hands together now fruitlessly; it would be a few days yet before the evidence began to fade. He ought to be more careful, use methods other than his hands to block off colour. He'd heard of being caught red-handed but this was ridiculous.

Sidling up to the door he put his eye to the peep-hole. The image on the other side startled him at first. It looked like a deformed vicar with a vast white collar. The figure blinked and swayed as though drunk. Kim suddenly realised, not entirely joyfully, that it was his father.

He unlocked the door and pulled it open. His father immediately snapped alert, though seemed to look straight through Kim as if he wasn't there. His swollen lips opened then closed; his bruised and battered face made his expression inscrutable. Kim had the sneaking suspicion that his father didn't recognise him. 'Dad, hi,' he said as a prompt.

His father didn't reply. He swayed to the right, brought his hands up to the doorframe to steady himself, and suddenly Kim noticed something that sent a cold spasm of shock through his stomach. His father's hands were covered with fresh blood. Kim looked beyond his father, and caught the barest glimpse of something green and shimmering sprawled in the front garden, half-concealed by the hedge. Then his father was pushing him back as he forced his way into the house, slamming the door behind him.

Kim backed away, disbelief pounding into his skull like nails. 'Aunty Claire?' he tried to say, but his mouth was so dry it felt glued shut. His father moved methodically, unconcernedly, like a machine. He twisted the key in the

51

front door, then pulled it from its slot and pocketed it. Kim just stood there, rooted by shock, as his father strode past him and into the kitchen.

When he heard his father yanking open drawers, making cutlery rattle, he began to tremble. As though in slow motion, feeling sick inside, he drifted over to the telephone. He reached for the receiver with fingers that felt nerveless as sausages. Then he heard a sound behind him and whirled round.

Bob had reappeared noiselessly and was now standing less than six feet away, holding the largest carving knife the Sterlands owned loosely in his right hand. Kim looked into his eyes and saw no warmth, no reason, saw only empty cold whirlpools, sucking everything that made sense into a formless black void where nothing worked.

'Dad,' Kim mouthed. The word that emerged was less than a whisper. 'Dad, what are you doing?'

Bob's cold, dead gaze focused on Kim, then flickered slowly down to the boy's hands. When he saw the paint on them his face became instantly, terrifyingly bestial.

'Dad, no!' Kim screeched as his father lunged for him. He jumped back, saw the knife slice through the place where his head had been a split second before, then he turned and fled.

With a howl, Bob launched himself in pursuit. Kim screamed so hard he tasted blood in his throat. Dad had suddenly become his every video nightmare rolled into one: Freddy Krueger, Jason Voorhees, Michael Myers. Kim glimpsed the flash of the knife as it arced towards him, and panic enabled him to put on an extra spurt of speed. If Bob had not been hampered by his injuries he would have caught his son easily. Kim screeched '*Muuuummmmm!*' and leaped at the stairs.

He bounded up them two, three at a time. His mother suddenly appeared on the landing just above him, clutching the baby, looking pale, confused, frightened.

'Kim, what's the matter?' she said. Kim glanced at her and saw her eyes widen as she looked behind him. '*Bob, no!*' she screamed.

It was that glance which probably saved Kim's life. He

threw himself forward onto the top step and rolled over. The knife thudded into the stair carpet, barely an inch from Kim's thigh. As his father loomed over him, Kim kicked out with his legs, a panic reflex. His right foot smashed into the centre of his dad's face. Though Bob's head snapped back, blood spurting from reopened wounds, Kim felt as though he'd kicked an iron post.

Bob pinwheeled his arms, but he couldn't keep his balance. Kim closed his eyes as his father fell backwards down the stairs. His body sounded as though someone was destroying the banisters with a sledgehammer. His mother was screaming, and Kim wished she'd stop. She'd deafen the baby, or terrify her, or both.

He opened his eyes and saw his father sprawled motionless in a star shape at the bottom of the stairs, covered with debris. Using arms that felt shaky as old age, Kim hauled himself onto the landing and tried to stand up. His leg hurt terribly; when he put weight on it, it flared in agony, making him cry out. His mother was quietening a little now, clutching the baby to her. The baby was blinking and mewling, wriggling a little in her arms.

'We've got to get help,' Kim said. 'You stay here, I'll ring the police.' Holding onto the banister he began to limp down the stairs.

Hilary shot out an arm and grabbed her son's wrist. 'What are you doing?' she demanded. 'You can't go down there. What if he wakes up?'

'The phone's down there,' Kim said. 'I don't think he'll wake up, Mum. I'll take this just in case.'

He curled his hand around the handle of the knife that was embedded in the stair carpet and tugged, but the knife wouldn't come free. Kim shuddered at the force his father must have used to drive it so deep.

'There's a phone in the bedroom,' Hilary said. 'Why don't you use that one?'

Kim looked at her. His mind was so scrambled with panic that he'd forgotten about that. He nodded and hauled himself back up the stairs. Led by his mother he limped towards her bedroom at the end of the landing. Just before entering he glanced down at his father's body. It was still motionless, limbs so splayed that it resembled a mannequin more than a human being.

When he entered the bedroom his mother was standing by the telephone on the bedside table as though keeping guard. Unbelievably the baby had fallen asleep again. Kim's bad leg was making him feel sick. He dropped onto the bed gratefully and snatched the receiver from its cradle. His finger had already dialled two 9s before he realised. He held the receiver away from him and looked at it incredulously, as if it had changed into a carrot before his eyes.

'It's dead,' he said, looking up at his mother. 'Dad must have cut the wires before he came in.'

'Oh no.' Hilary's body seemed to sag. She rocked the baby as if it needed comforting. 'What are we going to do?'

Kim was just as scared as Hilary, but his fear was forcing his mind to work, to race through alternatives. He crossed to the window and peered out. All that confronted him was a sheer brick wall, a twenty-foot drop onto a crazy paving path. He felt despair rising in him and gulped it down like nasty medicine. There was only one thing to do − sneak down the stairs, step over his father's body and escape via the back door in the kitchen. He outlined his plan briefly to his mum. She didn't like it but she had to agree. There was simply no alternative.

Kim led the way back onto the landing, senses alert. The house was quiet, apart from the squealing roar of a car chase caged within the TV. Kim crossed the landing and peered over the banister. Instantly a wave of terror, awful and absolute, coursed through him. He managed to turn his head and look at his mother. He tried to speak but his brain, his vocal cords, his entire head felt locked in ice.

'What is it?' Her voice rose in panic with each syllable, her son's fear infecting her. She stumbled forward, face creasing at the razor of pain between her legs. She looked over the banister.

'Oh God,' she whispered.

Bob was gone. Where he had lain were only bits of broken banister and a smeary pool of blood in the shape of Africa. Kim looked around and saw that the knife which had been embedded in the stairs was gone too. He tried to force his

54

mind to work, to decide on the best course of action. For now he and his mum had a clear run at the stairs. Could they risk it? Or was Dad lying in wait for them somewhere along the way?

Kim leaned over the banister as far as he could, craning his neck. He could not see his father anywhere. Maybe he had gone away, or even passed out again. Certainly there was nothing to be gained from waiting here. He explained this to his mum. She looked terrified, but nodded. They began to creep along the landing, both wincing at their own separate hurts. Kim winced too every time the floorboards creaked. In the quiet house, the tiny sounds of bending wood were like the bellowing blares of a Klaxon.

They were over halfway along the landing, only a few feet from the head of the stairs, when the door at the end of the landing crashed open. It was the bathroom door. Framed there was a monster that resembled Bob Sterland barely at all. Its face was a glistening mask of gore, its hair standing up in clotted spikes. Its eyes were black and dead like a shark's, its bared teeth slick with a pink froth of blood and saliva. Its shirtfront was a bib of red; dangling in its right hand, pointing at the floor, was the carving knife. It took a shaky step forward, and its hand came up until the knife was level with its face.

'Bob.' Hilary's voice was a pleading cat's mew. 'Please, Bob. Please.'

Bob took another step forward, then another. Deliberate. Slow. Robotic. He blinked blood from his eyes, swayed as if about to collapse. Then he recovered and took another step closer. He was no more than eight feet away.

Kim tugged at his mother's arm. 'Come on, Mum, in here.' He pulled her, limping, into his own bedroom and slammed the door. There was no escape, not really, but they couldn't just stand there and wait to be butchered. Hilary was wailing now, great racking sobs convulsing her body. In her arms the baby slept, oblivious.

In the split second before his father opened the door, Kim looked around for a weapon and couldn't find one. And then the handle jerked, the door swung back, and here he was, the mad slasher from a thousand drive-in movies come true. Hilary screamed. The baby woke up and began to cry. Kim positioned himself before his mother and the two of them began to back away.

Kim knew there was nowhere to go. Once they reached the wall that was it. He was so scared he couldn't even scream or cry. His father advanced unsteadily. His surgical collar, streaked with blood, resembled a carapace of exposed bone, the suggestion of a protective exo-skeleton like the thing in *Alien*. His dad's face was so mashed and covered in blood that individual features were almost indiscernible. He was not even showing his teeth any more, which made it look as though his mouth was gone.

Kim was just building up the courage to fly at his father, make a suicidal attempt to wrestle the knife from him, when his bad leg caught the sharp edge of the bedframe. The pain was so severe it was like being hamstrung. He howled, his knee buckled, and he fell onto his backside. Fresh pain flared at the base of his spine. Hilary screamed again as Bob made a gurgling sound of triumph and loped towards Kim's sprawled body.

Frantically Kim tried to crawl under his bed, but the space was too tight and there was too much debris under there. His hand closed around something metal. He drew it out. It was one of his spray-paint cans. Desperately he hurled it as his father. Bob barely flinched as the can rebounded off his shoulder. Kim drew out another can, this one heavier, almost full. He was about to throw it when a better idea struck him. He pointed it at his dad's face and pressed down hard on the spray-head.

A filmy jet of bright green paint leaped from the nozzle. It mingled with the blood on Bob's face, making him more hideous than ever. He looked like a zombie now, a car crash victim come alive, rot sliding down his face with the seepage from open wounds. Kim gritted his teeth and sprayed the paint directly into his father's eyes. Bob screamed and reeled back, like Frankenstein's monster scorched with flame.

As Bob staggered about the room, Kim dragged himself painfully to his feet. His mum had fallen silent and was simply staring at his dad with wide open eyes. Her mouth was open too, locked in a stillborn scream. The baby in her arms was struggling, uncomfortable in its mother's overtight grip.

'Come on, Mum,' Kim said, 'let's go now,' He took her arm, the muscles of which were rigid as a bodybuilder's. When he pulled at her, her eyes flickered and focused on him. Shuffling, face blank, she allowed herself to be led.

Bob was crouched on the floor, hands working at his eyes, trying to rub the stinging blindness away. The knife was by his side. Kim darted forward and snatched it up. He propelled his mother as fast as their injuries would allow out of the room, closing the door behind them. It was only when they were out of the house and Kim had pulled the kitchen door shut behind them, that he finally allowed himself to cry.

Bob saw the moon first, a slice of light which penetrated the black burning of his vision. But it was not a good light. It was sickly and evil, green as decay. His eyes still smarted, weeping tears, but little by little the world was coming back to him. As it did so he knew he had lost and he wished he had been blinded after all. The evil was everywhere, crawling over every surface. Bob held up his hands and saw they were thick with it, sticky and burning like fire. His heart was racing in his chest, threatening to burst, each rapid pump a stab of pain. He blundered to his feet, head spinning, knowing that the poison was already raging through his system.

He had lost. *Lost.* The notion was almost too colossal to accept. As he rose his reflection rose too, in a mirror across the room, confronting him.

'No,' Bob murmured, 'no.' Something flexed inside him, the last of his control, and then suddenly, shockingly, broke. *'No!'* he screamed. *'Noooooo!'* He ran full-tilt at the mirror and hurled himself towards it head-first.

The din of shattering glass was accompanied by a hot, pure pain that Bob almost revelled in. He was hoping it would be the last pain, the end pain, but it subsided all too quickly. His shattered thoughts swam like confused fish in his mind. His vision was a boiling kaleidoscope of green and red. Something glinted. Light. A promise of salvation.

Bob snatched at the light, swept it up. It was a triangle of glass. Ignoring the jagged edges, the slivers that cut through his skin and embedded themselves in the soft meat of his palm, he began to hack at his face, trying to remove the mask of evil. It was no good. The evil had sunk deep, like water into a sponge; even now he could feel it working its way to his core. If it took over his soul then he too was lost, would be in thrall to it forever.

Squirming, he hauled himself across the carpet of broken glass to the window. The evil moon leered at him, taunting him with its victory. Bob shook his head, moaning his defiance. He raised his arm, hand flopping onto the bar that secured the window, trying to lift it. Pain screamed in every muscle, the evil trying to dominate him. Bob felt something give and the window swung open. A freezing wind swept in, stinking of decay.

With a gargantuan effort Bob hauled himself onto the windowsill. The world was careering, spinning round and round, but Bob held on, refusing to be disoriented. His upper body was out of the window now. He kicked his legs, and suddenly he was falling. As the wind rushed past, the rags of his blindness were torn away and all at once he could see clearly. He screamed, but the trap was sprung, there was no going back.

The green man, waiting below, raised its arms to catch him.

The Fertilizer Man

Tosho leaned on his spade and looked out over his allotment with satisfaction, his old back throbbing with a steady pain. Two hours ago the allotment had been a weed-clogged patch of tired grey earth, but now the soil was rich, dark, moist — perfect for vegetables. He swept off his cap and wiped his forehead with a grimy sleeve, his face red and shiny. Digging over the allotment had been a slog, especially for a man his age, but Tosho didn't mind. He came from a family to whom the work ethic was important as mother's milk.

He looked up, past the allotments, past the council estate, to the squared-off peaks of the tower blocks beyond. That was the trouble with young people today, he thought; no moral fibre. Too many of them sat in offices, typing out reports that no one ever read, breathing air out of packets. He shook his head sadly. That wasn't the way to live, was it? God didn't create the land so that people could rot their lives away in office blocks.

He pulled open his shed door, making a mental note to oil the creaking hinges, and placed his muddy spade carefully on a sheet of newspaper in the corner. He stretched his stubby limbs, clenched and unclenched his meaty hands. His body had been locked into a digging position and he groaned as he straightened up, spine crackling.

The sound of approaching voices caused him to look out of his shed window. A group of teenagers, six or seven of them, were clambering over the gate that led into the allotments. They were looking furtively around, sniggering, putting their fingers to their lips. Their leader was tall and thin and wore a leather jacket. He had sharp nipped features as though someone had taken a long piece of white plasticine, pinched out a nose, and made the eyes and mouth with three strokes of a needle. A greasy quiff flopped over his forehead. He said something to the others and they laughed obediently. He led them to a greenhouse, said something else, and pointed at the ground. Immediately two of the boys stooped and began to pull small half-grown carrots from the earth. The thin boy went into the greenhouse where Tosho could see him through the glass, stuffing his jacket with tomatoes, jerking them off their plants with easy, languid movements, all the time his weasel-like face holding an arrogant leer.

Tosho felt a black wave of rage engulfing him. His chest constricted into bitter knots, his temples throbbed with anger. He snatched up his spade and yanked open the door.

'What the bloody hell do you think you're up to?' he bellowed. He clenched the spade firmly in both hands and lumbered towards them.

Heads snapped up. The two boys who had been stealing carrots dropped their loads and bolted away like startled rabbits.

'Come back here, you little buggers!' Tosho shouted, but at the sound of his voice the boys simply increased speed, leaped over the wooden gate with a fear-spurred agility and disappeared up the road. Angrily Tosho turned his attention to the other boys clustered around the greenhouse. One of them was shouting into the greenhouse whilst the others stood, fidgeting nervously, not daring to leave without their leader.

'I'll have you, you buggers!' yelled Tosho, picking his way carefully between the even rows of vegetables. The tall thin boy with the weaselly face emerged from the greenhouse, laden down with tomatoes. He looked unconcernedly in Tosho's direction, then began to stroll nonchalantly towards the gate, the other boys falling into step behind him. They tried to imitate their leader's arrogant swagger but were given away by their jerky movements and occasional backward glances. Tosho was still some way off and knew he could not catch them before they reached the gate, so, frustrated, he resorted to the next best thing — verbal threats.

'You just come back here, you bloody hooligans! I'll tan your bloody hides for you!'

The thin boy stopped, turned slowly, and regarded Tosho through slitty eyes. Apart from his perpetual leer his face revealed nothing. Then he mockingly raised a hand and jabbed a two-fingered gesture in Tosho's direction. 'Piss off, you senile old bastard,' he called in a thin whining voice. His words were met with a stringy burst of nervous laughter from the other boys. They crowded round their leader like baby chicks round a mother hen, watching Tosho warily. After a moment the thin boy jerked his head and they began to stroll away.

Tosho, watching them, was speechless with rage. His face and neck flushed a livid red, and for a moment he was so angry that he couldn't move. Then a strangled cry erupted from his vocal cords, he waved the spade in an arc above his head, and he charged, his anger making him oblivious to what lay beneath his feet.

The boys scattered for the gate, leaving a trail of tomatoes and carrots behind them. One by one they vaulted over it, stopping briefly on the other side to jeer at their pursuer before disappearing out of sight round the corner of the road.

Tosho thumped to a stop like a huge clockwork caveman. His anger seethed and bubbled impotently. His heart was thumping much too quickly, causing a biting pain in his chest. He suddenly felt very weary and the spade in his hands seemed to have become much heavier. He stared at the spot where the boys had disappeared but found it difficult to focus. Unpleasant cactus shapes blinked behind his eyelids in a red and green swarm.

'Are you all right, sir?'

The voice startled Tosho and he whirled round. A tall man in his thirties, wearing an immaculate business suit, was standing directly behind him. The man had chiselled tanned features, beautifully groomed hair and perfectly polished shoes. A slim briefcase was tucked neatly under his arm. Tosho gaped stupidly at him for a moment, mouth opening and closing like a worried goldfish. Where had the man come from? The allotments covered a large flat area and there was absolutely no way he could have crept up without Tosho knowing about it. It was as though he had suddenly popped up from the ground like a subterranean jack-in-the-box.

One of the man's perfectly shaped eyebrows raised a little. He had a friendly, yet strangely immobile face. 'Are you quite all right?' he repeated.

'Yes ... yes ... I, er ... just those bloody kids,' mumbled Tosho. His body drooped as the rage ebbed from him.

'I saw the whole thing. Perfectly dreadful,' said the man. He stretched out a supporting hand to steady Tosho's swaying body. His grip closed like a clamp around Tosho's forearm and he steered him effortlessly back to the shed. Once there, he went inside and reappeared with a wooden box which he set down on the ground. Tosho thanked him and sank onto it gratefully.

'Do you know who those boys were?' asked the man.

'Yes ... that is, I've seen them around. They're always in bother. Just a bunch of bloody troublemakers.' Tosho looked up as a thought struck him. 'You aren't from the police, are you?'

The man smiled and shook his head. 'I'm afraid not, sir,' he replied in his deep melodious tones. 'I am a salesman.'

'A salesman?' echoed Tosho, baffled. He looked at the man's shoes. He found it faintly disturbing that not a trace of mud was present on either.

'Indeed, sir,' replied the man, flashing a professional smile. His teeth were pure white and very straight.

'But ... but what do you sell?' Tosho enquired. It struck him that he wasn't particularly interested, but something about the man's manner had compelled him to ask the question. The man leaned a little closer and his smile widened. Tosho recoiled slightly. He felt uncomfortable and decided it was because of the man's eyes. They were very dark, almost black, and they were scrutinising him with an hypnotic unblinking steadiness.

'Let me show you an example,' said the man. He opened his briefcase, took out a white cardboard packet and handed it to Tosho. Tosho took it automatically and began to read the lettering on the front: *Gro-fast Fertilizer – Amazing*

64

Results Guaranteed. The rest of the lettering was too small for Tosho to make out without his glasses. He looked up, bewildered.

'Fertilizer?' he said.

'And a variety of other agricultural products,' replied the man smoothly. 'But this is our latest item. It is a specially formulated concentration of elements guaranteed to enrich the soil and produce the healthiest vegetables possible.'

Tosho frowned, suspicious. The man's wide smile was beginning to irritate him. 'How come I've never seen none of this in the shops?' he asked, matching the man's steady gaze with an accusatory one of his own. The man's face never altered.

'Normally we deal in bulk orders,' he explained, 'but this fertilizer is still in something of an experimental stage. We therefore decided to start by giving free samples to a number of accommodating landowners. To judge its progress and effectiveness, as it were.'

A small bell tinkled happily in Tosho's mind at the magic words 'free samples', and his red face crinkled into a friendly beam.

'I'll tell you what, mister,' he began in a manner that suggested he was doing the other a great favour, 'I'll take one of them free samples and put it on me own allotment. I don't mind doing some of your experimenting for you.'

The man nodded graciously. 'Thank you, sir,' he replied humbly, 'that would be most kind.'

'Wait on, though,' said Tosho as a possible loophole occurred to him, 'what if this stuff ruins me crop? I'll want compensation.'

'Absolutely no problem, sir. In such an eventuality you would receive the highest market value for all produce spoiled. Here is a guarantee.' The man unsnapped the catches on his briefcase, opened it no more than a few centimetres and withdrew a sheet of paper which he handed to Tosho. 'If you have any complaints whatsoever, don't hesitate to get in touch.'

Tosho glanced briefly at the sheet of paper, then folded it and shoved it into the pocket of his worn ill-fitting jacket. 'Well, thank you very much. Very kind, I'm sure,' he said.

'Not at all, sir,' replied the man smoothly. He looked up at the sky as though gauging the time by the sun, then said, 'Well, I must be going, though I shall call by again presently. Goodbye.' He extended a brown hand with elegantly manicured fingernails. Tosho shook it tentatively. The man's hand was pleasantly warm and his grip was firm. With a final smile he turned and strode away.

Tosho watched him until he disappeared behind a hedge, and then examined the box of fertilizer the man had given him. He ripped off the corner of the cardboard top and upended the box into his palm. A fine reddish powder trickled out. Tosho sifted it with his forefinger, then held it up to his nose and sniffed. Funny-looking stuff, he thought; almost like flour but red instead of white. He fetched his spectacles from the shed and read the instructions carefully. PLANT VEGETABLES AS NORMAL, THEN SPRINKLE LIBERALLY WITH GRO-FAST FERTILIZER. ALLOW TIME FOR FERTILIZER TO ABSORB INTO SOIL BEFORE WATERING. Tosho was a little disappointed. Was that all? Despite the fact that the box had been a gift, he couldn't help feeling somehow cheated.

He spent the rest of the day planting seeds in his newly dug garden. His mouth watered as he thought of the potatoes, carrots, peas, radishes, onions and other vegetables he would be bringing home in the following months. Vegetables always tasted much better when you grew them yourself, he always said, and this year looked as though it was going to be particularly good.

When the seeds had been planted, Tosho used the new fertilizer on them. He ripped open the packet and sprinkled the red dust over the earth with a heavy hand. It lay on the soil like a blanket of blood, and then as Tosho watched it seemed to mingle with the earth and become absorbed into it; actually seemed to become one with the soil. He was amazed. He had never seen anything like it! The fertilizer seemed to enrich and nourish the soil, gave it a red healthy sheen that caused it to stand out amongst the neighbouring plots of earth, even the most carefully tended of which looked dull

66

and sterile by comparison. Tosho was well pleased. If the stuff worked as well on vegetables as it did on the soil, he was in with a chance of making a clean sweep of the prizes in the vegetable section of that year's local Horticultural Society Show.

He whistled with the joy of a highly satisfied man as he pushed his old wheelbarrow into the shed at the end of the day. He was always reluctant to leave his allotment, but it was getting dark and he didn't want to be late for his supper. Besides, he was looking forward to boasting about his new wonder fertilizer to his mates in the local that evening. He locked the shed door and set off home, still whistling. By now the distressing episode with the boys that morning had slipped completely from his mind.

Colin Deakin remembered though. He was not too clever when it came to remembering historical dates or mathematical equations, but those people who had crossed him were meticulously filed away in his mind under the heading 'Hit List', and Tosho was one of those people. It was Tosho's fault that Deakin had not bought the motorbike that afternoon. It was Tosho's fault that that smarmy git in the showroom had sold it to someone else.

Deakin had needed those tomatoes: all of them. He had planned to nick enough vegetables from the allotments to raise a tenner down at the market. That was all he'd needed for the bike. Ten more fucking lousy quid. But now, because of that stupid interfering old bastard, he'd lost the chance to buy the machine he'd had his eye on for weeks.

Deakin wouldn't stand for that; he'd show that old shit. He got out of bed and quietly opened a drawer. Everyone was asleep by now and he didn't want to wake them. He took a black T-shirt, black jeans, black boots and black gloves from the drawer and pulled them over his pasty frame. He slicked his hair back out of habit with a few practised flicks of his oily comb and zipped up his leather jacket. Silent as sleep he went downstairs, furtively unlocked the front door, and crept out into the night. He headed towards the allotments, keeping to the darkest corners, sliding from wall to wall like a leather-clad eel. Finally he reached the gate over which he and his mates had jumped that morning.

His cruel pinched features surveyed the surrounding landscape. Satisfied that no one was around, he climbed nimbly over the gate. There were no street lamps here, and it took Deakin a moment for his eyes to become accustomed to the gloom, though fortunately the moon provided an ice-cold light. Other moons slithered over the greenhouses, pools of white seemingly trapped within the glass.

Deakin crept cautiously over the uneven ground. Here and there were small fences, little more than twine stretched between stakes hammered into the ground. In the half-light they were difficult to see, and Deakin had to move slowly to avoid tripping over them. Tosho's allotment lay over the far side, and the teenager cursed the old man every muddy inch of the way.

He was within thirty yards of the allotment when he suddenly stopped. Had he heard something? He strained his ears to listen, but all he could hear was the faint sound of a car receding into the distance somewhere. He was about to continue forward when he heard it again – the bump and thud of clumsy movement from somewhere in front of him.

Deakin dropped to his knees and became perfectly still, merging with the darkness. Squinting ahead he thought he could see a dim shape moving around near the old man's shed. Surely the old git wasn't senile enough to stay here until this late at night? Deakin peeled back his sleeve and looked at the watch he had stolen from Woolworth's: twelve twenty-three. He shuffled on all fours to a nearby hedge so that his black silhouette would not be seen against the silvery glow of the sky, and stood up slowly. He peered through the gloom towards Tosho's shed.

There *was* something moving about down there. It seemed to be scuffling around with weird jerky movements. But all Deakin could make of it was a vague white shape, like someone crawling on all fours.

He was intrigued, and a little scared, though he would not have admitted that to anyone. He crept closer, his body feeling as though it had seized into a taut knot of muscle, making his movements stiff and unnatural. He clenched his fists tightly and tried to blot out his unease. He saw the vague white shape bobbing through the air and round the side of the shed, out of sight. Somehow, not being able to see the shape made Deakin feel worse, not better.

He noticed a rake with a broken handle leaning against a wooden box and snatched it up. Immediately a feeling of security swept over him. He always felt strong and powerful with a weapon to hide behind. He picked his way over to the shed and tiptoed stealthily around its side, raising the rake slowly like an executioner with his axe. His jawbone was clenching and unclenching in an effort to keep the saliva from drying in his mouth. Though he was scared he was also angry. What was frightening about a white blob that moved in the darkness? he thought, and the answer came: Nothing, nothing at all. Yet despite his logic the fear was there, like an anvil in his chest, and it wouldn't go away.

There was nothing round the side of the shed. Nothing, that is, except ground and weeds and the shed wall, all cut into harsh black and white tones by the cast of the moon. Deakin realised he had been holding his breath and exhaled slowly. The uneven ground, dotted here and there with the occasional greenhouse or garden shed, stretched silently to the tall hedge which bordered the allotments. There were no white shapes bobbing in the darkness, and there were no thuds of movement either. Deakin smiled, stepped forward – and his foot plunged into empty space. As he began to fall he instinctively jammed the end of the rake into the earth to steady himself, but his ankle twisted and he crashed to the ground.

He lay for a moment, panting, his body jarred by the fall and his right foot dangling in space. His thoughts were wild and illogical. It was as though someone had snatched away a plug of reality from beneath his foot, leaving a rent full of nothingness. He pushed himself slowly upwards, wincing at the pain in his bruised ribs and ankle. He lifted his right foot gingerly out of the hole he had stepped into, stood up and brushed himself down. The hole was about three feet in diameter and seemed to tunnel under the shed wall. Deakin examined it curiously.

It looked like a foxhole, or ... or ... It came to him suddenly. A badger's set! Was that what he had seen in the darkness — a badger? Deakin pushed the end of the rake into the hole to see how far down it went. The hole was deep, plunging about five feet before curving round under the shed wall. It must be a bloody big badger, Deakin thought. Why, he could probably crawl through that tunnel himself.

Curiosity was getting the better of him now. He decided to have a look in the shed, see how big the badger really was. He had never seen a badger before, but he had heard they were vicious bastards if cornered. Gripping the rake and steeling himself, Deakin kicked at the lock on the shed door.

It wasn't quite as ramshackle as it looked and his pinched features creased as the impact caused pain to spear up through his bad ankle. Furthermore, the noise that his boot made on the wood was amplified by the stillness of the night, so much so that Deakin was sure the vibrations could be felt throughout the neighbourhood. He stood for a moment and listened, but heard nothing. Satisfied that his attack on the door had gone undetected he tried again. This time he hooked the end of the rake through the rusty padlock, stood round the corner of the shed, and heaved on the protruding end of the rake. Bit by bit the screws parted from the wood and eventually the entire lock came away with a tearing sound. The shed door swung open.

Deakin peered into the building, wrinkling his nose at the musty smell. Moonlight filtered through the grime on the tiny window, enabling him to make out a few vague shapes. There was a workbench along one wall, stacked with flowerpots, tools, and some small bags of weed killer. Larger tools such as rakes and spades hung on hooks on the opposite wall. Tucked in one corner was a wheelbarrow piled high with weeds. Although the shed was relatively small, the clutter provided ample room in which an animal could conceal itself. Deakin took a few cautious steps inside. He had a sudden uncomfortable feeling that eyes were watching him, sheltered in the blackness.

'Come out, you fucking rodent,' he hissed, jabbing savagely at a black bulky object in the darkness. His fear fed the flames of his anger. His voice rose. *'I fucking said come out!'*

He began to sweep the rake about like a practising swordsman, prodding and slicing into every possible hiding place. It was unnerving that there were so many pockets of darkness in such a tiny area. Suddenly Deakin heard a minute sound, like something pressing itself back into the shadows, and he stopped dead, listening. The sound was coming from somewhere in front of him.

He extended the rake with excruciating slowness. His muscles felt bunched and cramped in his body as though gathering themselves for action. The rake-head touched something solid; something that gave a small grunt of surprise; something that began to move!

Deakin felt the rake suddenly wrenched from his hands. He staggered backwards, aware of a shape looming from the darkness, reaching for him. He plunged out of the shed doorway, grabbed the edge of the wooden door which was swinging gently on its hinges, and slammed it shut. He held it closed with one hand and looked desperately around for something to wedge it. After a moment he heard movement again from within, then a burrowing sound. Curiously he put his ear to the door, but just at that moment the burrowing stopped. Deakin held his breath – and heard the soft pad of footsteps behind him. He had forgotten about the hole. *Oh God, oh God.* His spit congealed into a golf ball as he turned to face whatever it was that had come out of the shed.

It was a man. Just a man, Deakin thought, just a man. But the man was naked, and even in this light Deakin could see that his body was perfectly smooth and hairless, and where his genitals should be there was only a small mound of smooth, unbroken skin.

The teenager began to back away on rickety, spent legs. The man's handsome regular features were fixed in an immobile grin. His teeth gleamed white, his hair – despite his crawl through the tunnel – was beautifully groomed.

In his hand he carried a spade.

Deakin turned and tried to run. His insides seemed to slacken and slosh in his body. His foot caught on

71

something and he tripped and fell face-down into the mud, his gloved palms making a pitiful, hopeless smack as they hit the ground. He raised his head, his long face very white through the clumps of soil that clung to it. The man was stationary, hefting the spade in his hand.

Deakin's foot still rested on the half-buried log he had tripped over. With the intense horror of nightmare he suddenly felt the log squirm beneath him. He looked down and his mouth opened in a soundless scream. It wasn't a log at all; it was a human arm, and it was breaking through the soil of the ground like some gruesome plant. Deakin's thin lips began to form a silent word, *No*, over and over again. He looked up desperately at the white orb of the moon and his face crumbled into tears.

The soil seethed beneath Deakin, and another arm began to break free from the earth. Before he could move, the hand on the arm flexed, then whipped forward and grabbed his ankle. Deakin began to scream and thrash about but the hand simply tightened its grip.

Alerted by the struggle, the man with the spade jerked into motion again. Unhurriedly he strode towards Deakin's writhing form. Deakin's last sight before he blacked out was the man standing astride him, his perfect white teeth gleaming in the light of the moon.

Slowly, still smiling, the man raised the spade as though he was about to chop through something.

Which he did.

Very early the next morning, someone could be seen picking his way through the allotments: a tall man wearing an immaculate suit. He was the man Tosho had met just the day before — the fertilizer salesman.

Unhurriedly the fertilizer salesman made his way over to Tosho's shed, a vague smile on his handsome face. In his hand was a large trunk which he carried with effortless ease. He noted the broken padlock on the shed door and nodded in satisfaction. He opened the door and went inside.

Twelve heads turned as one. Twelve identical handsome faces smiled at him. The fertilizer salesman set the trunk down on the shed floor and opened the lid.

Inside were twelve brand new suits, just like his own.

Progeny

I miss you, Dora. I miss you so much. Why did it have to happen like this?

His first sensation was of an incredible lightness, as though, for him alone, gravity had lessened. He was vaguely aware of the floor below him, but had to concentrate hard before he had any perception of his own feet touching that floor. Even then he seemed ephemeral, as though he were suspended from the ceiling and could reach the ground only with his tiptoes. The room at first was like something in a dream: an impression. Something flimsy and insubstantial, like a hastily constructed set. Unpainted. Undetailed.

Gradually, however, a focus established itself. A bed. And, more importantly, the girl *in* the bed. He immediately felt guilt, shame, fear. At the sight of her solemnly sleeping face, her blonde hair spread over the pillow like a princess's, he felt anguish grip him. Seeing her like this, so serene, appeared to indicate that she had not been traumatised by what she had been through. Nevertheless he knew that she was changed. Irrevocably. Somewhere deep inside. He had seen the evidence, suffered it every day. They shared the scars, the hurt, the ever-booming echo of that dreadful, mindless moment.

The dependence. The incapacitation. That was the second thing he noticed. It had gone. All gone. Yet it seemed as though he was nothing but ... but an outline. A shell. Full of emptiness.

His brain, his mind, whatever it was up there, sent a

77

message to his arm, told him to raise it. Methodically he imagined the procedure, the arm coming up, the fingers straightening. His eyes (he must have eyes; he could see, couldn't he?) looked at the place where the arm should be. There was no sense of strain in the eyes, no foggy patina of approaching cataracts as there had been previously.

And yes, he *could* see the arm. Dimly, hazily, but it was there, wasn't it?

Well, wasn't it?

His uncertainty troubled him. Why did he feel so strange? He let the arm drop — or at least he thought he did. (The instant he stopped thinking about it, the arm seemed to . . . to go away. To be discarded. To . . . to . . . to dissolve?)

I don't think, therefore I may not be.

Sudden anger. The girl in the bed. She was the important one, not his bloody arm. He wasn't here to establish the fact of his own existence.

So what *was* he here for? What was he supposed to do? Surely not that? No, please God, he wouldn't. He just wanted all this to end. He'd rather die before he put her through that again.

I know what you think of me, Rachel, and I only wish that I could use my voice, or even hold a pen, that I could communicate my regret to you in some way. The last ten years have been hell, partly because of my situation but largely because I can see how it's eating you up, growing and blackening inside you, mutilating your mind. I never meant to do what I did, Rachel. You must believe that, though I know you never will. If only you could read my thoughts. If only I could talk to you. Just ten minutes, that's all I would ask for. I would give my life for just ten minutes of articulation.

Don't you think I've asked myself over and over again why I did it? Well I have. And each time I come up with the same answer — I just don't know. It happened, that's all, it just seemed to progress naturally, which in a way is the most horrifying thing of all. I was perfectly sane, perfectly clear-headed, or at least I thought I was. Mind you, they say the mad always think they're sane, don't they? It's only the sane who worry that they might be going crazy.

All I would like to do, Rachel, is to give you my version of what happened that day, to take you through it step by step. I wouldn't ask you to condone what I did, or even to understand it. I would just ask you to listen to me, that's all, to listen to my side of things. Maybe it would help, I don't know. Or maybe nothing would change. If I could go back and make things different, I would. Believe me, I would.

This is how it happened. I took you out around twelve, twelve-thirty that day. It was a sunny day and I was as happy as I could be under the circumstances. I know it seems that I planned it all from the start, but it's not true, Rachel, you must believe that. If you think I planned it, then it makes me a bigger monster than I already am, but nothing could have been further from my mind, *nothing*, and that's God's honest truth. So what *were* you thinking about? I hear you ask. Just how *did* you feel?

Well, like I say, happy enough. Just being with you made me feel that way, and there's nothing to be ashamed of in that. I loved your innocence, your exuberance. You didn't exactly make me feel young (in fact you quite exhausted me sometimes), but you made me feel as though the *world* was still young, as though there were still wonders in it, wonders that only children could see.

I suppose you reminded me of *my* childhood. Yes, that's it, I think. But not in a sad or wistful way like we sometimes remember our youth. In a happy way, a nostalgic way, as though you were living what I'd had to give up. Does that make sense to you? Because that's exactly how I felt, no more, no less.

The drive was uneventful, so I'll start from the funfair. I'm sure you think it was there where I started to get my ideas, but that's not true either. Oh, you can argue it was a warm day, there were lots of young girls in shorts and those T-shirts they wear without sleeves (halter-tops, are they called? Anyway, it doesn't matter), and lots of couples having fun, their arms around each other, some even kissing, I suppose. But honestly, Rachel, I never really noticed any of those things, and even if I did none of them affected me. None of them "got me thinking" or anything like that.

You were being your normal lovely self. Laughing a lot. Asking lots of questions. Pointing at things, your eyes as big as dinner plates.

I bought you an ice-cream and some candyfloss and a toffee apple, and I let you ride on whatever you wanted. I knew I was spoiling you but I thought: granddad's prerogative. I decided that the worst that could happen was that you would be sick on the big dipper or the ferris-wheel, and I thought that that was a small price to pay for all the fun.

The only ride we went on where there was any real physical contact was the Ghost Train, and that was because you got scared and grabbed my hand. There was nothing unusual in it, nothing funny. It was only a natural thing. When we came out of that tunnel, back into the daylight and the noise, all the other kids were holding their parents' hands too.

Should I stay here or move closer? What if she sees me and starts to scream? Oh God, won't someone please tell me what to do?

The room unveiled its details one by one, unwrapped them as though they were presents or secrets. It was a colourful room, gaudy even, filled with innocently smiling images that to him seemed somehow desperate. The Wombles cavorting on the curtains to his left seemed to be denying the existence of the black night. On the pink carpet objects were strewn − or perhaps arranged, carefully placed, like childish charms against evil spirits. There was a fluffy blue dog, a Raggedy Ann on its back, a storybook opened to a picture of the Sleeping Beauty, a pair of small white shoes laid toe to toe.

The shoes. He looked at them and a sensation overcame him. In other circumstances he might have started to shake. A lump might have obstructed his throat. Perhaps even tears might have fallen.

Yes, they were *the* shoes. There was no doubt about it. They were the shoes she'd been wearing on that day.

He moaned, or thought he did, and his gaze skittered, as

always, back to the girl. Once again he stared at her face, tried to discern some residue, some mark left by what had occurred. The fact that he couldn't profoundly distressed him. If she had let her feelings show — her confusion, her trauma — then perhaps the badness might have flowed out of her, left her for ever. But her innocence had buried the trauma, secreted it in the deepest, darkest part of her mind. Which meant that her scars ran deep, that somewhere in the bubbling brook that was her childhood a capsule lurked, a flimsy, fragile thing, ready at the slightest whisper to crack and spread its poison.

Why? he whispered (thought he whispered). Why oh why oh why?

The girl made a small sound, frowned, twisted slightly, as though a breeze had passed over her face.

He froze. A thought came to him: What *was* he doing here? Why *had* he come back? Surely the strength of his curiosity, his need to see, to know, had not dragged him here? No, he couldn't believe that of himself. Even after what he'd done he found it impossible. He was no slavering ghoul, no voyeur, no gloater. God knew, there were enough of them around, people who revelled in the misery of others, but surely he could not be counted amongst their number? Those people were disturbed, mad, spiteful. But that day, *that day*, he must have been too. And if he had been then, why not now? Why was he here, after all? *Why was he here?*

He moved a little closer to the bed.

Can you recall what we did after the funfair? We walked along the promenade for a bit and then we went down on the beach. Starmouth beach is lovely. Smooth sand, hardly any pebbles, a pier you can walk right underneath, and lots of caves and rock pools.

You loved it. You picked up some shells and some bits of glass. The glass was all rough and rounded, do you remember? I explained this was because the sea had moved it around a lot and the salt and the tide had worn it down. I said the glass had probably come from a foreign country, that it had been washed miles and miles, right across the ocean. You looked at me, wide-eyed. 'Which country, granddad?'

you asked. I told you America or China or maybe even Russia. 'Wow,' you said and looked out to sea, shielding your eyes with your hand. I think you thought that you would be able to see the coastline of one of those countries just peeping over the horizon.

I remember that moment so clearly: the way you looked. You had your blonde hair tied back in ... what do you call them? Ponytails? Bunches? Anyway, tied back with these little bits of elastic with plastic butterflies on them. Your dress was flapping around your knees because of the wind coming off the sea and your white shoes were covered in sand. I told you we'd have to clean those shoes before we came home or Mummy wouldn't be pleased, but you just shrugged and pouted. I remember teasing you, telling you what a little madam you were, making you laugh.

I think of that laugh now. So childish. So carefree. How could I have done what I did? What in God's name drove me to it?

Anyway, I'll carry on, tell you the rest.

We walked along to the caves and the rock pools. You wouldn't go further than any of the cave entrances, especially when I told you about the dinosaur skeleton they'd found in one of them. In a rock pool we came across a big crab with only one claw, half-hidden by an overhang of stone. You found a stick or a reed or something and lowered it down, right in front of the crab. I bet you remember that, don't you? The crab didn't pay any attention, so you swirled the stick around a bit, disturbing the sand. All at once the crab's claw shot out and grabbed the stick. You should have seen your face! You jumped and let go of the stick and let out a little scream. Then you looked up at me and started laughing and laughing.

We walked back along the beach. You took off your shoes and socks and started splashing along the sea's edge. You kept trying to kick water up at me but the wind caught it and scattered the droplets. We walked under the pier, which smelt all seaweedy, and then, believe it or not, you announced that you were hungry again so we made our way back to the promenade. I gave you the choice of doughnuts and lemonade or some proper fish and chips from a seafront

café. You chose the fish and chips, so after we'd found a
bench where you could brush the sand off your feet and
put your shoes and socks back on, we made our way to
a café.

I don't want all this to happen again. I don't. I truly don't.
My only crime — my only true crime — was that I loved
her far too much.

The girl's eyes opened. They looked straight at him. He
froze, suddenly more terrified, more ashamed, than he'd
ever thought it possible to be.

'Mummy,' the girl shouted. 'Mummy, where are you?'
She sat up, blonde hair falling to her shoulders, snatching
at the pillow and holding it to her chest like a shield.

Movement in the corridor outside. Mowgli and Balloo
and King Louie and Bagheera lay flat on the wallpaper,
framing a pink door. The door opened. Light fell into
the room. A woman entered, sleepy-eyed, tousle-haired,
a dressing gown draped over her shoulders like folded
diaphanous wings.

He felt, in that instant, a crushing, desperate, terrible
shame. To be found here, to be discovered by this woman,
the product of his own seed . . . No. No, it was too awful
to bear. He wanted to shrink, to dissolve, to burst. Felt he
would be struck down the moment he saw the lightning bolt
of accusation in her glaring eyes.

But he was spared all that. The woman didn't even look
at him. Instead she crossed straight to the bed, took the
girl in her arms, whispered, 'Sh now, sh. Mummy's here.
What's the matter?'

The girl clutched the woman. Held tight to her sleeves.
Half-buried her stricken face in the woman's breasts.
Through a mouthful of thumb she murmured, 'Someone
was here, Mummy. Standing by my bed. I think he came
out of the wardrobe.'

The woman turned. Looked straight at him. *At him!* He
felt like screaming.

He waited. For the anger. The hate. Perhaps even the
violence. But:

83

'There's no one there,' the woman said. 'You've had a bad dream, darling, that's all.'

He listened, amazed. No one there? What did she mean? Why was she lying? He heard her continue:

'Do you want to sleep in Mummy's bed where it's warm? Shall we go and wake Daddy up? Get him to read us a story?'

The girl gave a sulky half-nod.

'Come on then. My, you're getting to be a big girl, aren't you? Hold tight. Do you want Raggedy Ann to come too?'

Chatting quietly to her daughter, allaying her fears with a weave of words, the woman carried the girl across the room and out, closing the door behind her.

He stood for a moment, wondering. Listened to the murmurs finally dwindle to silence. Then he crossed to the bed, sent a message to his hand, saw – or thought he saw – the hand lying flat on the place where the girl had lain.

And suddenly he understood. Thought he did. Wasn't sure. He felt the girl's warmth, felt it dissipate little by little. Felt the bed become cool. Cooler. Cold.

I'm sorry, he said, though he could hear no sound. *I'm sorry, I'm sorry, I'm sorry.*

You had fish and chips and mushy peas. A child's portion. And bread and butter and a strawberry milkshake. Despite what you said about being hungry, you couldn't eat it all, which didn't surprise me after all that stuff at the funfair. You pushed the food around your plate with your fork until I'd eaten mine, now and then stopping to have a sip of your milkshake. You had a funny look on your face, a sort of faraway look, as if you were leading up to something, thinking about something you wanted to ask. Sure enough a few seconds later you put down your fork and looked straight at me. Then you said, 'Granddad, where's Nanna gone?'

Well, as you can imagine, the question threw me. I had to think about it a bit before answering. I wasn't sure what to tell you – how much you would really understand

and how much I wanted you to know. It surprised me, coming three months after Dora's death. I would never have thought a six-year-old would keep such a question bottled up so long.

Eventually I said, 'She's gone to Jesus, pet. Didn't Mummy explain?'

'Yes,' you said with a frown on your face, 'but I don't know where Jesus is.'

I nearly laughed at that but I stopped myself just in time. You looked deadly serious and I didn't want you to think I was making fun of you. I was about to tell you that Jesus was a person, not a place, but then I realised it would sound as though Dora had run off with the milkman or something. Eventually I said, 'Jesus is God's son, pet. They live in the sky. In Heaven. That's where your nanna's gone.'

You frowned. 'You mean with the angels?' you said.

'Yes,' I said, 'with the angels. Your nanna's one of them now.'

'But doesn't she want to come and see us any more?' you asked.

'Of course she does,' I said, 'but once you get to Heaven you have to stay there. You can't leave.'

'Then I think Heaven's horrible,' you said. 'And I think God's horrible too. She's my nanna, not his.'

I felt as though I hadn't explained things very well. Children do that to you sometimes. You try to be delicate, try to skirt round the real facts because you think you're protecting them, when all you're really doing is confusing them, avoiding taboos not for their sake but for your own, and succeeding only in tying yourself into knots.

Does that make sense? I hope so. The reason I'm telling you all this is because it was due to this conversation that I gave you a hug in the car. Again, I didn't mean anything by it. It was just a hug, that's all. I suppose I was frustrated because I couldn't explain things and because I just sort of loved you all of a sudden, loved your childishness, your innocence. Even now I wasn't thinking anything. You were just a little girl, my granddaughter, and I loved you only because of that.

We started to drive home. It was about six, seven o'clock.

You were pointing at things, asking questions, and then bit by bit the questions tailed off and you went very quiet. I thought you must be sleepy but when I looked over I noticed you were a bit green around the gills, so I asked if you felt all right. You said, 'No, I feel sick.' I drove another fifty, sixty yards, then pulled into a lay-by.

I unbuckled your seat belt, then reached over and opened the car door. We were in the countryside by now. There were fields and hedges and trees, a couple of distant farmhouses and not many cars on the road. You leaned right out of the car and were sick on the ground outside. And that's when it happened. Right there while you were bringing up toffee apple and fish and chips and candyfloss and ice-cream.

Your dress got kind of bunched up and I could see brown legs and white pants and something just sort of clicked inside me. I've been through it time and again in my mind and I just can't explain it any other way. One minute I was thinking what a nice day we'd had and working out what time we'd get home, and the next I was doing those awful things.

Even now when I think about those things it makes me want to die in shame. I hope you won't feel the same way for ever, but I think that you might, I truly truly do. In a way I still can't believe I really did anything. It's as though it was someone else there that day, someone who looked like me but wasn't me. Someone who pushed aside my control and who used my body and my brain for their own degraded purpose.

But saying that is crazy, and much too easy. Of course it was me. I have no excuse for what I did and no explanation. It happened, that's all. It happened. I just want you to know it wasn't planned, it wasn't premeditated. It was terrible, I admit that. It was unforgivable. But I'm sorry. I've suffered enough. I know what it's like to be a victim and now I just want some peace.

I'm drifting. Can feel myself going back. No, I don't want to. I can't stand it any more.

He woke with a jolt when the door slammed. For a moment the sound made him forget who or where or when he was.

The door was as wide and as blank as his mind. There was colour to the left of the door − pink flesh, blue denim, yellow and black bee-stripes.

Rachel.

He remembered then, and was struck, as he often was, by their separate perception of a shared world. Time for him was an endurance, a boulder he was forced to drag in his wake. For her it was nothing, or at worst a feather which she could blow from her cupped palm and watch float away. Was she really seventeen? It seemed inconceivable. And yet in her swift maturing he had crossed deserts of anguish, oceans of pain.

As best he could he regarded himself. He saw as always the blanket covering his wasted legs, his hands like roots entwined in his lap. If only he had some autonomy he wouldn't mind the wheelchair. But no; the stroke had been as merciless, as uncaring and as permanent as his actions over a decade earlier. Of course he'd rather have died, but that would not have been suitable retribution. He ached at the sight of her golden hair. If only. If only. If only . . .

She walked across the room, staring at him as ever with dreadful accusation. She never spoke but then she had no need to. Her hate seemed to spill like poison from her cold eyes. Monster, freak, beast, betrayer, pervert: he saw all this in her gaze. He could close his own eyes but that was somehow worse, knowing she was there, watching.

She sat cross-legged on the floor before the wheelchair and stared at him. She was motionless, expressionless. He could have believed she was an automaton, bled of all emotion, if he had not heard her laughing with her friends. This was the moment each day when their worlds conjoined, when time for them both ran parallel. This was their shared hour, a time for remembering. For him it was the longest hour of all.

Homeward Bound

If it had been summertime it wouldn't have been quite so bad. At least then it would still have been light when he locked up the shop at 6:45 and set off home. But it wasn't summer, it was rusty autumn, and David Jessel couldn't shake off the feeling that he was being watched.

He pulled the shop door closed and fumbled with the big bunch of keys that he kept inside his overcoat pocket. There were four locks in all, and Jessel looked round nervously as he secured each in turn, half expecting a rush of bodies from a nearby side street. Once or twice he had noticed the skinheads who hung around the park railings watching him. He was sure they were planning something.

But it wasn't the skinheads who worried him particularly. Their stares were hostile, certainly, but at least theirs was a tangible threat, something he had learned to live with. No, it was the unknown threat that disturbed Jessel, the feeling that he was being calmly observed by something that was cold, intelligent ... inhuman? He shook his head and told himself for the fifth time that week not to be ridiculous. How on earth had he latched onto this idea in the first place? It was simply overwork. A weekend in front of the fire and the telly would do him the world of good. By Monday morning it would all be forgotten.

He walked quickly across the street. The buildings were blue-black, the pavements and roads soaked in a depressing orange light. The moon glimmered faintly overhead, a dirty cheesy yellow as though it hadn't been cleaned for weeks.

Jessel walked along the pavement by the side of the

park. The railings whipped by, one after another, caging the looming trees and bushes. He sensed something there in the bushes, keeping pace with him. He stopped and looked down to his left, nervous of what he might see. There was nothing. He began to walk forward slowly, watching the bushes all the time. A vague shape, dark and orangey, was trailing him. He felt relieved. It was only his shadow, and the shifting emphasis of the street lamps on the leaves.

He heard scuttering footsteps behind him and whirled round. It was a playing card, the six of hearts, ticking as it cartwheeled over the pavement. He smiled uneasily: how stupid to think the sound resembled footsteps. As the card reached him, he stamped on it, flattening it into immobility. There, he thought with satisfaction; now, no more silliness.

He walked on, looking straight ahead, trying to turn his thoughts to brighter things. He thought of his little house, modest but cosy. In ten minutes he would be there. He would go in, hang up his coat as he always did, put on the fire and the telly and make himself a meal. Then, when he had eaten, he would settle down for the evening with two bottles of Guinness and a large bag of salted peanuts. Absolute bliss. What more could a man ask for?

He quickened his pace, anxious to get home now. His heart beat faster as he turned the corner by the park. This was the bit he didn't like. He had to walk down these two streets where some of those skinheads lived and then through an alleyway. After that it was plain sailing. The streets broadened out and became brighter, and there were usually people around; respectable people, not yobbos.

He looked at his watch as he always did at this point, and reassured himself with the thought that in three minutes from now he would be out of the danger zone and nearly home. He set off, passing a little row of run-down, boarded-up shops. There were three in all, the paintwork peeling from their faded signs, their grime-thickened windows protected from vandals by rusty wire mesh. As he passed the last one, Jessel started.

He looked back and his stomach did a forward roll. A grey, bloated face was peering at him from behind the glass. He walked back slowly, his legs trembling. The face didn't move.

Maybe it wasn't a face after all; maybe it was just his eyes playing tricks, conjuring the layers of dust into shapes. It was too dark and grimy to see properly. As he leaned forward for a closer look, the face melted away, back into the darkness.

Jessel turned and ran. The keys jangled in his pocket, his feet clacked alarmingly loudly on the pavement as though he were wearing tap shoes. At the end of the street he stopped and bent double, a stitch jabbing his side. His breathing was harsh and laboured, squeezing out as a thin white vapour which curled for a moment and then dissolved in the sodium glare of the street lamps.

He forced himself to calm down. His body felt drenched with sweat beneath his heavy overcoat. Maybe he should have kept running. Up the next street, up the alleyway, his legs pumping blindly. That way he would be home in two minutes.

But no, he thought, that wasn't the way. Why should he run? There was nothing – *nothing* – to be afraid of. Running was undignified and unnecessary, and if anything he would only draw attention to himself. But still his legs itched to run.

He compromised. He walked swiftly, arms swinging by his sides. He set his face sternly, and jumped only a little when loose pages from a newspaper wheeled madly across the street in front of him and wrapped themselves around a lamp post. Somewhere in the distance he heard people shouting, and then start up with the drunken chorus of a football song. This was followed by the muted crash of breaking glass and a ragged bout of cheering.

Jessel almost fainted when a black, glistening hand lunged from beneath a car and flopped onto his foot. He whipped his foot back, the scream catching in his throat, sharp as a fishbone. He looked down.

It was a dustbin liner. It sidled around the wheel of the car and mouthed at him mockingly. Jessel kicked out at it and walked on. His body felt stiff and unnatural, not part of him at all.

Now he came to the alleyway: the dreaded, hated alleyway. He stopped and peered down it. Stretching ahead like a long black throat, it contained so many hiding places. The walls on either side seemed to be pressing closer than ever, as though the two buildings had uprooted themselves in the night and edged together, leaving only the narrowest of passageways. He started down cautiously. There was a sickly smell, as though everything had turned wet and rotten. His heart began to thud – *ba-thum, ba-thum, ba-thum* – like a warning.

More black bin liners, bulky with sinister shapes, lolled against the walls, grouped together as though in some dark conversation. Up ahead something glinted. A knife? No, it was a broken padlock dangling on a chain, flickering as it reflected the dull sulphurous glow of the caged light overhead.

Jessel hurried on. The ground was slippery and littered with rubbish. Crisp bags crackled feebly; broken glass glittered like precious stones; pulpy shapes collected in corners made him shudder and look away.

He was halfway along now. He passed a doorway set back in the wall, flanked by dustbins. Someone was standing in the doorway, watching him. He turned. There was no one there. Only the elongated shadow of a dustbin.

Thirty seconds later and he was out. Home and dry, his heart seemed to sing, home and dry. He hurried along the tree-lined road to his own little house at the end. The street lights beamed at him, lighting his way. More light came from behind lace curtains. His own house was in darkness, but it was a haven. Soon it would be as bright as its neighbours.

He walked up his driveway, past the meticulous flower beds and clipped lawn to the front door. He whistled as he fitted the key into the lock and turned it. The door opened. He stepped inside, still whistling, and closed the door behind him.

He turned on the light.

And screamed.

'Welcome home,' said the thing that was waiting for him in the hallway.

Birthday

On his tenth birthday, Matt Price was given a full England football strip, a pair of Arrow Futuro boots (As Worn By David Platt!), and his first ever proper leather football. He was so excited he phoned his best friend, Anthony Rushworth, at once to tell him. Anthony, whose tenth birthday was still some three-and-a-half months away, sounded almost as excited as Matt himself, albeit a little envious. The two of them agreed to meet at the park in fifteen minutes for a celebratory kickabout.

'Now you remember to be back in good time. It's your party this afternoon, and you'll need a bath if you're going to be rolling in mud all morning,' his mother told him.

Matt pulled a face, making his little sister, Jeanette, smile. 'I know, Mum, but I've got to get my practice in. I'll never be a professional if I don't practise every day.'

Jeanette, who was seven, and who had managed to get most of the yolk of her boiled egg around her mouth but not in it, said proudly, 'Matt's like Gazza, Mummy. He can do twenty-eight ball juggles in one go.'

'Thirty-two now,' Matt corrected her firmly, and felt a swell of unalloyed pride when his father looked up from his newspaper and said, 'That's really good, Matt. You keep that up and maybe we *will* have another Gazza on our hands.'

Eager to impress his father still further, Matt continued, 'When we played Ely's lot yesterday, Dad, we won 10–6 and I scored five of our goals.'

'Don't boast, Matthew,' his mother said before his father

could respond. 'Pride comes before a fall, you know.' And at the door a few minutes later, as she saw her husband off to work, Matt heard her murmur, 'Don't encourage him, Frank. It's his schoolwork he should be spending more time on, not football.'

His father was already out of the door so Matt didn't hear his reply, but he could guess from his mother's scowl and the way she clattered pots, tight-lipped, in the sink that his father had not entirely concurred with her viewpoint. Lifting his new football as quietly as possible from its nest of wrapping paper, Matt said, 'Right, Mum, I'm off. I'll see you later.'

When she turned from the sink, Matt thought she was going to forbid him to go after all, but then she glanced at his birthday cards which were standing temporarily on the kitchen table and gave a resigned smile. 'All right,' she said, 'but don't be late. And be careful. That main road is busy.'

Matt was nodding as he sidled towards the door. 'Yes, Mum. Okay. I will.' He lifted his new football boots from their box, and plunged down the hallway before she could change her mind.

He waited until he was out of sight of the house before he put the boots on. They smelled brand-new, of leather and polish, and they felt smooth and supple in his hands. Matt relished placing them on his feet, tying the laces slowly and carefully as if undertaking some precise and delicate ritual. When he stood up the boots creaked a little. Matt wished he had a mirror to admire himself in. He strutted to the park, peacock-proud, tossing his football from hand to hand, occasionally bouncing it on his thigh. He was aching to kick it, to run and dribble and shoot, but he was making himself wait until he reached the grass. He didn't want to risk the ball bouncing into the path of a car or breaking someone's window. When he reached the main road, and could see the green expanse of park on the other side framed by trees, he had to hop from foot to foot at the pedestrian crossing in order to curb the urge to race right across, dodging the cars.

It seemed an age before the red standing man became a

green walking one. When it did, Matt breathed, 'At last,' and hared in front of cars, now motionless, which growled softly at him. The park gates were to his left. He ran towards them, studs clattering on the pavement. Inside, three paths snaked away in different directions. Between them, like vast wedges of green pie, were flat open areas of grass. Later, if today was as hot as it had been recently, teenagers would be lolling on the grass, smooching, or bellowing above the sounds of their ghetto blasters as they soaked up the sun. Now, though, the park was all but deserted: Matt could see only six people. Four of these (a jogger, a man walking a dog and an elderly couple out for a morning stroll) were on the path; the other two were a young couple on the left-hand lawn who were skimming a frisbee to each other. With a whoop of delight, Matt tossed his football into the air and booted it as hard as he could onto the right-hand lawn. He chased after it, feeling the wind rush across his face and through his hair. In his mind's eye he could see goal posts looming before him, a Wembley crowd urging him on, Maradona flagging at his shoulder, unable to match his pace.

He reached the ball, chipped it delicately over the advancing Argentinian keeper and into the roof of the net. The crowd erupted as he leaped in celebration, punching the air. He could hear the commentator's excited voice: *'And it's there! Price has broken the deadlock in the very last minute of the game! Surely now the World Cup belongs to England! This young man will be the toast of the country tonight!'*

Matt wished Tony was here right now; he couldn't wait to show him all his new stuff. He looked around, the roar of the crowd and the screech of the commentator's voice fading from his ears to be replaced by the soft chatter of birds, the rumble of cars on the main road. The park was nothing much if truth be told – an aesthete would have been dismayed by the litter, the dogshit, the weeds and the graffiti – but to Matt and Tony and their friends it was all they could wish for. It was Wembley or Wimbledon, an alien planet or a tropical jungle. Miniature sea battles had been fought in its pond, the adventures of Robin Hood re-enacted in its oak trees and herbaceous borders. The park had its monsters too: the Head Gardener, for instance, who the boys believed was an evil alien scout in the guise of a crusty old man. And its ghosts: the disused cricket pavilion, paint peeling, overgrown by weeds, was reputed to be the haunt of a tramp who had drunk himself to death there many winters ago, and whose rotting, fly-blown corpse had not been discovered for months.

Musing on this, Matt shivered and glanced about, suddenly afraid there might be something lurking in the bushes. Reassured to discover there wasn't, he skipped across to his football, flipped it up onto his right foot and began to juggle it from one foot to the other, counting under his breath, 'One ... two ... three ... four ... five ...' When he reached twenty-nine he thought he was going to break his own record – his new boots were improving his game already! – but then his eagerness caused him to lose control, and a bad contact made him lunge at the ball, which looped over his head. 'Shit,' he groaned, and spun round, not wanting to lose sight of the ball for even a moment. What he saw standing in the centre of the lawn was so unexpected that he gave a startled, high-pitched yelp and stumbled backwards with such suddenness that he lost his balance and plumped unceremoniously onto his backside.

He gaped, open-mouthed, at what had caused his shocked response. It had apparently materialised from nowhere, an antique wardrobe, rather over-elaborate in its use of curlicues and filigree. However, what differentiated this wardrobe from others like it, and what had shocked Matt almost as much as its actual appearance, was that it was made not of wood but of glass, and so resembled, in its flawless, highly polished transparency, something from a fairy tale – a princess's tallboy, perhaps, or a magician's cabinet.

Matt remained seated for perhaps thirty seconds, thoughts whirling confusedly in his mind. He wondered whether they'd been right about the Head Gardener after all; perhaps he really *was* an alien, and maybe this was his spaceship. Matt had once read a book about a glass elevator that flew through space, and then of course there was Doctor Who's TARDIS, which was bigger on the inside than on

100

the outside. Okay, so the wardrobe door was open, and Matt could see right inside it – right *through* it to the grass on the other side as a matter of fact – but this did not necessarily mean that the wardrobe *wasn't* a spaceship. Maybe the controls were so subtle they were invisible to the naked eye. Or maybe this wasn't the spaceship's true appearance; maybe it could change form or was concealing its true shape behind deflector shields or something. Matt had been exposed to enough pseudo-science in books and films to be half-convinced that much of it could actually be true.

Dry-mouthed he stood up slowly, hoping the 'spaceship' would not construe his movements as hostile and vaporise him with a laser beam. He was relieved when the wardrobe simply stood there, silent and inactive, the sunlight flashing on its glass sides, adding to its splendour. Matt's heart was still thudding, and his limbs felt strangely hollow, but gradually his fear was giving way to a sense of wonder. The wardrobe, for him, held the attraction of a sleeping crocodile: despite its potential danger he simply could not pass up the opportunity for a more thorough examination. He felt he had to reach out and touch it, try to discern some measure of its purpose, its nature, perhaps even convince himself that the wardrobe was real and not some kind of illusion.

He edged forward slowly, arm half-raised, fingers out-stretched. He wondered whether he should say something: he'd feel silly talking to a wardrobe, but then again it would show that he meant no harm, that he was simply curious. But what should he say? And wasn't it likely that the wardrobe, or whatever controlled it, would not understand his language anyway? Perhaps his voice might even activate its lasers or something, perhaps by trying to reassure it he would be putting himself in even greater peril. He glanced around again as the bushes rustled, half-expecting a leathery-skinned creature to emerge, or a robot bristling with weaponry. But it was only a breeze which moved the bushes; he could feel its coolness on his cheek. He took a few steps closer to the wardrobe, his stomach jumping as if full of frogs, his feet almost silent on the grass. His new football lay a few feet

101

from the wardrobe's open door like an egg laid by some enormous reptile.

When he was three feet from the wardrobe he stopped. Perhaps he ought to wait for Tony so they could examine this phenomenon together. It had surely been more than fifteen minutes since they'd agreed to meet here, but Tony was notorious for his bad timekeeping. Matt looked around once again, half-wishing some grown-up might appear onto whom he could shift the responsibility. But the park, for the moment, remained stubbornly deserted, and Matt's curiosity was already beginning to get the better of his trepidation. He took another small step; now, if he wanted, he could reach out and touch the wardrobe's smooth surface. He held out his hand once again, fingers hovering inches from the glass – and then, taking a deep breath, he touched it.

He had visions of his body becoming encased in a sudden unearthly light, or of being hurled backwards by some electrical discharge. He braced himself for such an outcome, hunching his shoulders, clenching his left fist, screwing up his eyes and gritting his teeth. But there was no need. Beneath the light pressure of his fingers he felt only cool, smooth glass. He expelled a breathy, relieved chuckle. He stroked the glass as if soothing it. Then he leaned towards the wardrobe's open door.

'Hello,' he said tentatively. 'Is anyone there?'

He felt vaguely silly; he could *see* there was no one there, though again he knew he shouldn't take things for granted. Maybe the aliens were invisible, or in some sort of different dimension, watching him, deciding whether or not he was a threat. Thinking of this Matt said hastily, 'I ... er ... I come in peace. As a friend. Er ... this is ... er ... a nice spaceship. Welcome to our planet.'

His words died, and broached no response. Yet again Matt looked around, suddenly, uncomfortably wondering whether he was simply the butt of some practical joke. He imagined Ely and his creepozoid friends rolling around in the bushes, trying to stifle their laughter as they watched him. He could picture Ely's pimply face in his mind, his snide voice saying, 'And then he started *talking* to the bloody thing. You should have seen him. What a *dork*!'

102

He blushed at the terrible prospect of that, tried in his mind to calculate how long he'd been ball juggling, how long he'd had his back turned, whether Ely and co. would have been able to carry the wardrobe onto the lawn, set it down and scoot away into the bushes without him noticing. To cover himself, Matt shouted, 'I know you're there, Ely. You didn't fool me, you know. I knew it was you all the time.' He decided to move away from the wardrobe, wait for Tony after all.

And then he saw the coin.

It sparkled as he stepped backwards as though eager to be noticed. It was at the back of the wardrobe, in the far right-hand corner, and it looked like no coin that Matt had ever seen before. It was star-shaped, and the metal had a pearly greenish hue. All thoughts of practical jokes fled from Matt's mind. There was no way that Ely could have bought or found or even made something like that.

As he stepped forward again, Matt could see the headlines in his mind's eye: ALIEN SPACECRAFT DISCOVERED BY TEN-YEAR-OLD BOY. Maybe there would be a picture of him in his England kit holding the coin; maybe they could even squeeze in something about his footballing exploits and his ambition to be a professional and to play for England. If some football manager read that, they might invite him to go for a trial. 'Boy who discovered aliens scores amazing hat-trick on debut,' Matt murmured, and felt a flutter of excitement in his stomach. He braced himself, then darted into the wardrobe, intending to pick up the coin and go.

He was nowhere near quick enough. The instant he entered the wardrobe the glass door sprang closed behind him. Matt whirled, fear dousing his entire body in a shocking splash of panic. 'Oh shit,' he wailed, and struck out at the door with the flats of both hands, remembering too late that it was glass and that it was more likely to shatter than to burst open. However, in the event it did neither. Instead it simply jarred his arms, drawing an 'oof' of pain from him.

It took Matt perhaps a minute to bring himself under control, but little by little calm, logical thought gained ascendancy over his initial primitive fear of entrapment. Okay, so the wardrobe door had closed behind him, but there was no need to throw a wobbler, was there? If he couldn't get out himself then he'd simply sit tight and wait for someone to come along. He rubbed his wrists, which was where the pain from his jarred arms had settled, and tried not to wonder *why* the wardrobe door had closed on him. The thing had not really been a baited trap; he had simply caught the door as he passed inside. Or his weight had unbalanced the cabinet and jolted the door shut on him.

Wrists still throbbing, he examined the door with his hands. There was no handle, nor even a lock, on the inside, and the gap between door and frame was so tight that Matt could get no more than the tips of his fingernails into it. What did disturb him a little was that there appeared to be neither handle nor lock on the outside either, though he tried not to let this worry him too much. Obviously there was some hidden mechanism, a spring or something, somewhere. And even if there wasn't, well, the stupid thing was only made of glass. A good whack from a sledgehammer would free him.

He sighed, pressing his nose and the palms of his hands to the glass. Tony should be here any minute now. Matt only hoped no one would nick his new football in the meantime. Though he obviously wanted to be out of here, his initial fear had been superseded by frustration and more than a little embarrassment. The number of times he'd read about kids his own age trapping themselves in freezers and trunks and had thought: what a stupid thing to do. This thought made him remember why he'd entered the wardrobe, and he looked down to his left, to the small green star-shaped coin still lying in the corner. Bending over was awkward in the confined space, but there was just enough room for him to do it. He picked up the coin and looked at it ... and was surprised when it started to crumble away in his hands.

Though the coin shone like metal, its texture was similar to that of old soap, dry and cracked, dissolving into soft splinters beneath his touch. This led him to the conclusion that the object was not a coin after all, but was perhaps something organic, part of a plant maybe, or even some sort of tiny desiccated life-form, like a brittlestar. Or food, he thought. He held the crumbling thing up to his nose but could detect not even the slightest odour. Seconds later, as if reacting to his body-warmth, the object crumbled away completely, became nothing more than a fine greenish dust which settled on the glass floor of Matt's makeshift prison.

Sighing again, he gave the glass a soft kick, more a gesture of impatience than a bid for freedom. The glass made a dull *clung* sound, though showed no sign of cracking. Cautiously Matt tried to rock the wardrobe back and forth, but although he was standing on its floor and could see the crushed grass beneath it, the cabinet remained solidly immovable. It was as though somehow it was set in the earth, had foundations securing it in the ground like a building. 'Open sesame, you stupid bugger,' he muttered, and turned slowly around, wishing Tony would hurry up and arrive. 'This isn't fair,' he informed the wardrobe, or the aliens, or God, or whoever. 'It's my birthday today. This shouldn't happen on my birthday.'

Just then, as if whatever higher intelligence he'd been complaining to had heard and taken pity on him and decided to send a saviour, Matt glimpsed movement from the corner of his eye. He turned and saw Tony, hands in pockets, clumping across the grass in his direction.

'Hey, Tone,' Matt yelled, waving his arms. His voice echoed around him in the confined space. Tony, however, failed to react to Matt's voice. Frustrated, Matt banged on the glass as hard as he dared.

To his surprise Tony did not even react to that, though surely he must have heard it. Or maybe he was just messing about, pretending not to hear, but in these circumstances it seemed a pretty strange thing to do. Once, Matt remembered, he and Tony and three or four others had been in the park waiting for the last in their group, Bonzer, to arrive. As a joke they had all agreed to ignore Bonzer completely, to act as if he was invisible. The joke had endured until Bonzer got so annoyed that he leaped on Tony's back and started pummelling him. But Tony surely couldn't be playing that game now? The first reaction to seeing a friend trapped in a glass wardrobe in the middle of a park would not be to pretend to ignore him.

Unless ... A suspicion began to form in Matt's mind. Recently his gang had begun playing practical jokes on each other on their birthdays. It had started off with the bumps and hair-pulling and stuff like that, but over the last year or so the jokes had become gradually more elaborate. The funniest – and the one they'd got most into trouble for – had been played on Tony himself. Matt had arranged it so that their entire class was early for school on the morning of Tony's birthday, and had instructed each of them to bring along a small tin of something edible – baked beans, spaghetti, ravioli or whatever. He had filled a bucket with this mess, propped the bucket on the top of the door, and when Tony had walked in – SPLATTO! Matt still maintained the cane, the week's detention, and even the withdrawal of his pocket money to buy Tony a new blazer had been worth it just to see the expression on Tony's face at the moment of impact.

Matt banged on the glass again and shouted, 'Okay, Tone, you win. Very funny joke. Ha Ha. Look, I'm laughing. Now let me out please, okay?'

But Tony, apparently, was not finished yet. It seemed he was determined to draw this out as long as possible. He was standing now in the centre of the lawn, some twenty feet away from Matt, pivoting on his heels as he looked around. Twice his gaze swept across the wardrobe, but despite Matt's attempts to make him laugh by pulling faces and doing a silly dance and flipping him the V's, Tony remained admirably composed. On the third circuit, Tony halted when facing him and his expression changed. 'About bloody time too,' Matt shouted. 'Let me out, Tone.'

As if to comply with his request, Tony began to walk towards the wardrobe. But, thankful that his ordeal seemed about to end, Matt was nevertheless still a little puzzled. He expected Tony to be laughing at him, taking the piss, wringing every last drop of fun from this situation. But Tony was frowning and, indeed, not even looking at him. And when he stopped by the football and picked it up and examined it, still frowning, Matt realised that the joke was not yet over after all.

He groaned and banged on the glass so hard it hurt his

106

knuckles. It would be Tony's stupid fault if the glass broke and he got cut and had to go to hospital. 'Come on, Tony, you wankhead, let me out!' he shouted. 'You've had your fun now. I want to play football.'

To his surprise and intense annoyance, Tony simply shouted back, 'Matt, where are you? It's me, Tone. I think I've found your football.'

'I'm here, you dork-brain, as you well know! Now fucking let me out! This isn't funny any more.'

Tony had a look of concentration on his face as if he was listening to some far, far distant sound. After a moment or two his face relaxed and he shook his head. 'Matt,' he shouted again, 'where are you?'

Matt was now getting so angry that his throat was tightening, threatening to choke off his voice. He felt tears prickling behind his eyes and thought: *I won't cry. I won't. I won't.* For a few seconds he couldn't speak. He simply banged on the glass with his clenched fist, swallowing to rid himself of a thick, acidic wad of rage. Finally the pressure in his throat began to ease and he said, 'If you don't let me out of here in two seconds, I'll kick my way out. I mean it.'

Tony simply sighed, took one more look around, still maintaining his baffled expression, and then he actually started to walk away. *'What are you doing, you wanker?'* Matt half-screamed. He twisted to follow Tony as his friend walked right past the wardrobe, no more than an arm's length from Matt himself. 'Hey, come back,' Matt shouted. 'Tony, you bastard, let me out. Bring back my ball.' But Tony continued to walk away, Matt's football in his hand. 'Right!' Matt yelled. 'Right, you asked for it!'

Bracing his back against the glass wall, he pistoned his leg out, kung-fu style, at the door. He hoped the glass would not shatter all at once; if it did it might well slice both his new England football socks and his bare legs to shreds. What he was hoping for was to kick a small hole in the door and to work from there until there was a large enough space for him to crawl out safely. As his studs made contact with the glass he half-spun away, shielding his eyes with his hand, but his studs simply slithered over the glass as though it was ten feet thick, failing even to crack it.

He squealed as his foot shot away from him, the studs and glass acting like a skate on ice. Searing pain lanced up through his ankle, blurring his vision with instant tears. Caught off balance he teetered back, his shoulder thumping into a glass corner, his head following the momentum through and banging hard against a wall. He fell down in the tiny space, jarring his elbow, the bare flesh of his leg squeaking down the inside of the glass with such force that a friction-burn sizzled the top layer off his skin. For a few moments he lay half-dazed, squashed into a space too small for a reclining figure, thinking: *pain, pain, pain, pain, pain.* He swiped the tears from his eyes and looked out furiously, only to find that his section of park was deserted. Then he started crying.

How long he sat there for, head between his hunched-up knees, sobbing with frustration and anger, he wasn't sure. When he finally looked up, wiping his eyes with the cuffs of his England shirt, the first thing he noticed was that the sun had shrugged off its muggy eiderdown of cloud and was beginning to blaze, as it had blazed almost incessantly for the past three weeks. Matt shifted uncomfortably, feeling the heat of it, like a cap, on the top of his head. He covered his hair with one hand and touched the wall with the other. It felt vaguely lukewarm, that was all. Matt wondered how long it would be before it began to get hot. He thought of his mother and Jeanette at home, getting everything ready for his party, and he had to bite his lip to stop himself crying again.

His body was a symphony of throbs and aches, especially his arms. When he moved his fingers it seemed to set off a muscular chain-reaction, flaring in his wrists and then shooting up to his elbow in his left arm, his shoulder in his right. But perhaps the worst pain, because it was constant and stinging, was the friction-burn on his right leg which started just above his knee and ended above his sock. It was like the trail left by a lick of acid, raw and oozing; when Matt touched it tentatively with his fingertip it felt like something was biting him with little needle-fangs.

Gritting his teeth, using the wall for leverage, he made himself stand up. The pain that sang in his ankle when he put his weight on it brought more tears to his eyes, but after a couple of minutes' tentative stamping the pain receded to a dull throb. Matt was sweating a little now. He could feel it on his forehead and throat and under his arms. He squinted up at the sun, which seemed to be glaring down on him alone. The glass walls of his prison now felt definitely warm to the touch.

For a while he simply stood and looked out at the park — at the grass and the trees and the parched mounds of beflowered earth at the borders of the lawn. He and his friends had always half-maintained that those mounds were where the Head Gardener had buried the murdered bodies of those who had stumbled across his secret identity. This belief had never previously failed to prompt a shiver of excitement in Matt, but now he didn't like the thought, didn't like it at all. One night, he and his friends had promised themselves, they would come with their shovels and they would dig until they found human remains. Matt rested his forehead against the glass, but removed it almost at once, leaving a smear of sweat, because the glass was too warm. 'We didn't mean it,' he murmured miserably. 'Please let me go and I swear I'll never tell.'

The sun inched higher in the sky, and little by little Matt's glass prison grew hotter. He blew upwards onto his face to cool himself, constantly pushed sweaty hair from his forehead. He couldn't believe how under-used this section of the park was. Since Tony had left he'd seen three people: a boy on a skateboard flashing by on the thread of path visible from his position, and a couple strolling hand in hand at the far end of the lawn, who hadn't even glanced in his direction when he'd started banging and kicking at the glass. They can't hear me, they're too far away, Matt had tried to assure himself, but a terrible suspicion (which in truth had begun to form after he had witnessed Tony's behaviour) was slowly crystallising in his mind. He constantly denied it, knowing it was impossible, but it nevertheless nagged at him. The thought was this: maybe Tony *wasn't* playing a joke. Maybe Tony could not see the wardrobe, and by entering it Matt had, in some strange way, been swallowed by its invisibility. This theory made Matt feel choked and sick and panic-stricken. He had to fight an almost unbearable urge to scream and flail and kick.

All that kept him from doing so was the hope and logic that he clung to. If he could see the world, he told himself, if he could hear it and even feel the heat of its sun, then somehow there must be a way of reversing that, making himself known to it. He kicked at the glass again, resting his weight uncomfortably on his bad ankle, but it was more a gesture of defiance than anything. He'd already realised that the glass was more than it seemed; though it looked like glass it was as strong as steel, perhaps stronger, for he couldn't even dent it. It was getting hotter. He swallowed and his throat felt thick and dry. He felt a tickle in his bladder and knew he would have to urinate soon. *Oh, please, please, let me out!*

He wondered how long it had been since Tony had left. It seemed like hours, though Matt knew it must still be mid-morning. The park always began to fill up around eleven, eleven-thirty, so it couldn't be as late as that just yet. He closed his eyes briefly, feeling the heat on his face which was making his body sweat, drawing out his fluids. When he opened them again four figures were walking towards him, two familiar, two in uniform – Tony, his mother and two policemen.

Instinctively Matt raised his arms and began to wave at them, trying to ignore the pain in his shoulder and wrists and elbow. 'Hey, Mum, I'm here!' he shouted, kicking the glass. 'I'm here, Mum. Let me out!'

It was obvious they could neither hear nor see him. Though they appeared to be looking in his direction their expressions did not change, nor did the pace of their tread. They stopped no more than four agonising feet away, Tony looking around, evidently lining up his landmarks. Matt saw that his mother's face was desperate with anxiety. He felt tears clogging his throat and building up behind his eyes once more. 'I'm here, Mum,' he wept, slapping the glass, almost enjoying the pain that flared in his wrist. 'I'm here, I'm here. Please, please see me.'

Her expression did not change. Nor did the policemen's which were maintaining a calm and careful neutrality. Taking one last look around, Tony said, 'It was about here.'

'You're sure?' the fatter of the two policemen said.

Tony looked momentarily uncertain, then nodded. 'Yeah, definitely.'

'Okay,' said the policeman who had just spoken, and pointing straight at Matt instructed his colleague, 'You have a quick shufti over there, Bob. I'll look over here.'

Bob nodded and walked straight past the wardrobe, so close that the dark material of his uniform sleeve brushed the outside of the glass. Matt knocked on the glass as hard as he could, face creasing with pain, right beside Bob's ear, but there was not even the tiniest flicker of reaction from the policeman. With dismay Matt watched as the police poked about in the surrounding bushes and trees, then he looked at his mother again, who seemed to be trying hard not to cry, her hands balled together in her midriff as if she had stomachache. Finally the policemen came back. The fatter one said, 'You're sure he won't have just met up with some of his pals and gone wandering off to play somewhere?'

Matt's mother shook her head vehemently. 'No,' she half-sobbed, 'he wouldn't have left his new football behind.'

'Kids can be absent-minded like that, Mrs Price,' the other policeman said in a Scottish accent. 'They get distracted, start chasing around, forget stuff. I always used to be doing it. The number of hidings I got from my mother for leaving behind satchels, blazers, all sorts.'

Matt's mother's voice was even higher-pitched, closer to tears, this time. 'He wouldn't have left his football. I *know* he wouldn't. He only got it this morning. He'd been pestering us to buy him one for weeks. It's his birthday today. We were going – ' The words choked off as she began to sob.

The policemen looked at each other, then the fatter one moved forward and patted Matt's mother awkwardly on the shoulder. 'Now then, Mrs Price,' he said, 'try not to upset yourself. It's early days yet. He's only been gone a couple of hours.'

Matt's mother looked up, face ugly with her grief. 'Where is he?' she sobbed. 'Oh God, *where is he*?'

In the wardrobe Matt felt sick with despair. He pressed

111

his face and his hands to the glass wall and whispered, 'I'm here, Mum ... I'm here.'

The police and his mother and Tony went away. Matt, feeling both physically and emotionally exhausted, sank down in the wardrobe, back sliding on the hot glass, knees coming up to meet his chin. His throat and mouth were dry and thick. His body was losing fluid through tears and sweat, but still he needed to urinate. The friction-burn on his leg was stinging, and Matt began, tentatively, to lick it like an animal. At first the pain got worse, but then it gradually eased.

He closed his eyes. He was hot and sick and his head felt muggy and dull. He used to feel like this on long car journeys when the family went on holiday to places like Cornwall and Southwold. Once, he remembered, he had leaned over his father's shoulder on the motorway and vomited copiously into his lap. It was now a funny story that the family told, but Matt couldn't recall anyone laughing much at the time.

Other memories drifted hazily in his mind, memories of the holidays themselves. Lying in a strange, exciting bed and hearing waves rushing up the beach at night; unwillingly trying some of his father's seafood platter and finding that he liked it; log-flumes and ghost trains, and giant slides which felt like the top of the world; hot dogs, fish and chips, candyfloss; the wonderful salt-smell of the rock pools; crazy golf.

Fragments, like jigsaw-pieces, were sifted by his mind until they seemed to form a spiral, a whirlpool, into which he felt himself being sucked. It was a slow, painless, comforting feeling. He allowed himself to be seduced by it, to be taken to a dark soft place where memories, smoothly and unobtrusively, evolved into dreams.

He awoke to the sound of voices. At first he thought they were directed at him and blinked away his sleep in excitement. Quickly, however, his disappointment returned. He realised that the owners of the voices — just like those who had been here before them — knew nothing of his presence. Looking around, Matt saw policemen, lots of them. Some were poking around in the flower beds and bushes, some were scouring the lawn for clues, some were standing around talking, and some were erecting a crude barrier of yellow tape and metal poles around the perimeter of this section of park. Matt felt frightened, almost as if he was playing a joke that had somehow got out of control. Was all this fuss really for him? When he counted the policemen he was shocked to discover there were a total of seventeen, fourteen of whom were in uniform, three in plain-clothes.

The voices he had heard came from two of the plain-clothes men and a uniformed sergeant who appeared to be having an argument. They were standing just too far away for Matt to be able to make out the words, added to which they were conducting their quarrel in an undertone, presumably to thwart the waggling ears of any nosey subordinate.

It was not until Matt tried to stand up that he realised how dreadful he felt. His body throbbed with developing bruises, his throat was swollen and sore and dry. His head was stuffed with a hot woolly ache that had evidently been caused by the sun. And despite feeling parched he needed to urinate, the urge so desperate that it was making him nauseous.

Cupping a hand under his genitals, as if relieving their weight might stem his urge to piss, Matt used his other hand to bang on the glass. Pain sang in his wrist. His throat felt full of sandpaper as he croaked, 'I'm here. Please ... help me.'

No reaction, which was what he had expected but which nevertheless filled him with despair. Perhaps subconsciously he had been hoping a nap would make his problem go away, just as a worry often seemed lessened after a good night's sleep.

He needed to piss. He needed to piss *now*. And if he didn't take down his new England shorts which he hadn't even had the chance to get muddied yet, then he would flood them.

Surrounded by policemen who couldn't see him, he pulled his shorts and underpants down to his thighs, turned to a corner of the wardrobe and began to urinate. He sighed as he did so, feeling his bladder deflate, then wrinkled his nose as the hot, pungent smell of his own urine touched his nostrils. He had been hoping the urine would pool only in the corner he was pissing into, would not spread out too far, and he was therefore dismayed when it began to exceed the boundaries he had envisaged for it. It inched across the floor towards him, covering half of it, then three-quarters, and then finally meeting the opposite wall of the wardrobe, running into and filling all the corners. Now Matt had no choice but to stand with his new football boots in his own urine, the stink of which rose about him like swamp gas.

He began to sob again. He leaned forward to rest his sweaty forehead on the glass wall, then jerked back. Shit, the bloody thing was too hot! Outside his prison, the police were still milling about, looking purposeful. The trio who had been arguing had broken up and gone about their separate businesses, some resolution apparently having been reached. Matt's new shirt was sticking to him. He ached all over. Today, he thought, I have been on this planet exactly ten years. The thought frightened him. It somehow made his life seem like a neat package which was now destined to be crushed and tossed away. He glanced wriggling black movement to his right and looked. A young labrador had scampered onto the lawn and was cavorting around the policemen who were crouched on the grass, looking for clues. Some of the policemen were obviously irritated by the dog whilst the others were lunging for it playfully when it came close, laughing as it gangled out of reach, its tail whipping from side to side.

Matt kicked the glass again, trying to ignore the pain which jerked up through his system. 'Hey, dog,' he croaked. 'Hey, dog, can you hear me?'

He did not expect a response, and was therefore astonished when the dog stopped dead, stiffened, pricked up its ears and slowly turned its head towards him.

Matt felt his mouth go completely dry, his head begin to spin. He blinked his eyes, urging himself: *don't faint now, for goodness sake.* Maybe it had been a fluke, maybe the dog had heard something else and not him at all. Vaguely Matt was aware of a young blond-haired policeman looking amusedly at the dog and saying, 'What is it, boy? What have you heard? Go on, boy, fetch.'

Urgently Matt began to thump on the glass, clenching his

114

teeth against the pain. 'Here, boy, come on,' he rasped. 'Make them see me. Please, *please*.' The labrador began to lollop towards the wardrobe, its expression seemingly one of bemusement, the hackles on its neck rising warily. It was not wagging its tail now, but that didn't matter because it could see him, *it could see him!*

Matt crouched down as the dog walked right up to the glass, barely aware that he was half-laughing, half-sobbing. He opened his left palm and pressed it flat against the wardrobe's transparent door, defying its heat. The dog leaned towards it, nose twitching as it sniffed, though it presumably would not be able to pick up his scent through the glass.

Now the labrador began to circle the wardrobe, sniffing at its base and whining. 'That's it,' Matt said, still half-laughing. 'That's it. Tell them. Let them know.' Eagerly he looked across to the group of crouching policemen, a few of whom were now straightening up and looking curiously at the dog. 'Come on,' Matt urged, 'come on.' The blond-haired policeman who had been playing with the dog began to stroll across. 'Yes,' Matt whispered, clenching his fists. 'Oh yes. Come on.'

'What is it, boy?' said the policeman. 'What have you found?' The dog looked up at him briefly and wagged its tail, then continued sniffing round the wardrobe's base.

'Has he found something, Mike?' one of the other policemen called across.

Mike shrugged. 'Dunno. I can't see anything.'

'What about the grass?' Matt croaked from inside the wardrobe. 'It's all flat, you dork. Are you blind or something?'

The policeman held out his hand to the labrador, which twitched its tail briefly but continued circling the wardrobe.

'It's this patch of grass here. He seems to find it interesting for some reason.'

Now a couple more of the policemen were walking over. 'Probably just the smell of a lady dog which passed this way,' one of them suggested dismissively.

'Or maybe there's a bone buried there,' another said. He only realised the implications of his words when the others

115

looked at him. Frowning he said, 'Nah, can't be. In broad daylight?'

'Maybe we'd better get some shovels, just to make sure,' Mike said.

Inside the wardrobe Matt's joy was turning to frustration. Kicking the glass again he said, 'The grass under the wardrobe is flat, you morons. There's a perfect square of squashed grass. Can't you see it?' It was only as the words left his lips that it occurred to him that maybe the policemen couldn't see it. If whatever controlled the wardrobe could make it and him invisible, then there was no reason why it shouldn't be able to make the grass appear normal to the policemen's eyes.

He watched as a couple of the policemen went away to collect shovels, wondering what would happen when they tried to dig. Would their shovels meet with some invisible obstruction? If so, how would they react? Matt wanted to believe that they would quickly put two and two together. They would conclude that the missing boy was most probably trapped inside the invisible box and they would devise some means to break it open. If they were as smart as that then he could be free within the hour. He might even be free in time for his party. His stomach clenched excitedly at that prospect.

The wardrobe was now so hot inside that Matt felt he was being slowly baked. The heat was causing the stench of his urine to turn increasingly sour; each breath he took was like inhaling the unflushed dregs of a toilet bowl. This combination of heat and smell was making him light-headed; events outside his prison seemed to be happening in a hollow and slothful manner. His thoughts felt as if they were contained in a balloon-like membrane which was threatening continually to float out through the top of his head. He was sweating so profusely that his skin felt slimy, like the putrefying flesh of old vegetables.

Two policemen returned carrying three shovels apiece. Behind them, scowling, strolled one of the plain-clothes men. 'Just a couple of feet and that's that,' Matt heard him say. 'If someone *is* buried there, then I want you to be as careful with the turf as whoever did it obviously was.

116

Though why we're paying any attention to the actions of a bloody mongrel ...' He shook his head, apparently too disgusted to complete the sentence, and watched sullenly as the shovels were distributed and the policemen readied themselves. The young labrador, which was still circling the wardrobe, still sniffing and whining and occasionally scrabbling with its claws, was grasped by the collar and pulled protestingly away.

Now, Matt thought, now we shall see. As the policemen approached he felt an involuntary trembling in his body, starting at his feet, working up through his legs and stomach and chest, branching out into his arms, flowing into his head. He thought it was anticipation, excitement, but when he looked down he realised the movement was coming not from him but from the wardrobe. It was vibrating as if affected by an earth tremor, and the surface of the yellow pool that was Matt's urine was trembling minutely, tiny waves slapping against the wardrobe's corners, confirming the movement.

When the first of the policemen was perhaps two feet away, and placing the blade of his shovel on the ground in preparation to dig, the glass wardrobe rose into the air like an unsupported lift. Shocked, Matt slithered and almost fell in his own urine, but managed to regain his balance despite the pain that shot through his bad ankle. He banged the wardrobe's glass wall simultaneously with both fists, reawakening more pain, and screamed, *'No! No! No!'* His protests had no effect. The wardrobe rose steadily until it was perhaps twenty feet above the ground. Then it stopped and hovered in mid-air, like some bizarre bubble lifted by the wind.

Below him, through a glass floor filmed yellow with his piss, Matt saw the policemen begin to dig. Utterly despondent, he sank to a crouch, closing his eyes in frustration and despair, feeling like wailing but unable to summon up the energy to do even this. He could feel hope trickling away. He was never going to get out of this. Never. He would be here until he starved to death. The digging sounds from below made him feel his grave was already being prepared.

He crouched for an age in the rising stink of his urine, sweat plastering his hair to his head and his clothes to his body. His limbs throbbed, his throat felt lined with cardboard. For the time being he felt sick to his stomach, but soon hunger would begin to gnaw at him, and his tongue would swell through dehydration. The heat of the sun was now making his head beat thickly, jarring his thoughts, and all feeling seemed to be retracting from his extremities, as if the life-energy which filled him was shrivelling, curling inwards like the petals of a dying flower. He tried to waggle his fingers but there seemed little sensation there. Opening his eyes he saw them twitch briefly but that was all. He seemed divorced from himself. Enervated, his eyes drooped closed again.

When he next woke his headache was so bad it seemed someone was beating him about the head with a frying pan. He moaned and raised an arm, which felt stiff and tight with pain. The smell of urine stung his nostrils; it was pungent as a long-neglected public toilet. Worse, the back of his new England shorts were soaked from where he had sunk into a sitting position in his sleep.

He rose with immense difficulty, his limbs feeling frighteningly weak. Despite his aching head the sun was no longer strong; indeed, it was setting in a spectacular wash of pinks and crimsons, leaving shadows to coagulate and strengthen on the earth. Matt's throat and mouth seemed indistinct now, a thick wad of rubber in which a suggestion of pain occasionally spasmed. He could feel the coldness of his own stale urine running from his drenched shorts down the back of his legs and into his socks, which he remembered had been crisp and new-smelling and startlingly white when he'd dragged the wrapping paper from around them that morning. He felt an emotion rising in him, but it was not until it reached the surface that he recognised it as rage. And then he was screaming raggedly through his parched throat, and he was kicking and flailing at the glass walls around him, the adrenalin of his fury superseding the pain.

His assault on the walls of his prison stopped only when his foot skidded out from under him, and for the second time he fell. He smashed his head against the wall again, almost blacking out. His body splatted in urine, which immediately soaked and stained his new clothes. This time, he knew, he would not get up. He had lost the strength and the spirit. He had been reduced by the relentlessness of his ordeal to this, an animal grovelling helplessly in the stench of its own waste. He closed his eyes and let his head fall back. He wasn't going to get out and so he wanted to die. Now. He felt himself sinking and wondered if this was what dying was. Then there was a slight bump and the sensation ceased. Reluctantly he opened his eyes.

The wardrobe had descended back to earth, that was all. It was standing on the grass of the park again, a few feet away from a neat square hole in the ground which had been ringed with lights, a police barrier and a warning sign ordering people to: KEEP OUT. POLICE INVESTIGATION. Of the police themselves there was no sign. Matt was about to close his eyes again when he glimpsed a suggestion of movement in the darkening hedges to his right. Slowly he turned his head, and saw three hunched shadows detach themselves from the surrounding gloom and begin to shuffle towards him.

Matt heard a voice, crackly and shrill with age. 'I told ya he'd still be alive, boys.'

There was a deep chuckle, then a new voice said gloomily, 'Don't seem to be much fight in him, though, do there? Me, I like 'em with a bit of spirit.'

'Aw, stop whingeing,' said a third voice, the one which had chuckled. 'That's all you ever do. Moan, moan, moan.'

Voice number two snorted indignantly. The hunched shadows came close enough now for Matt to make them out.

They were old men, midgets, their faces gnarled and bewhiskered, their clothes simply colourless rags. Their eyes were milky-white and flashed like metal, though they did not appear blind. Matt saw that their hands were enormous, spidery, the fingers obscenely long and jointed in at least five places. He whimpered and tried to raise himself, but found that he could not.

The gloomy-voiced midget was dragging what appeared to be a metal trunk on castors behind him. The trunk jounced and bumped over the uneven ground. It looked heavy, but the midget did not appear to find the task a strenuous one. A few feet from Matt the trio stopped, looking down at him with their milk-white eyes. The one who had first spoken tapped the lid of the trunk with one of his hideous fingers. 'Come on then,' he said. 'Let's see what you've managed to cobble together.'

The gloomy-voiced midget shot him a pained glance. 'Please,' he said. 'I'm a craftsman. I take great care and pride in my work.'

The other two sighed. One of them cackled. 'Just show us,' said the other. 'Let us be the judges.'

Scowling, the Craftsman unwound the rope that encircled the trunk, picking at the knots with his grotesque fingers. When the task was complete he groped around in the folds and flaps of rag that clothed him, finally producing a key which he inserted into the trunk's lock. Matt heard the key grinding as the midget turned it. Then there was a resounding click and the other two midgets craned forward, eager despite their banter to see their companion's handiwork. The Craftsman turned briefly to look at Matt, his creased face wrinkling into an unpleasant smile beneath his unkempt beard. Matt shivered at the smile and at the coral-white eyes whose surfaces seemed to swirl lazily like the patterns in an oil-slick.

'Get on with it,' one of the midgets grumbled. The Craftsman scowled at him, then turned back to the trunk. Curling his long fingers under the rim of the trunk's lid he lifted it and threw it back.

The other two midgets murmured their approval at what was inside. 'It's *nice*,' said one, whilst the other reached out and stroked the trunk's contents, multi-jointed fingers crackling.

'Where are you going to put it?' purred the stroker.

'The pond, I thought. They'll probably be dredging that tomorrow.'

The other two nodded. 'It looks perfect in every detail,' the stroker crooned.

'Of course it's perfect,' said the Craftsman a little indignantly. He stepped back from the trunk to pick up the rope which he had tossed carelessly aside, and in that terrible, tantalising moment Matt raised his head with a gargantuan effort and caught the barest glimpse of what the trunk contained.

He saw – was certain he saw – a pale hand and an England football shirt streaked with slick red stripes. His whole body seemed to shrivel with terror. His stomach clenched with genuine pain, causing tears to spark in his eyes before he could see if there was a face.

He heard the lid of the trunk clanging shut, soft movement coming towards him, and then a voice which said, 'Pretty boy.' When he blinked away his tears he saw those opaque eyes staring down at him greedily, saw the Craftsman doing something with the wardrobe door and then pulling it open. Matt wanted to scream but could only whimper and writhe like a fish tossed onto a rock. The first thing he felt was the wind on his face. The second thing, their hands on his body.

Warts and All

It started as nothing more obtrusive than a small bump between the second and third knuckle of the index finger of Jason Platt's right hand. It itched ever so slightly, and Jason rubbed at it as he lay back on his bed and stared out of the window. It was the summer holidays. The days were white-hot. Jason watched the tops of the trees nudge the undersides of wispy clouds like cattle prods. Birds were chirping. Faintly he could hear the pigs snorting in the sty. He sighed as he heard the back door slam, and was pulling on his baseball boots even before his mother's footsteps began to clump up the wooden stairs.

He was tying the second shoelace when her head appeared round the door. She looked weary, the skin around her eyes dark, her hair scraped carelessly back.

'Jacey,' she said in a tired voice, 'could you feed the chickens and fetch in the cows for milking? I'm going to have to phone the vet. Ermintrude's come down with something again.'

'Sure, Mum,' Jason said, springing from his bed as though in the hope that a show of vitality would somehow rub off on her. Since his dad had run off with 'that woman' they had had to deal with one crisis after another. First their prize pig, Lizzy, had died of bloat. Then some of the cows had eaten some fungus in the top field which had affected milk production. Then the farm's plumbing, which had been on the way out for years, had finally packed in. And now Ermintrude, the goat, whom his mother adored, kept coming down with these mysterious illnesses.

125

'What's wrong with her this time?' Jason asked, crossing the room.

Beth, his mother, shrugged. 'Oh, I don't know. Diarrhoea. Bringing up her food. And her eyes look ... funny. Cloudy.'

Jason didn't like the sound of that but he tried to keep his voice casual. 'It's probably just a bug she's got. Mr MacDonald'll give her something and she'll be right as rain in the morning.'

Beth's lips twitched into a smile. 'I hope so. But I'll still have to pay his bill, won't I?'

Jason placed a hand on her arm, tried to instil as much earnestness into his fifteen-year-old voice as he could. 'We'll get by, Mum, don't worry. We'll be all right.'

His mother smiled, touched his hair briefly, but her eyes showed she was unconvinced. 'Course we will,' she said, then started down the stairs.

Jason followed, watching the way her shoulders slumped, the way she stooped like an old woman. He saw a few errant white hairs among the chestnut that he was sure had not been there a month ago. He loved his father achingly, but he also hated him for what he had done. Love and hate: sometimes Jason got so confused that they seemed like the same thing. Scowling, he trailed his mother through the kitchen and out the back door. Almost unconsciously he rubbed at the bump on his index finger.

'Nettle sting?' Beth asked.

Jason looked up almost guiltily, unaware that she had been watching him scratch. It was now night and the animals were quiet. The two of them had struggled through another day. Jason liked this time best – the quiet hour before bed when his mother sewed and he read his book. Sometimes the two of them played cards together or Trivial Pursuit or Scrabble. Or sometimes, though not often, they watched a film on the black and white TV, whose reception in winter made programmes take place in a snowstorm.

'No,' he said and held up his hand on which the bump was now the size of a pimple. 'It's this thing. It itches like mad. I noticed it this morning. I can't stop scratching it.'

Beth put aside the cardigan she was darning and took his hand. Her own hands were delicate, long-fingered, but work-rough. 'Hmm,' she said, 'it's a wart. You shouldn't pick it, it'll spread. Look, you've made it bleed already.'

She bathed the wart in TCP, which got under the broken skin and bit like ants. Then she peeled the backing from a plaster and placed it carefully over the growth.

'Now, leave it alone. Tomorrow I'll get you something from the village.' She reached for the cardigan again, then her hands were deflected to her mouth which opened in a yawn. Blearily she looked at the clock and straightened, placing a hand in the small of her back. 'I suppose I'd better go and check on Ermintrude,' she said tiredly, 'Would you make the cocoa, love? I'll only be five minutes.'

'Yes, Mum, course,' Jason replied.

They stood up together.

Jason tossed and turned, unsure whether he was asleep or awake. He seemed full of a hideous, grinding itch, which he scratched and scratched and scratched but which still did not go away. He suddenly jerked upright with a cry, his eyelids ripping open. He saw insipid light crawling over his curtains, a pink dawn staining the room. He looked down at his bed, saw smears of half-dried blood striping the sheet and the pillow. The plaster his mother had placed over his wart the night before was screwed up like a small roll of pink flesh. Jason grimaced, his head thick, his stomach slightly nauseous. He rubbed his right hand on the edge of the bed, trying to soothe the itching which had escaped his dreams.

He was unable to do so. The itching persisted, biting-jabbing-rippling over his skin. Clenching his teeth, he held up the hand in front of his face and examined it. The original wart had been reduced to a raw, bloody wound by his fingernails. Jason was dismayed to see three more warts clustered close to the original like offspring. His mother had told him that if he scratched the wart it would spread, but Jason hadn't reckoned on the process being this rapid. He toyed with the idea that he'd contracted measles or chicken pox, but then discarded the notion. No, he'd had both of those by the time he was eight, and he didn't think you could catch them twice. Hissing breath through his teeth, his right hand clenched into a fist, Jason hurried down the landing and into the bathroom.

Almost feverishly he put the plug in the wash basin, then twisted the cold tap. The water spattered up off the enamel, wetting his pyjamas, but Jason didn't care. He plunged his hand into the cold water and immediately gasped in relief. The warts stopped itching as though shocked by the temperature, or as though the itching had been a layer of sensation that the water had sloughed off. With his left hand he rummaged through the bathroom cabinet above the basin, found TCP, a lotion called Bug-Away (which was really for insect bites but which Jason thought might help ease his itching) and a roll of bandage. He drew his hand from the water, dried it carefully on a towel, then put TCP on the damaged wart. The stinging made his eyes water, caused him to clap his left hand tightly to his mouth. When it began to ease a little he applied the Bug-Away, then wrapped the bandage awkwardly around his hand, tying it in a clumsy knot with the aid of his teeth. That done he returned to his bedroom, sat on a chair (he was too repelled by the blood-smeared sheets to return to bed) and drifted into an uneasy sleep.

He woke a little later to the sound of weeping.

'Mum?' Jason said. 'Mum, what's the matter?'

He felt an internal fist squeeze his stomach and chest. His mother was slumped over the kitchen table, her head in her hands, her eyes red and swimming with tears. Her hair hung down like curtains, exposing the back of her neck. Jason stared at the soft down on her skin, the delicate nubs of vertebrae, and his eyes too filled up. He had never seen his mother look so vulnerable, so ... exposed as she did at that moment. His right hand, which had begun to itch again, but only slightly as if it were a sluggishly awakening wasps' nest, now jerked as though enlivened by her wretchedness. Holding it tight to his chest like a frightened kitten, Jason dragged up a chair and sat beside her.

'Mum,' he said tightly, 'Mum, please don't cry.' He laid his left hand self-consciously on the curve of her back. 'Talk

128

to me, Mum, tell me what's wrong. I don't like to see you like this.'

He grimaced as she sniffed and raised her head. She looked like a witch, haggard and ugly. Something crackled in her palm. Jason had thought it was a handkerchief she'd been pressing to her face but he now saw it was a piece of paper.

'The electricity bill's come,' she said in a reedy voice. 'And I just don't know how I'm going to pay it. That ... that bastard left us with nothing, Jacey. A farm that costs more than it earns and bugger-all else. We're ... we're going to have to sell some of the animals, that's the only solution. Even with you off school this place is too big for us to manage on our own ...'

She choked on a sob and wiped her face with her sleeve. For the millionth time that summer, Jason said, 'We'll manage, Mum, you'll see. We'll get by, the two of us. We've got to really, haven't we?'

His words received no reply and after a few moments he stood up and wandered over to the cooker. He filled the kettle, lit the gas, and began to potter about, making breakfast. His hand was itching but he tried to ignore it; yet he held it as a dog might hold a paw pierced with a thorn. Behind him he heard the creak of the chair as his mother sat up, the sound of her blowing her nose. He sensed she was watching him but he didn't turn to look at her. At length she asked, 'What's the bandage for?'

Jason picked up the teapot and carried it to the table. He felt oddly embarrassed by the question, as though she'd asked him something deeply personal, or like the time he'd been examining his newly sprouting pubic hair in a small hand mirror in the bathroom and she'd walked in. He put down the teapot, pulled a chair from under the table and sat on it. Awkwardly he said, 'It's that wart. I must have been scratching it in my sleep. When I woke up this morning it was all bloody. And there were three more on my hand.'

Beth raised her eyebrows. 'Three? Are you sure? They don't usually spread that quick.'

'Well, these have,' said Jason, 'and they itch like crazy. I feel like chopping off my hand just to make it stop.'

He poured the tea and reached for the Cornflakes. Beth said, 'I'll make an appointment for you with Doctor Miles. He should be able to fit us in sometime this morning. It's not normal for warts to spread like that. And they don't usually itch either.'

Jason nodded and spooned Cornflakes into his mouth. He felt clumsy holding the spoon in his left hand. His right hand he held tight to his stomach, balled into a fist like something asleep.

Doctor Miles was an avuncular man in his sixties. He wore a waistcoat and a watch on a gold chain, and had bushy mutton-chop whiskers like a character from Dickens. He had been Limefield's doctor for over thirty-five years, and seemed as permanent as the dark stone buildings and the brooding hills. When the Platts were admitted into his surgery, he stood up and lumbered towards them, hands outstretched.

'Elizabeth, my dear, how are you? And young Jason – my you're a big lad. I expect you'll be a six-footer just like your ... hmm ... yes, well, it's good to see you.'

He covered the faux pas quickly, and without losing his joviality, yet Jason still saw his mother's lips purse, the skin tighten around her face as though she were drawing in her defences. Miles waved them to seats which looked moulded from glazed liquorice, perching himself on the edge of his colossal desk. Toying casually with the end of his stethoscope, he said, 'Now then, Jason. Your mother informs me you have some rather unusual warts.'

Jason nodded, and repeated what his mother had already told Miles on the phone while the doctor carefully snipped the knot on the bandage and peeled it from Jason's hand. As the bandage came away, Jason's voice tailed off, and he and his mother both stared at what lay beneath the material.

There were now five, six, seven, eight, *nine* warts on Jason's hand! *Nine!* Which meant that five new ones had sprung up in the last four hours! The original wart was a crusty, lumpy scab. The others ranged from small white-tipped bumps to hard dry nodules like split peas. For a long moment nobody said anything. Even Miles was silent, his eyebrows raised quizzically. At last Beth murmured, 'It can't be. They can't be spreading as fast as this.' She glanced at Miles. 'What exactly *are* they, doctor?'

Miles hummed and hawed. He examined the warts closely, probed at them with what looked like a plastic blunt-ended toothpick. His brows were beetled. He clucked his tongue. At last he said, 'Well, I'm ashamed to admit I'm baffled.' He sat back, frowning. 'They certainly *look* like warts, but if what you tell me is true ...' He paused. 'You're quite sure you only had four of these when you woke up this morning?'

Jason nodded.

'And when did you say you noticed the first one?'

'Yesterday morning.'

'And that was this one here?' Miles said, pointing at the scab.

Jason confirmed that it was. Miles shook his head and dragged a notepad towards him, taking a pen from his breast pocket with his other hand.

'Well, what I'd like to do, with your permission of course, is to make you an appointment with a colleague of mine. He's a skin specialist, his name is Stephen Lester, and he's based in Leeds. In the meantime I'll make you out a prescription for something that *should* cauterise the warts and something that *should* stop the itching. If you find that what I've prescribed works, then let me know and I'll cancel the appointment. How does that sound?'

Jason glanced at his mother. It sounded okay to him, but her expression was one of reluctance. Knowing pride would keep her from explaining why, he said, 'Well, the thing is, doctor, it's a bit tight for us at the moment, and I'm not sure we can really afford – '

'Nothing *to* afford,' Miles interrupted, holding up a hand. 'It's all paid for on the National Health. All you have to do is show up.' He reached for the receiver. 'So are we agreed? I really do think you need to get those things seen to, Jason.'

They both looked at Beth, who nodded. 'Of course,' she said, and added indignantly, 'even if we do have to pay for it.'

Miles made his call. Putting down the phone he said,

'Well, that's that. Your appointment is for next Tuesday at 2 p.m. Here's your prescription. And remember what I told you – any improvement, you let me know.'

Jason smiled and thanked him. After Miles had carefully applied a clean bandage to his hand, he and his mother left and made their way to the chemist's to pick up the prescription. The stuff to cauterise the warts was like white glue, the lotion to ease the itching a greasy yellow. In the bus on the way home the itching got so bad that Jason had to rip off the new bandage and smear the yellow stuff over his hand. He reapplied the bandage with his mother's help, then leaned back, closing his eyes, gritting his teeth. He felt a little thick-headed, a touch feverish, but put this down to the stiflingly hot bus, the jolting and grinding of gears as the driver negotiated ruts in the road. Thankfully the yellow stuff seemed to act quickly and within minutes the itching was little more than a subdued tingle.

When they got back the first thing they saw was Ermintrude the goat lying on her side in her pen.

This was not unusual in itself; Ermintrude slept often, especially in the heat. But there was something about the way she was lying that immediately drew the eye. Maybe it was the fact that she was so, so still. Or maybe it was the flies, buzzing around her motionless form, clouds of them landing on her face then taking off, like a busy airport in miniature.

The reason, however, was not important. The fact was, as soon as Jason saw the goat he felt a blend of dread and weary inevitability. Beside him he heard his mother mutter, 'Oh my God,' then the two of them were through the gate and stumbling up the slight grassy incline beside the house.

Up close the truth could not be denied. Ermintrude's tongue lolled from her mouth; her eyes, implacable as dark glass, were half-open. The collar she wore round her neck, and the long chain attached to it and secured to a peg in the ground, looked like some slack and clumsy torture device.

Beth dropped to her knees and abruptly began to cry, trembling right hand frantically stroking the goat's fur as though to massage life back into it. Jason stood at his mother's shoulder, staring down, listening to the flies whose incessant drone was like the empty idiot hum of death itself. The sun beat on their backs, its apparent optimism like a mockery of their situation. Though he knew it was pointless, Jason could not help thinking that this was his fault. If only they'd stayed at home and not gone to the doctor's about his stupid warts, then maybe Ermintrude might still be alive.

Though she did not blame him for what had happened, Jason felt that his mother's silence was accusation enough. The two of them went about their tasks with barely a word to each other for the rest of the day, their eye contact reduced to a bare minimum. For Jason, however, guilt was not his only problem. Coupled with it was an increasing physical discomfort, the root of which, he felt sure, lay in his itching hand. The yellow stuff had done its job for a while, but now the itching was returning, and not just that but it seemed more voracious than ever and had spread as far as his elbow. Also the stuffy feeling in his head had worsened, as had his feverishness. It was almost five o'clock when Jason stumbled back to the house and up the stairs to the bathroom. He decided to change the dressing on his hand, take a couple of aspirin and have a lie-down before supper.

He unwound the bandage slowly, both hopeful and fearful of what he might see. He tried to convince himself that the white stuff the doctor had given him must be working, that the itching had increased because the stuff was getting inside the warts and burning them away. A pulse was jumping in his throat which he tried to swallow but couldn't. He smiled at his own nervousness. His left hand was trembling slightly as he tugged the last of the bandage away.

The smile froze on his face. For the first time fear jumped into his mind, slid down through his body like a rain of sparks. Jason cleared his throat and tried to tell himself that what he was seeing was not as bad as it seemed. It was the stuff the doctor had given him that made his arm look such a mess. Once he had washed all the gunk off it would be okay.

He placed his arm in the sink and let cold water sluice over it. As before he felt relief from his itching, though this time it was not so absolute; he felt the itching biting back, fighting against his attempts to drown it. He dried the arm carefully with toilet paper, then examined it again. The pulse hammered in his throat, he felt sick to the pit of his stomach. There were – it took him almost a minute to count them – twenty-four warts on his hand and forearm. *Twenty-fucking-four*! Almost an average of one every hour since yesterday morning.

Jason shook his head. No, it couldn't be. Apart from the warts, some of which were growing together like clumps of fungus, his arm looked ... sickly. Wasted. As though all that lay beneath the skin – blood, muscle, bone – was turning mushy like old banana.

He shuddered at the thought and closed his eyes to stop himself from puking. It was just his imagination. After all, there was no pain, just this bloody awful itching. Stubbornly he applied more of the white stuff, more of the yellow stuff, and smothered it in clean bandage. He tied the bandage tight, as though to contain the ... the infection beneath the constrictive material. By this time tomorrow, he assured himself, the white stuff will have begun its work; his warts would be shrivelling away. He looked at himself in the mirror and was reassured that his face looked normal, if a little flushed. Next moment he gripped the edge of the sink convulsively as his name came screeching up the stairs at him:

'*Jaaasonnn*!'

Jason turned towards the sound. Of course it had been his mother's voice, and preceding it had been a hideous screeching, squealing noise which was still going on. He thought wildly of something huge, like a juggernaut, careering out of control, slamming on its brakes as it ploughed towards the house. Then he realised what the noise really was: it was the pigs. They were screaming with terror, as though a lion had been let loose in their sty.

Jason raced downstairs, out the back door and round the corner of the house. He saw his mother leaning over the wooden wall of the sty, screeching as loudly as the pigs, brandishing a broom in her hands. Her eyes were stretched wide; spittle was flying from her lips. Reaching her, Jason too leaned over the sty wall to see what was going on.

It was Napoleon, father of many, the oldest, dirtiest, fattest pig that they owned. He was going berserk, charging about the sty, chomping, trampling, in a random and terrifying act of destruction. One of the younger pigs, Boxer, was a crushed mass of torn flesh. The others were huddled together, squealing, tumbling over one another to get away each time the huge boar charged.

Beth was using the broom as a bludgeon, bringing it down again and again, clubbing guilty and innocent alike.

'*Mum!*' Jason yelled at her. '*Mum, stop it! It's not doing any good!*'

She turned to face him, startled as though from a dream. Jason took the broom from her and climbed up onto the sty wall. He dug his feet between the wooden slats and leaned over as far as he dared. Napoleon was snorting and rolling his eyes − black stone-eyes, empty and merciless, like a shark's. Creamy froth was dripping from the pig's gnashing mouth, bubbling from his flared snout. As Jason watched, Napoleon teetered slightly as though drunk, then let out an enraged bellow and charged head-first into the opposite wall.

The impact caused the sty to shudder, the pigs to squeal anew. Jason clutched the top of the wall to stop himself losing his balance. Napoleon grunted and shook his head, then seemed to sense that someone was watching him and swung slowly around. Choosing his moment, Jason raised the broom, then brought it swiftly down. The broom-head made a sickening crunch as it impacted with Napoleon's skull.

Jason felt a judder pass through his body, but it seemed at first that Napoleon had been unaffected by the blow. The pig stood where he had been hit as though in measured and silent contemplation. His snout twitched; more froth drooled from his mouth. Then in a horrible kind of slow motion his legs buckled, his eyes glazed, and he rolled heavily onto his side. His flanks heaved − in, out, in, out − and he grunted softly as though in the midst of a contented dream.

Supper was cancelled. Beth seemed too traumatised by this latest episode to even consider preparing any, and Jason

135

felt too ill to eat anyway. Between them they managed to drag Napoleon's unconscious body out of the sty and into Jason's father's tool shed. Jason covered the pig with a blanket, locked the tool shed door, then called Raich Tanner, known as the Meat-Man, who promised to drop by and pick up Boxer's carcass in the morning. He was about to call the vet too, to come and look at Napoleon, when his mother stayed him with a hand on the arm.

'Leave it until tomorrow.' she said. 'I can't face seeing anyone else today.'

Jason felt inclined to argue – Napoleon might need immediate attention – but the look on his mother's face discouraged him. In the end he simply said, 'Okay, Mum,' and replaced the receiver with a soft ching. That done, he did what he had planned to do earlier. He went upstairs, took two aspirin, lay back on his bed and slept.

He had a strange and all too vivid dream. He was walking in the woods that bordered the farmland, his right arm itching horribly. He was looking for something, perhaps something to ease his discomfort, a herb or a plant or a root. It was early evening. Sun was dripping through the trees, dappling the ground, but soon Jason knew it would grow dark; the trees would turn black as though sucking the darkness in. He stumbled over rocks, around bushes, around trees, until suddenly he was in a clearing. This was where he was supposed to be ... yet still he couldn't say what he was looking for. He walked forward cautiously, head turning this way and that as though afraid of ambush. Something caught his eye: a butterfly perched on a leaf, delicate red wings shimmering like petals of blood. 'Butterfly,' Jason murmured, and was entranced by the word, as though really hearing it, relishing its lilting cadences, for the first time. He walked forward, saw the butterfly's antennae trembling, its eyelash-thin legs poised as though to spring. He moved closer. 'Butterfly,' he whispered again as though the word was a charm that could glue the insect to the leaf. Still the butterfly didn't move. Now Jason was only an arm's length away. He stopped and breathed, 'Butterfly,' for the third time, then slowly raised his bandaged right hand. He extended his index finger and brought it slowly, tremblingly, towards the fragile insect. The butterfly remained where it was. Jason's finger touched one of the wings, began to stroke it gently. He smiled, enraptured, and began softly to coo. Without warning the butterfly crumbled to black ash and was scattered by the breeze.

The ceiling looked blurred. Jason gazed at it but could not pinpoint exactly what it was that made it seem ... different. He was lying on his back, fully clothed, on top of his bed. Sunlight that contained the freshness of morning poured in through the window.

His arm hurt. Badly. Not just itched but really *hurt*, as if someone had come along and broken it in the night. The itch was still there but now it seemed swamped by the pain. Or rather, not swamped but squeezed upwards along his chest and the right side of his face.

He opened his mouth. The itching fizzed along his jaw, in and out of his ear, cut a trail across his cheekbone and the rim of his eye socket. Shit, it felt as though hornets were hatching out inside his skull. But his arm, that was the main thing. His arm hurt *so bad*.

He tried to move it and found to his relief that he could. He clenched and unclenched his hand, wincing against the prospect of further pain, but the ache remained constant; movement seemed not to affect it. He shuffled into a semi-sitting position and brought his right arm slowly round where he could see it. Beneath the bandage the arm looked ... misshapen, somehow pulpy. The thought made him nauseous. He plucked at the knot and unwrapped the bandage with fumbling fingers. The thing revealed beneath was so horrible, so utterly awful, that for a few moments he could do nothing but gaze at it.

It was hard to believe that the twisted, emaciated limb smothered in warts had ever been a human arm ... and it was even harder to believe that the obscenity was still attached to Jason's body. A cold clinical part of his mind furnished him with a memory, an approximation: a dead tree branch he had found in the woods a few weeks ago that had been yellow-white with insects' eggs. He whimpered as he moved his hand. The fingers were like fat, lumpy white worms, the arm itself boneless, fluid as a snake. He swung his legs to the floor, putting his left hand out to the wall to support him.

He froze. Fear raced through his body, slamming doors, blocking off air. The wall beneath his hand was ... bumpy, as though there were pebbles beneath the wallpaper. And the carpet beneath his feet. And his bed. They were bumpy too.

He looked. Stared. Properly for the first time. Everything in his room – *everything* – was covered in ... in lumps.

In warts.

No! No, it was impossible!

Jason slid to the floor and brought his knees up to his chin. He began to snigger, then to laugh, and then finally to scream. When he had done his throat felt sore and tender but his mind felt clear, his thoughts almost unnaturally lucid. He looked around the room – warts on the cupboard, warts on the chair, warts like soap bubbles in the glass of his window – and he thought, Mum. What about Mum? Oh shit, what about Mum?

He stood up, his legs weak and trembly, and stumbled out of his bedroom. Warts were popping up everywhere – on the landing, on the banister, even on the ornaments and plants and books and ... everything.

He went into his mother's room. It was empty, the bed covers thrown back. The bed was full of warts, which from this distance looked like white beads.

He came out of his mother's room and went into the bathroom.

She was not there either. Jason felt like going back to bed, warts or no warts. His arm hurt – fucking hurt – and his fluey symptoms (stuffy head, fever) were galloping through his body.

He half-turned and caught a glimpse of himself in the mirror. Reflective blisters flawed the glass but there was still enough of a smooth surface for Jason to see what his face had become. He stared at the image – his right cheek reduced to lumpy porridge, his ear a cluster of fleshy bubbles – and he shouted, '*No! No! No!*'

Instinctively he struck out with his left hand. The mirror

138

burst, a spider's web that exploded into slivers of discordant tinkling music. A stripe of blood welled up over the back of his hand. He ignored it, let it drip.

'Mum,' he moaned. 'Mum, where are you?' He sat on the edge of the bath. 'Why are you doing this to us, God? It's not fair. It's not fair.'

No answers came, not from God or anyone. Over the past couple of months Jason had come to learn that often in life there *were* no answers. Things happened, bad things, and when you asked why, when you pleaded to be told what you'd done to deserve them, you were presented only with the blank and uncaring mask of Fate. There was no way round the mask, no way inside it, no way of examining Fate's motives, trying to make sense of its randomness. All you could do was accept its actions and carry on. Because the more you picked and probed and questioned, the more infected the wound it had left in your life became.

Jason wanted, at that moment, to sleep, to die, to sink into a black and silent oblivion where he could forget this awful, awful ... *thing* that in less than two days had taken over his life. But first I have to find Mum, he told himself, I have to make sure she's okay. I have to get her away from here.

He stood up, walked slowly along the landing, down the stairs, into the kitchen. There were warts everywhere – on the bread, the cooker, the cutlery, the mugs – but still there was no sign of his mother. His right arm hung limply, unbandaged, by his side. He felt so ill, so very very ill, but in a way he felt he'd gone beyond that, as though physical pain was somehow only a minor by-product of a greater horror. He walked to the back door, pushed it open, went outside. The sun blinded him, swathed him in heat, as though in a last desperate display of beauty, warmth, life.

'Mum!' Jason shouted. 'Mum, where are you?'

He heard movement to his left, round the corner of the house. He turned towards it as a voice, his mother's, spoke the first syllable of his name, 'Jay,' as though pointing out a bird. Then, before the name could be completed, it bubbled up into a high, ratcheting scream.

'*Mum!*' Jason yelled and forced himself to run towards

139

the sound. He heard another scream, then a single sobbed word, 'No,' then a further scream, abruptly cut off. His body felt sluggish and it hurt — *it hurt* — but Jason pushed it to its limits. The corner of the house lay ten feet away ... seven ... four ... one ...

Then he skidded round it, saw the yard, the sty, the milking shed, the barn ...

And caught a glimpse, just a glimpse, of something scuttling, shapeless, *warty*, dragging his mother into the barn's gloomy interior.

'Oh God, no,' he moaned and sprinted towards the barn's open door. As he ran he thought crazily, Don't touch the butterfly, don't touch the butterfly, don't touch the butterfly. Halfway across the yard he slipped on a cobblestone and fell sprawlingly, hands raised as though in surrender. He bumped his head, jarred his hip, but clambered to his feet and carried on.

The barn was dark after the sunlight. Shadow lay on shadow in a sombre and confusing collage. The smell was a blend of cows and hay — rich, sweet, musky. Gashes of light lay on the walls like luminous cuts.

Jason walked forward, aware of his rustling footsteps, his breath like tearing paper. He saw mounds of hay, tools against the walls, a wooden ladder leading up to a hayloft. At the far end of the barn, cloaked in shadows, was what he could only think of as a *construction*.

It was eight feet high, five feet across. It resembled a kiln built of papier-mâché, or a colossal wasps' nest. It had grown, or been made, within the last twenty-four hours. Jason had come into the barn yesterday morning and there had been no sign of it then.

'Mum,' he called. 'Mum, please answer me.' His voice boomed hollowly and received only silence in reply. He walked towards the construction (*the hive*, he thought suddenly), his arm hurting, his body feverish, black fear gnawing at his stomach. Each moment he expected something to fly at him out of the gloom, to come screeching out of the dimness, but nothing did. When he was six feet from the hive he stopped, the itching crawling over his face, making it twitch, and said again, 'Mum? Mum, are you there?'

140

He heard something from behind the hive. A small but persistent sound that had him inching his way forward, straining his ears. It was a delicate sound − wet, smacking, repetitive − like a baby stamping its tiny feet in water, or ... or ... An image bloomed suddenly in his mind ... Bess, his father's sheepdog, slurping her way through her midday bowl of Pedigree Chum.

'God, no,' Jason breathed. 'Oh God, please no ...'

He tried to shout, '*Mum!*', but the word dissolved in his mouth, became a choking sob. He took a lurching step towards the hive, then stopped as the slurping sounds were replaced by silence. He began to back away as a looming shadow, darker than the rest, sidled round the edge of the hive and seeped across the floor.

Something followed the shadow. Something hunched, fat, bulbous with warts. A sickeningly pungent smell spiked Jason's nostrils, and he turned his head away as he felt his gorge rise. When he turned back a second later the thing was staring at him unblinkingly.

Staring at him ...

(*No, it couldn't be! It couldn't!*)

... with Napoleon's eyes.

'Ne ... ne ... ne ... ne ... ne ...' Jason mumbled idiotically, his legs leading him a strange backpedalling dance. He thought of the broom crashing down on the pig's skull, the dead weight of the vast body he and his mother had dragged into the tool shed. The pig's eyes were black. Mean. So cold, so ... so *soulless* that a flash of any kind of emotion, even hatred, would have been welcome in them.

'Napoleon's locked in the shed,' Jason whispered as though his words could make it so. The warty thing growled at him softly, a black wound opening below its eyes to reveal crooked chomping teeth. It oozed forward, though at first made no move to attack, as though it were merely protecting its lair.

And then, without warning, it let out a hideous screaming bellow and charged.

Jason turned and fled, hot needles blazing through his body, ground glass speeding through his veins. Yet, despite

141

his ailments, he ran faster than he had ever run in his life before. His brain seemed to jolt in his skull, dislodging his thoughts. The sun glared at him. The yard seemed to stretch forever. Jason's feet flew over the cobbles. Once he almost slipped and offered up a brief, despairing prayer before regaining his balance. At last he reached the corner of the house, and seconds later was bursting in through the kitchen door, turning and slamming it behind him.

He stood, his back to the door, sweat pouring down his face. He was not sure how close to him the Napoleon-thing had been, nor even if it had followed him out of the barn, for the grinding, pounding, roaring machine of his own body had drowned out all other sound. That machine was winding down now, breaking into its constituent parts: pain, itch, fear, fever. Suddenly exhausted, Jason slid to the floor, leaving a smeary, sweaty mark on the door's warty wood, and closed his eyes.

Time passed. Jason was not aware he'd been thinking but when he finally opened his eyes again he realised he had come to a decision. With difficulty he dragged himself to his feet, looking round the warty kitchen until his eyes alighted on the big box of Swan Vestas his mother kept handy to light the gas. He picked up the matches, grimacing at the feel of warts on the box like blisters beneath the cardboard, and put them in his pocket. Then he crossed the kitchen and dragged open the heavy door that led into the cellar.

He went down the cellar steps, feeling warts of stone pushing against the soles of his feet, warts of rusty iron on the banister. The cellar was cool and quiet and dark. Jason switched on the light at the bottom and everything jumped into brightness. He sat on the bottom cellar step, suddenly overcome by a feeling of horror and depression. He sunk his face into his left hand and started to sob and shake his head. After a while he began to murmur, 'I'm sorry, I'm sorry,' over and over again through his tears.

Once his quiet hysteria had run its course he stood up and crossed to a set of shelves that were affixed to the opposite wall. He took down a rusty cobweb-strewn can of petrol, held it to his ear and jiggled it. Liquid sloshed inside. Not much but enough for his purposes. Can in hand, matches

142

in pocket, Jason ascended the stairs to the kitchen.

He looked out of the kitchen window. There was no sign of the Napoleon-thing, so he opened the door a crack and peered out. He half-expected something to come at him squealing, but nothing did, so he opened the door wider and stepped into the sunshine. He left the door ajar, and as a precaution unscrewed the cap of the petrol can and threw it away. It hurt his right hand to do all this but he gritted his teeth against the pain and thrust the hand into his trouser pocket. It felt like someone was grinding his bones to a pulp, but he managed to close the hand around the box of Swan Vestas and pull it out. Then, with a deep breath, he began to walk towards the corner of the house.

Actually turning the corner into the yard was the worst part. He had to force his legs to perform the action. He wondered how quickly he could splash on the petrol, take the match from the box, strike it and throw it, especially with his gammy arm. The procedure seemed time-consuming and cumbersome. He suspected that if the Napoleon-thing came for him again he would simply throw whatever he was holding at the creature and run. He sniggered at the thought despite his fear. His laughter died and he looked around with wide eyes as he entered the yard.

It was empty. The only sound he could hear was the lazy drone of summer. For the first time he noticed the door of his father's tool shed, the bottom half shattered like matchwood. He swallowed, or tried to. The pulse in his throat was jumping again. His body felt like a clumsy burden as he crossed the yard and re-entered the barn.

Silence. Gloom. So deep, so profound, that Jason felt almost like jumping and shouting to counter it. At the far end the hive sat in its nest of hay and shadows like a giant egg. The Napoleon-thing was nowhere to be seen.

Jason began to walk forward. The petrol sloshed at his side; the matchbox felt solid and comforting in his wart-encrusted right hand, despite the pain. If that thing comes for me, he thought, I'll turn it into bacon rashers — and this time he tried not to think of the awkward procedure that this would involve.

He could smell the petrol. Could smell something else

too, something besides the hay. It was a hot smell, raw, unpleasant. Bacon rashers, he thought desperately, fucking bacon rashers. He walked right up to the hive, heart gibbering, and began to jerk petrol around its base.

Something moved behind the hive. Shifted. Grunted quietly. 'Bacon rashers,' Jason muttered and waited for the Napoleon-thing to emerge. He waited long moments until the grunting softened and the movements ceased. Wary of the smell of petrol, he thought. Either that or the thing's asleep.

He splashed petrol over the hive itself, unaware that he was humming softly. The chemical smell made his stomach turn, but Jason ignored it. When the can was empty he tossed it onto a mound of hay and fumbled open the box of matches. He was about to reach in for a match when he thought: I wonder what it feels like.

The thought seemed unbidden, almost startling, like something scuttling from beneath a rock on the beach. 'I wonder what it feels like,' he said out loud, and next moment had transferred the box to his left hand and was reaching out with his gnarled right arm. He stretched his fingers, like white-barnacled worms, and laid his palm flat on the hive's exterior. It was warm. Dry. Alive. And more . . . more than that . . . it spoke to him . . .

It was not an actual word, but a boom, a throb, a pulse that resounded throughout his entire body. Jason's itching flared, then stilled, like fire doused with water. He felt suddenly . . . free. That was the only phrase to describe it. Free as a bird, free as the wind, free as . . . free as . . .

Free.

'Free,' he said. And smiled. The word sounded good in his mouth.

Free. That single word somehow, magically, seemed to embrace a complete and perfect philosophy.

'Free,' he said again, and chuckled delightedly. 'Free.'

Then he threw the matches away, squatted back on his haunches, and waited.

Playing God

I done something amazing. I done something wich milions of peple have bene trieing to do for milions of yeres. Ill be a hero, Ill probly get an OBE or something from Her Majesty (God Bles Her). Peple will chere me in the stretes and ask for my ortagraf and all that.

Ill tell yoo what I done and how I done it. It was qite esie realy, qite strateforwerd. Maybee thats wye no ones ever bene abel to do it before, becase it was so esie no one thoght to do it that way. But Im geting ahede of myself arnt I, Ill take yoo throgh it step by step. Im riting it down like this as I supose a kind of testerment, a sort of record for fewture generasions, a bit like the Bibel realy.

Anyway this is what hapened. Were I live its like a bedsit in a howse. Its a bit manky, the toylet lekes and theres like all damp on won of my wals but I put a poster over it, Cobra with Silvester Stalone, have yoo sene that film, its dead good. Anyway if I look owt of my window I can see this park over the rode were all these peple go joging, yupees and all that, and theres sometimes some realy nise berds and plenty of fat peple hoo look like there goeing to drop dead of hart atakes. (only they wont anymore now becase of what I done)

Anyway this won nite, I think it was last Wenseday, yes it was becase the chinky was shut so I had to have boreing old benes on toste for tee. Anyway I desided to go for a wark in the park and look at all the berds joging and that and so I went owt and warked acros the rode and went in throgh the gates. It was stil qite lite becase its Agust and it

147

dosent get dark til 9 or something and it was qite warm so I just wore my tee shirt, my best won with Comando on it that I got in virgin megastore in town and my best jenes. Anyway I was warking arond and there were a few peple joging but not many, no realy fit berds like I wanted, and then all of a suden I got like this bad pane, realy bad, in my arm and then in my chest.

Anyway it was realy horibele and my legs went like jely and I thoght id pewke so I nelt down on the grownd and wated for it to go away and sudenly I saw this like flash of wite owt of the corner of my iye and I looked up and there he was. Only I dident no it then, it wasent until later on that I started puting too and too together. At the time I just looked at this person and I showted 'help' but he ignored me, he just ran past. He was yonge, abowt twentyfive or something, with this wite trake-suite and all blond hare. He looked like an angle realy wich was his joke I supose.

Anyway I think becase Id sene him, maybee becase I was stronger than he thoght I was, he caried on runing and after a bit the feleing stoped. I stil felt sike and all that and swetey and my hart was banging like a drum but I manajed to get to my fete and wark home. I went in and Mrs Miller hoo lives downstares, shes old and shes got arthrites realy bad and I think shes a bit senile in the hede, anyway she says to me 'yoo look realy pale Michael are yoo ill' and I says 'no Im alrite thanks Mrs Miller Ive bene joging'. Shell beleve anything yoo tell her, pore old cow.

Anyway I went upstares and made a cup of tee and drunk it but after a bit I pewked it all bake up agane so I went to bed. The next morning I woke up and I was fine.

Anyway a weke pased or something and I was ok, fit as a fidel, and then on the next friday I think it was I desided to go in the park agane and look at all the berds joging. So of I went as well as can be expected and warked arond a bit. I saw some kids playing footbal and wached for a bit but then won of them ponted at me and sade something and the others all laghed and they gave me this funy look like I was won of them sex perverts or something so I warked of but not before scowling at them and puting them in there plase.

Anyway then I saw these too berds, dead fit Im not joking.

148

Won of them looked like Samantha Fox and the other won looked like Linda Luserdy. They both cold have bene paje 3 girls no mesing. Anyway they were joging along chating and everything and there tits were bobing up and down like Heven. Anyway won of them (the Linda Luserdy won) turned rond and gave me the iye Im not joking. I smiled at them all sort of sexy and they gigled and so I started joging behind them abowt a few yards away, ten or so.

Anyway next thing I no it hapened agane, a big masive pane shooting up my arm and into my chest. I went cold all over then hot then I fell over, the grond just came up and hit me like the werld had gone upsidedown. I felt sike and awful and the pane was bad, everything clowded over and I thoght this is it but then some time pased althogh I dont remember much but it must have becase when I opened my iyes all these peple were lening over me, lots of jogers with swetey fases and some other peple and too men with uniforms on hoo put me on a strecher and then lifted me into an ambulense. Ther was lots of peple tarking and runing arond and flashing lites and all that, but what I remember most is looking up and seeing him there agane in his wite trake-suite, that yonge man with the blond hare all good looking like an angle. He was looking at me Im sure but when I looked at him he turned away and caried on joging. I tride to tell won of the ambulense men but he dident understand.

Anyway I was in hospitel for a bit, abowt a weke. I had won visiter Mrs Miller. If yoo ask me it shold be her in hospitel not me. All she torked abowt when she came to see me was creme crakers dont ask me wye. The doctors sade Id had a hart atack and Id bene very lukey. They sade I had to stop smoking and drinking and cut down on fat and take more excersise but I mene I was joging when it hapened so that shows what they no doesnt it. Anyway I no what it was cased that hart atack. Id bene doeing lodes of thinking lieing there and Id come to an amazing conclushen. My hart atack had been cased by that man in wite that joger. Twise Id seen him and twise Id bene struke down in my prime. I new this was more than a coinsidense, I just new, it just came to me like God had sent me a mesaje or something. (maybee

149

he had). That man looked like an angle but that was all a trike. In trewthe that man was not just an ordinery man at all. I new now withowt a dobt of shadow that he was 'Death' in person.

I no it sonds daft but if yoo think abowt it it isnt realy. The thing is peple always think of 'Death' as beeing something importent like some big skelerten man all dressed in blake with won of them big curvy blade things. But hes not like that at all, hes just like yoo and me, he just blends in, its like camaflaje. No one ever nos hoo he is even thogh Ill bet lodes of peple have sene him.

Anyway when I got home I made a plan, I rote it all down rele prefeshernal like a bownty hunter like what Silvester wold have done, what Id nede and everything. I always rite things down, that way I never ferget things. Anyway I got it all sorted and a few days later I was in the park agane only this time I was redy. I was croched behind a bush wating, I felt strong and good like I had a frend from above looking down on me if yoo no what I mene.

Anyway I wated for abowt a long time, an hore or so but he dident show up. Lots of peple ran past my hideing plase and never won of them gesed I was there I was that qite. I was like a panther rely I supose wating for its pray all silent and I was even all dresed in blake and I had burnt cork on my fase so Id blend in. I wated and wated never moveing even thogh my foot was goeing to slepe and I was borde as hell.

Anyway at last it started to get dark and I was thinking of caling it a day when my pashense was rewarded. Like before the first thing I saw was that flash of wite, that bloody trake-suite that never semed to get derty. (wich prooves another pont). Shore enogh it was him ('Death') joging along like he dident have a care in the werld he even had a sony walkman on can you beleve his cheke. I cold see his blond hare boncing up and down and he dident even look swetey but only a traned iye like me cold have piked up a detale like that. Anyway he joged down the path litle noeing what lay in wate for him. (ie me). I let him get a litle way in front of me and then I berst owt of the bushes like a posesed deemen or something and I jumped on him.

Anyway after that things semed to go in slow moton, maybee that was his trike his way of trieing to escape but it dident fool me o no, I was too strong for him, I had him on the flore and I was on him like a ton of brikes. He was qite wedey realy and he looked dead scared and he says 'what are you dooing leve me alone' but I hit him in the mowth and made him blede and he shut up. Anyway I pined him down and I says to him 'weve all had enogh of yoo, yore not goeing to case no more troble ever agane'. He says 'I dont no what yore tarking abowt' but he did no, I cold see it in his iyes. Anyway I hit him agane to kepe him qite and I reched into my pokete and I got owt my garote. I says to him 'Im goeing to do to yoo what yoo tride to do to me' and before he cold bat an iyebrow Id wond the garote rond his neke and I was draging him into the bushes.

He dident look so pretey now I can tell yoo. (Ha Ha). His tonge was stiking owt and his fase was goeing all a funy color and he was making horibel noses like gurgling and coghing and his hands were clawing at his throte and his nise wite trake-suite was all mudey. I just laghed at the noses he was making and I says 'see how yoo like it yoo basterd' and then I finished the job there in the bushes and I enjoyed it.

Anyway that wasent the end of it becase Id sene these films were vampires and all that come bake from the dead so I thoght Id beter do the job good and proper. I wated in the bushes with 'Death' until it was dark and everywon had gone home and there wasent nobody left arond and then I lifted 'Death' onto my bake, he was qite lite realy for what he was, and I caride him owt of the park and acros the rode and up to my bedsit withowt not a sole spoting me.

Anyway I had the next bit all planed owt. I took 'Death' into the bathrome and put him in the bath and then I put all bin liners and newspapers and all that on the flore. I had a new ax and a new sore wich Id boght that day from a shop in town and I put them to good use that nite I can tell yoo. I choped and sored 'Death' into litel peces, it was hard work, harder than choping wood and by the end of it my arms were kiling and I was sweteing like a bukete and there was blood everywere but it was worth it. Another thing Id thoght of was geting lots of plastic bags from asda so I got all those and I put 'Death' in them and put all selotape rond the top and then put all the litel bags into a bin liner and put lodes of selotape rond the top of that won as well.

Anyway when I done all that I washed the bath owt and the flore and the walls of all the blood and I washed my hands and my fase and I chanjed my cloths and put the old wons in another bin liner and then I took the too bin liners and put them in the dustbins owtside redey to be colected next morning. When Id done all that I had a last cheke rond to make shore everything was shipshape then I went to bed, I was tiered but hapy.

Anyway next morning (wich is this morning becase I only woke up too hores ago or something) I wated for the dustbin men to come becase they always come on a Tewsday, Id planed it that well. I ate my brekefast, sasage sanwich and a cup of tee and I sat on my chare and looked owt of the window.

Anyway at last just when I was geting nervose I here this big rumbling nose and then this big yelow dustbin lory comes rond the corner. All the men got of and I cold fele the buterflise all in my tumy, then they come up ower path and I felt like I wanted to screme or something. Anyway I nedent wory becase this won, this niger felow with them dredelokes in his hare opened the bin with 'Death' in it and starts to lift owt the bag. I cold see he was haveing troble, 'Death' was qite hevey I admit it, so he cals won of his mates over, this ginormose bald felow to help him. Then the too of them lifts owt the bag and caries it up the path and withote bating an iyebrow chuckes it in the bake of the lory. I see them big tethe cheweing up the rubish and I see it cheweing up 'Death' and I see some blood but not won of the men semes to notise. Anyway I felt a big wate lift up of my sholders and I got my jakete and went owt for a wark arond, I even says 'morning' to the men as I go owt but they ignord me and then I here a few of them laghing behind my bake but I smiled to myself and I thoght Ill be yore hero soon enogh yoo just see.

Anyway that all hapened a litel wile ago and now I admit it Im a bit woried. You see I pased a paper shop and I notised in the daley miror it says '50 die in plane crash' and Im thinking if I kiled 'Death' how cold this bee. But maybee I thoght they were dead before I kiled 'Death' in wich case everything is fine but how can I be shore. Ive desided that theres only won way, I have to do a litel experement. Ive desided to try it on Mrs Miller. (shes old and a bit senile and shes got her arthrites so if Im ronge things wont be so bad). Im goeing down there now to pretend to have a chat but when Im in there Ill get my garote owt of my pokete and do the bisnise and well see what hapens. If Im ronge Ill have a bit of a problem to dele with I admit it but hope-fuly that wont be the case. Im shore anyway Im rite, the daley miror must have got it ronge, it userley does. Ill be bake soon to rite down what hapens.

Down To Earth

'This is going to be the one,' Clare said. 'I've got a feeling about it.'

Martin looked at her only a little sceptically. Over the six years they'd been together her 'feelings' had often turned out to be uncannily accurate.

'Don't get your hopes up,' he said. 'It's probably just desperation setting in.'

Clare shook her heard, her auburn hair sweeping across her cheeks. 'No, this is going to be it. I'm certain.'

They had been house-hunting for over two months now. In that time Martin had lost count of the number of houses they'd seen. It must have been two, maybe three dozen. Before they had started, they had sat down together to stipulate their requirements. Clare had got her diary and her pen and had made one of her famous lists: nice area, bigger garden, three bedrooms (at least), bigger kitchen, cellar for storage, et cetera, et cetera. They had worked out their finances and set themselves a price limit too, but had already had to revise that upwards once they saw what the market had to offer, much to Martin's concern.

Now, as Martin eased the Citroën through the narrow main street of the village, he said, 'Remember what we said about us both having to like it. We're not going to have an argument if I don't think it's right, are we?'

Clare turned wide, innocent eyes on him. In the April sunlight they looked momentarily green as grass. 'Course not,' she said. 'But you will like it, Martin. I promise.'

The estate agent was waiting for them when they arrived,

157

a spotty youth with greased-back hair and a double-breasted suit that looked one size too big for him. He gave Clare a brief lascivious glance, then offered Martin a damp handshake and introduced himself as, 'Mr Parry'. As he produced a set of keys and turned to push open the front gate, Martin and Clare stood on the pavement and appraised the house.

It was one of a row of limestone cottages, each of which had a small front garden and a porch like a sentry box. The cottages either side of the vacant one were pretty and well cared for, and the street itself, at the far edge of the village, was quiet and leafy, bordering on farmland.

As Parry pushed the front door inward, causing an accumulation of junk mail to slither across the tiled floor of the porch, Clare took Martin's arm and grinned at him. He raised his eyebrows at her non-committally; he recognised that grin all too well. She was determined to like this place, and not only that but she was determined that he would like it too. 'The stone's a lovely colour, isn't it?' she said. 'I could plant some Virginia creeper to climb up the front of the house. It'd look lovely against that pale background.'

'Let's look at the inside first, shall we?' Martin said.

She rolled her eyes, huffed out a sigh. 'God, you're no fun.'

They went inside, stepping through the porch and an inner door into a small entrance vestibule. A set of stairs led upwards directly in front of them. To their left was a stripped pine door, which was standing open. The place smelled musty and echoed with emptiness. When Martin wrinkled his nose and muttered about damp, Parry, waiting for them in the sitting room, said quickly that a damp-proof course had been recently installed and all the timbers treated, and that guarantee certificates were available on request. Clare smiled smugly.

The sitting room was spacious and contained a fireplace which had been all but filled in with grime-encrusted York-shire stone and a marble surround which Clare cooed over, and which even Martin had to admit was impressive.

'We could open up the fireplace,' she said breathlessly, her voice bouncing off the walls. 'We could get a nice Victorian

158

grate and hood with a tiled insert, or an Art Deco one. We could have a real fire in the winter. Just think of what it'd be like at Christmas, Martin, with our tree in the corner and logs crackling on the fire and us cuddled up together on the settee.'

Despite himself, Martin found that visualising the scene gave him a pleasurable wriggle of warmth, before he remembered that he was supposed to be the voice of reason here. Sometimes Clare would get so carried away with an idea, she would tend to view it through rose-tinted spectacles, would refuse to look at it practically, to acknowledge potential pitfalls. Martin didn't want to be a killjoy, but sometimes she needed someone to temper her enthusiasm.

On the other hand, sometimes *he* was over-cautious, and needed Clare there to gee him up. It was a partnership that worked well. Together, they kept things on a pretty even keel.

'It's a nice idea,' he said, 'but how much is it all going to cost? I mean, the house is already seven or eight thousand over what we wanted to pay, and if you're talking about putting a fire in, you're talking about probably another three or four hundred, even more if the flue's no good.'

'Yeah, but we don't have to do it straight away, do we?' Clare said. 'We'll just do it gradually, as we can afford it.'

Parry, hovering behind them, chipped in, 'There's plenty of potential here as you can see. The house itself is structurally sound and really doesn't need very much doing to it, if anything. As well as your damp-proof course and timber treatment, you've got your central heating and double-glazing. Once you've paid for the house itself, I think you'll find there won't be any other essential outgoings. Between you and me, I reckon this place is a pretty sound investment.'

Clare was nodding, but Martin turned to Parry coldly. 'You would say that though, wouldn't you? We'd only have to carpet the place top to bottom for a start.'

Parry looked away, unable to hold Martin's gaze. 'Well, that's up to you, isn't it?' he mumbled.

'You mean you think we could manage without carpets?'

159

Martin didn't know why he was beginning to feel quite so aggressive. Perhaps because he didn't like the thought of Clare joining forces with this slimeball to gang up on him.

Parry's cheeks were flushed. Though he was standing still, Martin got the impression he was squirming inside. Before the estate agent could respond, Clare released him by saying, 'How long has the house been empty?'

The quick smile of gratitude Parry gave her infuriated Martin. 'About a year.'

'And the people who lived here before were an old couple?'

'Yes, Joe and Dorothy Fleming. They lived here about forty years.'

'Right. Well, I think we've seen in here, haven't we, Martin? Let's have a look at the rest of the house.'

She took Martin's arm and led him through into a small dining room and from there into a spacious fitted kitchen where all the surfaces were gritty with dust.

'This is great!' exclaimed Clare, letting go of Martin's arm and rushing to the window above the sink which looked out onto the back garden. It was a long narrow strip of land, not huge but certainly much bigger than they were used to. In the last couple of years, Clare had got into gardening in a big way, and had become increasingly frustrated with the tiny plot in front of their modest back-to-back just a mile outside Leeds city centre. Martin knew she had big plans in the gardening sphere. Even before they'd started house-hunting, she'd been talking of 'a proper lawn where kids could play' (*Kids!* he had thought, alarmed), a greenhouse, a rockery, a vegetable plot. He knew the instant she got home, she would get out her diary and draw a long narrow rectangle to represent the garden here and would start planning what was going to go where. She had already done this with a couple of the other places they had looked at, even though they had both known that the houses themselves had been unsuitable for them.

'I could do a lot with this,' she said, as she always did.

Martin pulled a face. 'It's a jungle.'

'I know,' she said with relish, 'but there's such a lot of

potential, Martin, just like with the house. What do you think?'

Martin was all too aware of Parry still hovering behind them, ready to jump in, to chip away at any sign of weakness. 'I don't know,' he said. 'I'd have to see upstairs first.'

'Come on then,' she said, grabbing his hand and tugging him back through the dining room and sitting room to the staircase.

They clumped upstairs, Parry remaining downstairs at Martin's request, their footsteps echoing on bare wood. At the top of the stairs, directly to their left, was a surprisingly large bedroom overlooking the road at the front of the house, and at the back, overlooking the long garden, was a small square bedroom and a bathroom.

'Lovely tiles,' remarked Martin sardonically in the bathroom. The place was tiled floor to ceiling in pale green; each tile had a flower basket motif on it.

'These will all have to come off,' Clare agreed. 'We can plaster the walls and paint them blue, and put lots of pictures up and panel the side of the bath. And we could get one of those old bathroom cabinets and put it up on the wall there, above the toilet. And maybe we could have some shelves behind the door ...'

'More expense,' groaned Martin.

'I don't mean straight away,' said Clare, frowning. 'We can stand this for a while, can't we, until we get some spare cash together?'

'Sure, if you like looking at walls that look as though someone's phlegged all over them.'

She released an exasperated sigh. 'What's wrong with you, Martin? This house is everything we need. Why don't you like it?'

Immediately Martin felt a little ashamed. 'Oh, I don't know, Clare. It's not that I don't like the house. It's just that you're so over the top. I don't want to get caught up in your euphoria and maybe overlook glaring faults, things that are going to cost us money we hadn't planned on spending.'

'Such as what?'

'Oh, I don't know. What if the roof needs replacing or something?'

161

'Then that would show up on the surveyor's report, wouldn't it? There's nothing to stop us putting an offer in, though, is there? If we find out later that the place is falling down we can always pull out.'

Martin nodded slowly, then conceded, 'Yeah, I suppose you're right. As usual.'

'Besides, doesn't the house *feel* right to you? Don't you get good vibes from it?'

Martin couldn't feel anything except a mild sense of panic at the prospect of such a huge financial commitment, but he said, 'It certainly seems to be the most suitable place we've seen so far.'

'God, sometimes I think you've got no romance in your soul,' said Clare, rolling her eyes.

Martin smiled. 'That's what you get for marrying an accountant.'

Between the bathroom and a storage cupboard with a wooden door, a final set of steps twisted upwards. This led to the third bedroom, the attic bedroom. Martin and Clare reached the top of the stairs and found themselves in a room with a low sloping ceiling and a central beam.

'Wow!' exclaimed Clare. 'This is brilliant! We could sleep up here, Mart. It'd be like being in a big tent.' She crossed to a velux window set in the roof through which sunlight poured in a broad beam, opened it and stuck her head out. 'Just smell that fresh air. We could lie here at night and look up at the stars. Oh!'

Martin was about to comment on the fact that there wasn't much cupboard space and that they would never get their wardrobe up those narrow twisty stairs, but now he turned to look at Clare. 'What is it?'

She was craning her neck, her eyes screwed up to peer at something presumably at the bottom of the garden. 'I thought I saw someone moving in the shed,' she said.

'What shed?' Martin joined her by the velux and stuck his head out too. It was just big enough for them to stand there side by side, cheeks pressed together.

From here they could see down into the back garden and over the high fence that bordered it into their potential neighbours' gardens and the fields beyond. Martin hadn't noticed it the first time, but now he saw that there was a dilapidated shed at the end of the garden, all but obscured by long grass and some kind of vine that sprawled across the roof.

'See that window?' Clare said. 'Well, I thought I saw someone moving behind it, inside the shed, but it must have been a cloud passing across the glass or something.'

'Maybe a tramp's been sleeping in there,' suggested Martin. 'Shall we go and see?'

They closed the velux window, then clomped downstairs and back into the sitting room, where Parry was waiting, rocking back and forth on his heels, looking bored. He turned on a smile when they appeared. 'Happy?' he asked.

'We just want to go out into the garden,' said Clare. 'Is the back door unlocked?'

Parry unlocked it for them, telling them to take their time, and they went outside. The air smelt fresh and green. The garden seemed even more overgrown close to, and soon they were striding through a tangle of weeds and waist-high grass. Lining the tall left-hand fence which separated the empty cottage from its neighbours were a tightly packed row of fir trees.

'They'll have to come down,' Clare said casually as if the house was already theirs.

'Why?' asked Martin.

'Because they take up too much room, they block out the light and they suck up all the goodness from the soil.'

They reached the shed, which was in an advanced state of disrepair, covered in mould and cobwebs, paint peeling from its rotting wood panels. Martin's suggestion that a tramp may have been sleeping in here seemed unfounded, after all. From the looks of things, no one had come anywhere near the place for months.

He and Clare trampled down the grass around the door, then Clare took hold of the rusty handle and tugged. The shed creaked alarmingly, the walls seeming to shift a little. Martin took a nervous step back as dust from the roof sifted down over them.

'Careful,' he said, 'the place looks as though it could

163

collapse around our ears at any moment. We'd probably have to get the council to come and take it away.'

Clare's look of triumph made it obvious she considered his words a sign that he was weakening.

'Just open the door,' he told her.

She did so, a series of calculated tugs bringing the door juddering open inch by inch. Inside the shed, the dust was so thick it seemed to teem like smoke. On either side of a central aisle just wide enough for one person to walk up and down, a jumble of boxes, small cupboards and old mismatching drawers, which looked as if they had been fished from rubbish skips, had been stacked haphazardly on top of one another. A battered chest of drawers dominated the back wall, the top forming a work surface on which long-dried soil was scattered. Sagging shelves bracketed to the walls were heaped with rusty tins, flowerpots and various other bits and pieces. The whole lot was festooned with a spiders' ghetto of grimy cobwebs. As sunlight crawled across the walls and floor, Martin got the impression that lots of small, black, many-legged creatures were scuttling for cover.

'We'd have to sort through this before the council came,' Clare said, stepping tentatively inside. 'There's probably loads of good gardening stuff we could use.'

'*Who'll* have to sort through it?' said Martin. 'As far as I'm concerned, the council can just take the lot.'

'What are you always telling me? That spiders can't hurt you?'

'They can't, but I still don't fancy them crawling all over me. Besides, there are bound to be some big buggers in here. Look at that one.'

He pointed to a web in the corner above the window. The spider sitting in it was so large they could both clearly make out the bristles on its legs.

Clare shuddered and backed out of the shed so fast that Martin had to hop aside. She shut the door with a firmness that made the building shake like the scenery in an Australian soap opera. 'We'll leave that for another time,' she said, 'like when we've got ourselves some radiation suits.'

They struggled back up to the house through the long grass. That evening, over pasta at a cheap and cheerful restaurant they both favoured, they discussed the pros and cons of the house, and even Martin, naturally reticent though he was, had to admit that the pros had a landslide majority. The next day he rang the estate agent from work and made an offer two thousand pounds below the asking price. After speaking to the daughter of the previous owners, the estate agent rang back to let him know that if he increased his offer by another thousand pounds the house was his. Stomach churning, Martin acceded, then rung Clare at her studio to let her know what had happened. She whooped with delight, half-deafening him, and insisted they go out for a celebratory lunch. Martin knew she'd been rushing to finish the painting of a house that a customer had commissioned her to do for his wife's birthday the following week, but once Clare decided to do something there was no budging her. When he pulled up at the door to her studio, a unit in an old textile mill that had been converted to craft workshops, and got out of the car she burst out of the front door and threw her arms around him. 'Oh, Martin,' she cried, tears running down her face, 'we're going to be so happy.'

They spent the next few weeks packing things into boxes and dealing with solicitors, estate agents and mortgage consultants. The surveyor's report came through, and revealed that there were a few minor repairs to be made to their new house but nothing drastic. On their last day in their old house, Clare toured the empty rooms and said goodbye to each one before climbing into the car beside Martin with tears in her eyes and her throat too clogged to speak. Martin too felt oddly as though he was deserting an old friend as they turned left out of the street for the last time, pursued by the rumbling mass of the removals van, and started the twelve-mile journey to their new home.

On their arrival, Martin handed the house keys to Clare, who ceremoniously opened the front door. 'Ta da!' she cried, then squealed as Martin scooped her up and staggered with her over the threshold. The removals men and Martin spent the next hour carrying stuff in, with Clare directing operations. As soon as the removals men had driven away, Martin collapsed onto the settee with a groan.

'Wimp!' Clare exclaimed, and pounced on him.

165

Martin cried out as she slammed all the air out of his stomach, then, recovering, croaked, 'Get off me, you bully, I'm knackered.'

She jumped up and peeled off her T-shirt. She was not wearing anything underneath. 'How knackered?' she asked him, jiggling her eyebrows up and down provocatively.

'Well, maybe not that knackered,' he said, and chased her upstairs, she squealing, he grunting like an animal. In the attic bedroom, they quickly unfolded the futon, stripped one another's clothes off and made frantic, passionate love. Just before climaxing, Martin thought he smelled tobacco smoke, which reminded him instantly of his college room-mate's roll-ups. Then he forgot all about it, his senses overwhelmed by the rapture of ejaculation.

They spent their first evening eating curry out of foil containers because they hadn't unpacked any crockery and trying to tune the television in. By ten o'clock they were dozing off and so staggered up to bed. Clare fell asleep almost immediately, but Martin, despite the fact that his limbs were heavy with fatigue, lay staring up at the sloping ceiling, listening to the silence, which seemed somehow different to the silence of their old house. At first he couldn't work out why, then he decided that it was because this silence was absolute, a proper countryside silence, whereas in the old house they had slept to a background of city sounds — mainly car engines, he supposed — which he had grown so used to that after a while it had seemed subliminal. It's quiet, he thought to himself in a Jimmy Cagney accent, too quiet. He turned over restlessly, then decided that was even more uncomfortable and slumped over onto his back again. He sighed loudly, half-hoping that Clare would wake up and ask what was wrong.

Then he heard a sound downstairs and felt something cold lurch in his stomach.

It was an unmistakeable creak of wood, which gave him an immediate mental picture of someone moving stealthily around the house. One of the reasons they'd wanted to move further out from the city centre was because the crime rate in their area had been going up and up, so to get burgled in their first night out in the country would be the ultimate irony.

Martin wondered whether to wake Clare, just to make her aware of what was going on, then decided against it. He got up, dragged on the boxer shorts, jeans, T-shirt and slippers that he'd dumped exhaustedly on the floor by the side of the bed earlier, and then blundered across the room, trying not to fall over any of the boxes that were strewn around like boulders.

He reached the top of the narrow twisty staircase and paused to listen. He couldn't hear anything now. Perhaps it had just been the house settling. After all, the floorboards must have been subjected to more weight in the past few hours than in the past year. Nevertheless he wished he had something solid in his hands, something he could use as a weapon if needs be, but everything that he might have used – Clare's hockey stick, his snooker cue – was still packed up, God only knew where.

He crept down the stairs, gritting his teeth each time the wood creaked beneath his weight. On the landing he groped for the light switch and eventually found it. Immediately light blinded him; for a few seconds he could see even less than he'd been able to in the dark. His heart thumped rapidly as his eyes adjusted. If there had been someone hiding in the bathroom or either of the bedrooms on this landing, they could have walked up to him in those five or ten seconds and cut his throat while he was standing there squinting.

Eventually the glare faded, and he started down the main staircase, pausing every couple of steps to listen. The house was silent now, but might that mean that the intruder had heard him and was hiding somewhere, ready to jump out? If this had been daytime, Martin knew he would not have been half so paranoid, but the darkness and his tiredness and the unfamiliar surroundings were combining to create an atmosphere of menace, at least in his own mind.

He reached the bottom of the stairs and paused to listen at the door to the sitting room, but again he could hear nothing. Nevertheless, no matter how often he told himself not to be ridiculous, he couldn't shake the mental image of a grinning, wild-eyed figure crouching behind the door, holding a meat cleaver above its head. Abruptly, perhaps because he felt his imagination would be worse than any reality, he pushed down the handle and shoved open the door.

It swung open onto blackness, but Martin didn't enter the room immediately. He hovered on the threshold, listening, and again heard only silence. Only when he could stand the suspense no longer did he step forward, thrusting out his left hand, groping for the light switch which he seemed to recall was on the wall there somewhere. He was right; his hand slapped the switch and the light came on. He allowed the shudder that had been building inside him to escape when he saw that the room was empty.

He stepped inside, his eyes darting to every corner, but there was no possible hiding place. He was just beginning to feel relieved when he smelled tobacco smoke, which reminded him of the faint waft of it he'd had earlier when he'd been making love to Clare. It smelled rich and sweet, like pipe-smoke, like the kind of tobacco that came loose in tins. It smelled as though someone had been smoking in this room just minutes before. Martin's heart, which had slowed momentarily, once more began to quicken.

Nose twitching like a dog's, he wandered around the room, trying to locate the area where the smell was strongest. He crouched before the fireplace, taking such deep breaths that after a few moments he began to feel dizzy. Perhaps it was the wind blowing down the flue, he thought, or something coming through from next door, some fault in the brickwork. Now that he had what appeared to be strong evidence that someone had been in the house, he couldn't honestly believe that that was the case.

At last he did what he should have done immediately, but had been putting off; he crossed to the door that led to the dining room and opened it. If someone had been in this room they'd have been able to see him crisply silhouetted against the light. He had a bad few seconds while he groped to his left for the light switch, imagining knives flying at him out of the darkness, something flashing from the shadows to pin his hand to the wall, or even sever it. Then the light came on and he saw that this room too was empty and seemingly undisturbed. He crossed to the closed door that led to the kitchen. The faint smell of smoke still lingered on the air.

He followed the same procedure – open door, grope for

the light switch. The kitchen too was empty, apart from a leggy spider galloping around the sink. He was at first startled, and then a little embarrassed, when he caught sight of his reflection in the window that the blackness outside turned into a mirror. His face looked pinched, his eyes wide and hair awry. The smell of tobacco smoke was so faint now he could almost have believed he'd imagined it.

He checked the back door, which was locked, and then the door in the corner of the kitchen that led down to the cellar, which was bolted from this side, top and bottom. Then he chuckled as though it would convince him how silly he'd been, and went back upstairs, switching off lights as he went, trying the front door on his way past to ensure that that too was locked. Perfunctorily he checked the big bedroom at the front of the house, the bathroom, and then finally the small bedroom that overlooked the back garden. On a whim he switched off the light in the small bedroom and crossed to the curtainless window to peer into the garden below.

It was a spiky collage of dark shades − black, blacker, blackest − beneath a sky that was barely any lighter. Was there something moving down there or were the vestiges of his hyperactive imagination imposing themselves on the blackness, trying to convince him that a thick clump of vegetation over by the shed was a hunched, shuffling shape? He opened the window wide and leaned out. A cool summer breeze lifted the brown smell of earth to his face. Something whispered in the blackness below: the wind through long dry grass. That, he assured himself, was the only movement. He closed the window and trudged back up to bed.

The next day was Saturday. Martin decided not to tell Clare about his nocturnal wanderings, partly because it seemed silly in the daylight and partly because he didn't want to risk giving her the creeps before they'd hardly had chance to move in. They spent the morning cleaning the place from top to bottom, and then after a lunch of fish and chips, Martin started to unpack whilst Clare did what she'd been itching to do since leaping out of bed, buzzing with excitement, early that morning − she went out into her garden. Martin smiled to see her striding out of the back door armed only with her trowel and secateurs, her hands encased in green gardening gloves. Now that they had a proper garden, they were going to have to get some proper tools for it. Already Clare had asked Martin to buy her a wheelbarrow for her birthday in August.

Time drifted by as he unpacked. Each box he emptied and flattened seemed like a small victory. He was in the back bedroom which they were planning to use as a study when he next looked at his watch and was surprised to see it was almost four o'clock. Tea-break, he thought, and wandered over to the window, intending to shout down to Clare. It was obvious from the state of the garden that she had been attacking it with great gusto. A good half of the lawn had been hacked down to ankle-height and the clippings stuffed into two bulging bin liners. He could even see the dark earth of one of the flower beds for the first time, the weeds that had been uprooted from it forming a sizeable mound on the cropped lawn. But there was no sign of Clare herself ... and then he noticed that the shed door was open. He could just make out a dark figure moving around inside the building. So she had decided to tackle the giant spiders alone, after all, had she? Living in the country must be toughening her up already.

He went downstairs to put the kettle on. Walking into the sitting room, he was surprised to hear voices coming from the kitchen. He was even more surprised when he walked into the kitchen to find Clare shovelling coffee into a trio of mugs as she chatted to a dumpy middle-aged woman who was leaning against the sink with her arms folded.

'Extra-sensory perception or did you smell the coffee granules?' Clare asked, turning to him, her face flushed, eyes sparkling.

'What?' said Martin bewildered.

'Never mind. This is Joyce, our new next-door neighbour. Joyce, this is my husband, Martin.'

'How do you do?' said Joyce, smiling.

'Hi,' said Martin, stepping forward to shake hands.

'Look what Joyce brought for us, Mart. House-warming present. Isn't that nice?'

Clare indicated a battered trug full of strawberries so red and plump they looked unreal.

170

'Oh wow, that's brilliant!' exclaimed Martin. He popped a strawberry into his mouth; it tasted as sweet as it looked. 'This is really kind of you, Joyce. Thanks.'

Joyce blushed a little, which Martin couldn't help but find endearing. 'Think nothing of it. They're really a present from the whole family. We went strawberry picking this morning and picked far too many as usual. They're actually just an excuse for me to come round for a nose.'

'Well, you can't have mine, I haven't finished with it,' Martin might have said if he had known her better, but instead Clare told him, 'Joyce has been telling me about the Flemings, Mart.'

When he looked at her blankly she elucidated, 'The old people who lived here before us?'

'Oh, right,' said Martin. 'Actually that reminds me. Were you in the shed just now?'

Clare shook her head. 'Should I have been?'

'No, it's just that I thought I saw someone moving around in there. And the door was open too,' he added.

'Are you sure?' said Clare, and turned to look out of the window. 'Well, it's not now. Look.'

Martin looked. Sure enough the shed door was closed.

'Maybe we've got a ghost,' she said in a mock-hushed voice, wiggling her eyebrows.

'What makes you say that?'

'Oh relax, Mart, it was a joke. Honestly, Joyce, sometimes my husband takes things so seriously.'

Joyce smiled, albeit uncertainly. Frowning a little, Martin said, 'What about the Flemings anyway?'

'Oh, it's not much of a story really,' said Joyce as if apologising. 'I was just saying that Dot — Mrs Fleming — became too ill for Joe to look after her properly, and in the end the two of them were more or less forced by their daughter to go and live in a nursing home in Harrogate. I honestly think she thought it was for the best, but Dot was so upset on the day they had to leave I could hardly keep from crying myself. They loved this old house. They'd been here all their married life, you know, over forty years.'

'Yes,' said Martin, 'the estate agent told us.'

'And he loved his garden too, did old Joe. It's been

171

heartbreaking watching it all go to rack and ruin this past year or so.'

'Well, you can rely on us to restore it to its former glory,' said Clare, handing out the coffee. As she opened a packet of Hob Nobs, she said enthusiastically, 'Hey, maybe when we've got it looking half-decent again, we could invite the Flemings over for the afternoon, just to show them we're taking care of the place.' Then she frowned. 'Or do you not thing that's a good idea, Joyce? Might it upset them to come back and find someone else living in their house?'

Joyce nibbled her biscuit, lifted a finger to prevent a crumb slipping from the side of her mouth. 'It's a sweet idea, but an impossible one, I'm afraid. Poor old Joe and Dot are both dead now.'

Clare looked genuinely upset. Martin had always thought her expressiveness one of her most attractive features, perhaps because he found it such a strain to portray his own emotions.

'Oh no!' she said. 'When was this?'

'Oh well, Dot was on her last legs when they took her away, poor old thing, and she died a couple of months later. From what I can gather, it seemed that once she was gone Joe just pined away. Mrs Chinnery who lives on the end used to visit him regularly, and she said that the only things he really cared about were Dot and his house and his garden, and once he'd lost those there wasn't really much else to live for as far as he was concerned.'

'What a sad story,' said Clare. She looked out at the garden and sighed. 'I feel a bit like an interloper now.'

Immediately Joyce looked regretful. 'Oh dear, I certainly didn't mean to make you feel like that. I'm sure Joe and Dot would have been delighted to have had such a nice young couple picking up where they'd left off, so to speak, especially since you seem to be as keen on gardening as Joe was.'

'I'm still learning,' Clare admitted, 'but I hope Joe, wherever he is, won't mind if I make the garden my own.'

'I'm sure he won't dear,' said Joyce.

'The shed'll have to come down, I'm afraid, and we're

172

planning on digging the fir trees up. I can't understand why Joe planted them actually. They block out the light and they suck up all the goodness from the soil.'

'Ah, well, I think that was Mrs Hall's doing. She was the lady who owned this house before we did. She was a funny old stick, by all accounts. I don't think she and the Flemings got on. She was fanatical about her privacy, and insisted that Joe build the high fence between the two properties and then plant the trees along it for good measure.' She looked thoughtful as if there was more to tell, but instead of telling it she finished her coffee. 'Well,' she said decisively, 'it's time I was going. It's been lovely to meet you both. I hope you'll be very happy here.'

Exhausted by two days of lugging boxes about and one night of interrupted sleep, Martin slept well that night. The next day, at his suggestion, he and Clare trudged down the garden to clear out the shed. After Clare's comment about the ghost the day before, he felt spooked enough to avoid looking at the shed each time he found himself close to a window that overlooked the back garden. As far as he was concerned, the sooner the council came and took the shed away the better. He planned to ring them tomorrow at work to arrange a mutually agreeable time.

'You first this time,' said Clare, placing her green-gloved hands on his shoulders and marching behind him as if to shield herself against an arachnid ambush.

Martin tugged the shed door open carefully. Nothing seemed to have changed since their last visit.

'We'll just carry out anything portable and put it on the lawn, shall we?' he said. 'It'll be easier to look through then.'

Clare agreed and the two of them set to work. For the next ninety minutes they carried boxes, drawers and rusty tools out of the darkness of the shed and into the sunlight, stacking them on the cropped part of the lawn.

Clare only had a couple of spider-associated panic attacks during this time, the worst being when a large spider which had been clinging upside-down to a drawer full of screws she was carrying decided to scuttle up the side of the drawer and over her gloved hand. She screamed and threw the drawer

173

away from her, which, because the wood was so dry and rotten, splintered despite its soft landing, scattering screws everywhere.

'Oh great,' Martin said, coming out of the shed to see what all the noise was about. 'We'll probably be picking those up for the next three years.'

By midday they were more or less finished. They had accumulated such a stack of stuff it looked like they were building a bonfire. They had some lunch, then spent the afternoon sifting through what they had carried from the shed, salvaging what they could.

There wasn't much: a few rusty gardening tools which Clare said she could clean up, some rawlplugs, a wicker basket and some other bits and pieces. In one drawer Martin found a tin of Old Holborn rolling tobacco and some cigarette papers. He sniffed surreptitiously at the contents when Clare wasn't looking, but the stiff brown curls of tobacco were too dry and old to smell anything like the smoke he'd smelt in the house a couple of nights before.

'I'd better take this lot to the tip, I suppose,' he said when they had finished. He didn't much relish the prospect of carrying everything round to the car. The combination of physical work and fresh country air had made him bone-weary.

'Why waste it?' said Clare. 'We can use it for firewood.'

'But we haven't got a fire.'

'No, but we're going to get one, aren't we?' she said stubbornly. 'We can break it all up and store it in the coal shed by the back door. It'll be dry enough in there.'

'Well ... okay,' said Martin, 'but I can't be arsed to start breaking wood up now. I might do it after supper, if I've got the energy.' They both knew he wouldn't have the energy.

He was drowsing in the bath later that evening, a flannel over his face, when he got the impression that someone was standing silently in the room, watching him. He jerked upright, slopping water onto the floor, and snatched the flannel from his face.

There was nobody there, of course, but he thought he could detect the faintest whiff of smoke, was even

174

half-certain he could see a thin grey haze of it in the air, intertwining with the steam from his bath that was speckling the window with condensation.

'Clare!' he shouted, and then again, louder, to combat the Sting CD she was playing downstairs. There was a pause and then he heard her call up, 'What?'

'Come up here a minute, will you?'

He heard her clumping up the stairs, muttering to herself. 'What?' she said again a little impatiently as she walked into the bathroom, and then flapped a hand and exclaimed, 'Bloody hell, Sauna City!'

'Can you smell anything?' he asked her.

She sniffed the air. 'Like what?'

'Well ... like smoke or anything?'

'No, why? Have you been setting fire to your pubes?'

He gave her a look. 'I thought I could smell smoke. I've smelt it a couple of times before.'

She sniffed the air again, nose twitching like a rabbit's. 'No, I can't smell anything. Maybe it's coming through from next door.'

'Yes, that's what I wondered. Oh well, never mind, it's probably just me being paranoid as usual.'

'Probably,' she said wisely, then leaned forward and kissed him on the nose. 'Don't stay in there all night. We don't want you going all wrinkly.'

Martin had always been envious of Clare's ability to fall asleep the instant she closed her eyes. She managed it again that night, their third in the house, was breathing deeply before he had even found a comfortable position on the futon. He remembered his mother always telling him that a person who had no trouble sleeping was a person with a clear conscience. Presumably the inference was that he was guilty of something, though of what he couldn't imagine.

The house creaked and murmured all around him now. He lay listening to it in the dark. He wasn't sure whether the sounds the timbers made as they cooled and settled were soothing or a cause for concern. He still maintained that the creak he had heard two nights ago was different to these sounds; that had quite definitely, in his own mind at least, sounded like someone putting their full weight onto a creaky floorboard. Finally, after lying on one side and then the other, he rolled over onto his back and pushed the duvet down to his stomach. He closed his eyes, and almost immediately felt himself being sucked down into sleep.

It was still dark when he awoke, and for a few moments he couldn't get his head around what had woken him. Someone was tapping out a message, or perhaps just knocking gently on the ceiling in an attempt to rouse him. He realised how nonsensical that was at the same instant he realised he still had his eyes closed. His eyelids felt as if they'd been stuck together with glue that hadn't quite set. He sat up and used his fingers to pull them apart.

Immediately he saw that it was raining, droplets of water pattering on the velux window set in the ceiling. But he instinctively felt that it wasn't the sound of the rain that had woken him. He had always found that a soothing sound, had always felt that it emphasised the comfort and security of being curled up in a warm bed rather than detracting from it. No, something else had tugged him from sleep. There was some other source of anxiety. And then he realised that he could no longer hear Clare deep-breathing beside him. He stretched out a hand to her side of the bed. It was empty.

He threw back the duvet and lurched to his feet, raising a hand to prevent himself banging his head on the sloping roof. His heart was thumping quickly as it had two nights before. He told himself he was over-reacting, that he was still disorientated from sleep, but he pounded naked down the twisting staircase as if the house was on fire. 'Clare,' he called in a voice gravelly from sleep, 'Clare.' There was no reply. She'll be in the bathroom having a pee, or down in the kitchen making cocoa. But the house was in darkness, and silent except for the faint scuttling of rain, which made him think of thousands of spiders crawling over the outside of the house, trying to get in.

She was not in the bathroom. He grabbed his dressing gown from the hook on the inside of the door and wrapped it around himself. He switched lights on as he went, then padded down the uncarpeted main staircase, expecting at every moment to feel the needle-shock of a splinter sliding into one of his bare feet. 'Clare,' he called again as he

176

descended, and then at the bottom of the stairs, 'Clare, where are you?' The door to the sitting room was ajar. Unhesitatingly he shoved it open and entered, scrabbling for the light switch.

He saw immediately that both doors leading into the kitchen were open too, the one between dining room and kitchen swaying gently back and forth. He could feel the breeze that animated it now; it was too gentle even to ruffle his hair, but it made him shiver. He moved swiftly through the dining room into the unlit kitchen, yellow light from the sitting room trailing behind him, dragging brown shadows that were objects from the obfuscation. He was aware that the back door was open – he could hear it bumping gently against the frame – but it was to the window that his eyes were drawn.

Even through the blur of rain and a blackness that seemed as close to absolute as it was possible to get, Martin got the impression that there was something moving out there. Not Clare, but something else: something huge and shuffling, something that seemed to have no definable shape. Even as he told himself that it was an optical trick, a phantom created by his mind out of his anxiety for his wife, his stomach was clenching and freezing, and he was running for the open back door, shouting her name. He ran out into summer rain, which almost immediately blinded him. Through his swimming vision he saw a white-grey blur of flesh that was Clare. She appeared to be prancing naked on the lawn, like a primitive celebrating after a drought. Just for an instant, Martin got the impression she was dancing with someone, a dark flapping figure that creaked and rustled.

Then he swiped rain water from his eyes and he saw that she was alone, after all. He moved closer, to the edge of the lawn, his bare feet splatting through puddles in the pitted concrete. Though her movements were abandoned, her face was set, trance-like.

'Clare!' Martin yelled as if furious with her. 'Clare, what are you doing?'

She didn't jerk as if she'd suddenly woken up, but she did stop dancing and turn to face him. When she didn't answer,

177

he shouted again, more frantically this time, 'Clare, what are you *doing*?'

She walked slowly across the lawn towards him. Beyond her, rain seethed in the long grass. She walked right up to him, looked into his face with wide blank eyes, and then, still moving slowly, almost casually, she went into the house.

When Martin entered the kitchen she was standing naked in the middle of the floor, water running down her body, dripping off her hair. A puddle was widening around her feet. Martin peeled off his wet dressing gown and tossed it onto a radiator, even though they hadn't had the central heating on yet, and wouldn't until they'd had it checked over. He dried his feet on a tea towel, then told her, 'Wait here,' but she seemed not to hear him. When he returned with two dry bath towels thirty seconds later, she was still standing in the same position, her head cocked slightly to one side as if listening for something.

He dried her thoroughly, and even when he scrubbed at her hair, turning it into a frizzy mess, she didn't protest or come to. To be frank, she was giving him the creeps just standing staring like that. Although her eyes were open he had to assume she was sleepwalking, which she'd never done before in all the years he'd known her. Finally he led her over to a chair and made her sit down so he could dry her feet. In the semi-darkness her skin looked white and felt cold and clammy as fish-flesh. When he crouched and began to towel her feet, she turned her head slowly to observe him, and in a voice he barely recognised, said, 'Is that you, Joe?'

He stared up at her, a shiver rippling down over his naked shoulders and back, and then he suddenly got the feeling that she hadn't been talking to him at all, but to someone standing behind him. He whirled, his bare feet squeaking on the lino floor, and almost overbalanced. There was no one there; *of course* there was no one there. He glanced up at the window. Rain slithered like a blossoming germ culture on the glass.

'No, Clare,' he said gently. 'It's me, Martin.'

She seemed satisfied with his response. Her eyes closed, her body relaxed. Martin virtually had to carry her upstairs. Her head lolled on his shoulder, she murmured words that

178

were unintelligible, for which he was oddly grateful. When he laid her down on the futon and pulled back the duvet over her, she muttered once, then turned over and immediately fell into a deep sleep. Martin, on the other hand, lay staring at the rain writhing on the velux window until the sky tore, revealing the pink fire of dawn, whereupon he slept fitfully until his alarm woke him two hours later.

He was filling the kettle at the kitchen sink, the dull sound seeming to drum inside his aching skull, when he noticed the garden. The wood they'd collected from the shed and piled in a heap on the lawn the previous day was strewn all over the grass, and the dustbin liners that Clare had stuffed with grass cuttings and weeds were torn open and their contents scattered too. Had Clare done that in her sleep? The only other possibility was that the wind had been stronger than he'd realised, but he couldn't really believe that. The bin liners had been torn to shreds as though in a frenzy. Bits of them were clinging to the fir trees like flapping tongues of tar.

Martin took Clare a cup of tea. She came awake sleepily when he kissed her forehead, seemingly none the worse for her night's exertions. When he told her what had happened, she looked at him sceptically.

'I didn't do that. I'd have known about it.'

'Clare, I *saw* you! I dried you off, put you to bed.'

'Well, I don't remember. Maybe you were dreaming.'

She became sulky, withdrawn, refused to talk about it. In the end Martin had to leave it, had to rush to work, his head throbbing with sleeplessness, his stomach sour with frustration.

The familiar humdrum surroundings of the office distanced him a little from the unsettling events of the weekend. By lunchtime, munching a tuna salad baguette as he sat on a bench in the park, he had almost managed to convince himself that he was making far too much of a series of odd but not inexplicable events. So what if the house creaked? So what if he smelt smoke now and again? And Clare's behaviour could be put down to a bad dream or unfamiliar surroundings; wasn't he always reading that moving house was one of the most traumatic experiences of a person's life?

179

Back in the office that afternoon he phoned the council and asked them to come and take his shed away, telling them he thought it might have an asbestos roof. He was quoted a price of ninety pounds and promised that the job would be done 'sometime within the next couple of weeks'. When he asked whether it could be done sooner, the council official made him feel as though he was demanding the impossible. Martin drove home determined to put the weekend behind him, to make a fresh and positive start.

Locking the car door after parking the Citroën in front of the cottage, Martin heard the whir of some electrical implement. He didn't associate it with his own house until he went inside and realised it was coming from the back garden. He put down his briefcase and walked through the sitting room and dining room to the kitchen, dragging off his tie as he went. When he looked out of the kitchen window an astonishing sight met his eyes. Clare, dressed in a pink vest and white shorts, was wielding an electric saw which she was using to cut down the row of fir trees. She had already cut down half a dozen of the trees and only had two more to go. Even as Martin watched, the penultimate tree sagged, and then with the gristly sound of tearing wood, toppled over to join the others, which lay in a row on the lawn, reminding him uncomfortably of bodies laid out on the street following some disaster.

He saw her stand back, looking at the tree in satisfaction as it fell. She was sweating and covered in bits of twig and what looked like thin red scratches on her arms and legs. Her hair was dark with sweat, hanging over her face like rats' tails; she raised a green-gloved hand and pushed it aside. Despite his resolution to start afresh, Martin found the sight of her a little unnerving. She looked unkempt, almost primitive. She gave the impression of gaining great delight in hacking down such huge living things. He walked to the back door, opened it and went outside. She'd switched the electric saw off now, was yanking at the flex to release it from the clutches of a green feathery limb. Even so, she didn't look up until he called her name.

At first she didn't seem to recognise him. The expression on her face was blank, almost hostile. Then almost instantly she grinned and said, 'Hi, Mart. Look what I've done.' Now she resembled not so much a primitive as a little girl, dirty, exhausted and happy. Martin walked into the garden, which seemed suddenly wider now that all but one of the trees had gone.

'Where did you get that?' he asked, nodding at the saw.

'I hired it from the village. It was only five pounds for the day.'

Martin half-smiled, shaking his head. 'This is amazing. What time did you get home?'

'I've been home all day. You don't think I did all this in the last hour, do you?'

'So you haven't been to your studio at all today? What about those card designs you were moaning about? I thought they had to be in by Friday.'

Clare frowned. 'I decided that doing this was more important.'

Martin didn't want an argument the minute he got home, but he couldn't seem to stop himself saying, 'This doesn't bring in the money we need for our vastly increased mortgage, does it?'

She glared at him. For a moment she seemed too angry to speak. Then she sucked in a breath and hissed, 'Is that all the thanks I'm going to get? I've tidied up the garden, including putting all that rotten wood into bin bags that *you* were supposed to put in the coal shed last night but which is now too wet to use for firewood.' She leaned forward, eyes narrowing. All at once she looked wild again. 'Well, fuck you, Joe. Fuck you!' She threw down the electric saw, which bounced on the springy branches of one of the felled fir trees, then stormed past him into the house.

She was through the kitchen and out of sight before he realised what she'd called him. His belly spasmed coldly. If she hadn't been so furious he'd have gone after her, demanding to know why she'd used that name. He stared at the felled fir trees and discarded saw, feeling sick. The stumps, wet and raw, that jutted from the dark soil looked somehow obscene. The final tree stood upright like a defiant prisoner awaiting execution. Martin sighed deeply, ran a hand through his hair, then went inside.

181

The hammering of bath water on plastic was like the sound of her anger. Martin crept upstairs, silently because he thought if she heard him ascending it would enable her to gather her fury and give vent to it the instant he showed his face. The bathroom door was open, her clothes lying in a small heap beneath the towel rail. Martin sidled into the room, an abject look on his face. Clare was sitting in the bath with her head bowed, her knees bent up to her chin, her arms wrapped around her calves. Water was swirling and frothing around her feet as the bath filled.

'Sorry,' he said.

'Fuck off,' she replied, her voice muffled.

She wasn't shouting; that at least was an encouraging sign. Martin knelt beside the bath on the bare floorboards.

'I'm a total git,' he said, 'I didn't mean to have a go at you. As usual, I spoke without thinking. Sorry, Clare.'

She raised her head and looked at him. She looked tired now, her vigour gone. Her face was a mottled red, her eyes sludgy green.

'I'm only trying to make the place look nice.'

'I know, I know, I appreciate that. I'm just a bit uptight about the money aspect of it, that's all.'

She raised her eyebrows but didn't say anything. Martin sat back on his heels. For ten seconds or so neither of them spoke, then Martin said, 'You've certainly been working hard.'

'Thank you for noticing,' she said dully, sliding beneath the water, her hair fanning out across the surface like weeds.

'Where did you get all those scratches?' Martin asked.

She looked at her arms as though she hadn't noticed them until now. 'Oh, they're nothing. They'll go away.'

Martin wanted to ask her why she had called him Joe, but the words stuck in his throat. He told himself it would be too much like backtracking after he'd promised himself he wanted to make a fresh start, but really he knew it was because he was too afraid of the reply. Instead he asked her if she wanted to cut down the last tree as she'd done all the rest.

'No,' she said wearily, 'it doesn't matter. You can do it.'

182

'Are you sure?' he said, which made her wrinkle her forehead in a frown.

'I'm tired now. I've lost my momentum. I just want to go to sleep.'

'Okay,' Martin said, rising to his feet. 'You enjoy your bath and I'll go and cut the last tree down, then I'll make us something to eat.'

Clare closed her eyes in lieu of a reply.

It only took Martin five minutes to fell the last tree. As he was doing it he thought he caught the faint lingering smell of smoke. He glanced towards the shed, but the pale shape moving beyond the glass was only the reflection of a cloud filling the corner of the pane as it slipped from sight.

Though Martin kept telling himself they'd made up, there was a tension in the air that evening. He kept stealing glances at Clare as they watched a Michael J. Fox film together. Her eyes were fixed on the screen each time he looked, but he got the impression her thoughts were elsewhere. Probably thinking about what she was going to do in the garden tomorrow, he thought, suppressing a wriggle of irritation.

The film was almost over when he registered something black and scuttling somewhere over to his left. He looked down and saw a spider, far larger than any they'd ever encountered in their old house, perambulating across the floor by the left-hand wall, keeping tight to the skirting board.

'Spider alert,' he said, pointing. 'No need to freak out. I'll get it.'

He went into the kitchen to fetch a pint glass, and returned in time to see Clare swoop and pick the spider up with her right hand. When she rose he saw two long legs wriggling frantically from a gap in her clenched fist. Without a word she went into the hall, opened the front door and tossed the spider out.

'What?' she said, in response to his flabbergasted expression.

'You ... you just picked it up!'

'So?'

'You've always been terrified of spiders.'

She shrugged, looked momentarily uncomfortable. 'And

you've always told me that they won't hurt me. I don't see what all the fuss is about.'

'But ...' Martin didn't know what to say.

'Oh, don't go on, Mart,' said Clare. 'I want to see the end of this film.'

She sat down, fixed her eyes back on the screen. Suddenly Martin felt that he didn't know her at all.

They didn't talk much for the rest of that evening or the next morning. Martin was munching toast, ten minutes away from the time he should be setting off for work, when he said, 'If you look sharp I'll give you a lift to your studio.'

Clare looked up, her eyes seeming to focus as if she'd been concentrating on something else. 'What?'

'I said I'll give you a lift if you can be ready in the next ten minutes.'

'Oh ... no thanks. I'm not going in today.'

Martin felt a tightening in his chest. 'Why not?' he said neutrally.

Clare shrugged and looked down, her hair falling over her face. 'I've got stuff to do here.'

'In the garden?'

'Yeah.'

'But what about your card commission? If you don't deliver, you won't get paid, and they won't use you again. They'll think you're unreliable.'

She looked up again sharply. 'Who are you, my fucking agent or something? *I* know how much I've got to do. Just relax, Martin, all right.'

The confrontation had soured Martin's appetite. What remained of his toast as he dropped it onto his plate clattered on the porcelain like a small bone. He drove to work on automatic pilot, his mind obsessively reviewing the events of the past few days. Back at the house, in Clare's presence, he felt too close to what was happening to see things clearly.

Why were he and Clare bickering all the time? Was it just that they were tired after the move, trying to divide their time too thinly between work, their new house and each other? He could understand her eagerness to stay at home. Moving house *was* exciting; it was only natural to want to get things straight as quickly as possible. But equally you had to establish your priorities – or was that just him being too sensible as usual?

When he thought about it, what really bothered him was not that Clare wanted to stay at home, but the fact that doing so seemed to be having a detrimental effect on her. The first couple of days she'd sparkled, buoyed by the energy of a new challenge, but now she seemed listless, preoccupied, unpredictable. Or was he making too much of this too? So she'd sleepwalked for the first time since he'd known her – so what? It had been a disturbing episode but a one-off surely, easily attributable to the upheaval of the last few days.

But she called you Joe, his mind whispered at him. She called you Joe *twice*. This disturbed him, he had to admit, but again was it really so significant? The story of the Flemings' departure from the house they'd loved for over forty years had saddened her, he knew that; perhaps it had affected her more profoundly than she'd admitted.

And all the other things – the smoke, the constant glimpses of a dark figure in the shed, the creak of someone moving around downstairs, the huge shuffling shape in the garden on the night Clare had sleepwalked that had seemed made of . . . what? Wood? Vegetation? Or simply shadows and imagination? What of all those things?

'Maybe I'm the one going loopy,' he muttered out loud, surprising himself.

At work that day he found it difficult to concentrate. For a while he toyed with the idea of secretly approaching Joyce, their next-door neighbour, to ask her more questions about the Flemings. But what would he ask? Were they good people? Were they *nice* people? The thought of her puzzled, suspicious face as he tried clumsily to draw information out of her caused him to abandon the idea before he'd even set it in motion. Besides, what would his motivation be for asking such questions? Did he really think the Flemings were reaching out from beyond the grave, trying to take back the house that they felt still belonged to them? If there *were* such things as ghosts, why should the Flemings be hostile ones? In life, they'd been a normal loving couple as far as he was

185

aware; why should death change them? But did morality matter when a longing so intense it overwhelmed everything else was involved? Perhaps that was what had lived on – their yearning to reclaim what was theirs.

'Stop this,' he ordered, speaking out loud once again – louder than he had intended, in fact, for Tanya, one of his colleagues, said, 'Stop what?'

Martin felt himself blushing. He mumbled something self-deprecating in reply. Tanya looked at him sympathetically (unless Martin had been reading the signs wrong, she had fancied him for over a year now) and said, 'You look tired, Martin. Moving's a drag, isn't it? What you need is a night out to cheer yourself up.'

Martin wondered whether she was suggesting he go out with her. He just smiled and said, 'Yeah, you're probably right.'

When he got home he found Clare turning over the soil in the flower beds with a spade that looked new. She indicated a row of tools leaning against the wall under the kitchen window. 'They were Joe's,' she said, 'the ones we got out of the shed. I cleaned them. They've come up well, haven't they?'

Something bothered Martin but he couldn't work out what. Putting it firmly aside, refusing to dwell on it, he said, 'Hey, I've got a surprise for you.'

'What?'

'Just come inside and I'll show you.'

She pulled a face. 'Aw, Mart, I wanted to finish this.'

'Come inside,' he ordered, gently but firmly. 'That can wait.'

Grudgingly she took his hand and he led her inside. He presented her with the flowers he'd bought for her on the way home and two tickets for that evening's performance of *Swan Lake* by the English National Ballet.

'What's this?' she said, showing him what he suddenly thought was the first genuine smile he'd seen for days.

'I thought we deserved a night out,' he said. 'We're going to the theatre and then afterwards I've booked a table at the Mandalay, so look sharp, we leave in an hour.'

The evening was everything Martin had hoped it would

186

be. Away from the house, and more particularly the garden, Clare seemed her old self – animated, cheerful, chatty. Only when Martin asked her what she'd been doing in the garden did she become a little evasive.

'Oh, just pottering about, tidying up. Try some of this chicken mughlai, it's delicious.'

She only fell silent in the car on the way home. The hedges flanking the roads looked like coal in the darkness. Martin was slowing to take a corner when something black and thin streaked across the road in front of them, caught in the scoop of their headlights.

'Wow, did you see that?' he said. 'I wonder what it was.'

'A hare,' Clare replied without hesitation.

When Martin glanced at her he saw slivers of light gleaming on the whites of her eyeballs like tiny crescent moons. The certainty on her face seemed to defy argument.

Back at the house she became playful again. She coaxed him out into the back garden, saying she wanted to look at the stars.

Martin complied only because he knew he would be accused of being unromantic if he didn't, though entering the garden at night didn't much appeal to him. It was black out there, the shed and the bushes, the high fence and the far wall melding into a darkness that defied the eye.

'Isn't that beautiful,' Clare breathed, looking up and tottering round and round in a circle until she giggled and stumbled and made a grab for him. 'Ooh, I feel dizzy.'

'Too much wine,' said Martin. 'Come on, let's go inside.'

'No. Make love to me, here in the grass.' She began to tug at his belt, still giggling. He heard the tiny unmeshing of metal teeth as she pulled his fly down.

'*Clare*,' he said, looking around as if afraid of being observed, holding up his arms to fend her off.

'Oh come on. Don't be a boring bastard.' She took a step back from him, peeled off the red top she'd been wearing and tossed it aside. She looked monochrome in the darkness – pale grey skin, black bra.

'Come on, Clare, get dressed. We'll do it inside.'

'No, here,' she said stubbornly. She unhooked her bra,

releasing her breasts, quickly unzipped her skirt and stepped out of it as it dropped to the ground.

Anywhere but here and Martin would have been aroused. All he felt, however, was a mounting panic he couldn't put a reason to that churned like acid in the pit of his stomach.

'Clare, please,' he said and lunged for her.

She squealed as though interpreting his approach as playfulness and turning her back on him ran towards the darkness that had swallowed the far end of the garden.

'Fuck,' Martin muttered and went after her. He put out his hands as though the darkness was of such substance that he thought he might have to tear it apart. At first he heard Clare giggling and panting, the swish of her stockinged feet as she ran through the chopped-down grass. Then the blackness of the night seemed to enfold her, to throw up a wall of silence. Martin slowed, began to wade forward more cautiously.

'Clare,' he called, and when she didn't reply, 'Come on, Clare, don't be silly.'

He slowed to less than walking pace, putting one foot in front of the other very carefully, trying to make as little noise as possible. He sensed the shed looming before he actually saw it. Then he heard it creak as though someone pressed flat against one of its walls was tensing themselves. Just for an instant he smelled the faintest hint of smoke on the air which he immediately assured himself was his imagination.

'Come on, Clare,' he said angrily, 'this isn't fun – '

And then the word choked off, his body jerking in shock, as something black and flapping swooped at his face.

Or at least, that was his immediate impression. The clump of material hit him full in the face, momentarily blocking his vision, and even as it was sliding across his skin, dropping to the ground, he instinctively stuck out a hand and caught it in mid-air. Heart pumping, he raised the silky garment and looked at it, immediately recognising the black pants that Clare had been wearing.

Stuffing them into his jacket pocket, he hissed, 'For fuck's sake, Clare, stop messing about. You nearly gave me a fucking heart attack.'

There was no reply. Martin stood there for a few seconds, waiting for one, his breath quick with anger. At last he said, 'I've fucking had enough of this. I'm going inside. If you want to act like a stupid arsehole, fine.'

He turned and began to walk back towards the house. At once he heard quick, light footsteps behind him, and before he could even fully turn his head felt arms entwine around his neck, the full weight of Clare's naked body slamming into him. He stumbled sideways, knocked off-balance, and was borne to the ground. Prickly grass jabbed at his neck and face. Clare was all over him, her mouth wet on his, her hands fluttering, tugging at his clothes.

'Fuck me,' she urged, 'fuck me, fuck me.' Her hand reached unerringly through his open fly and closed around his cock. Despite himself, Martin felt himself responding, and he rolled onto his back, his hands sliding over her naked flesh, cradling her buttocks, then sliding lower, fingers finding the warm, damp crevice between her legs. She cried her pleasure into his open mouth, tore frantically at his clothes, he now aiding her as she stripped him. She writhed on him, frantic, slippery; he had never known her so eager, so desperate. The intensity of her passion fed his arousal, caused his reticence to dwindle. He closed his eyes and gave himself up to the moment. He smelled earth and her perfumed sweat and the hot musk of their sex. When he entered her she screamed her rapture so loudly that he giggled and smothered her mouth with his eel-slippery fingers, afraid that neighbours would come running from all sides to investigate the commotion.

Once he was spent, the magic wore off quickly. Clare clung to him, head on his chest, her sweat-damp hair forming dark question marks on her exposed cheek. She seemed happy to bask in the after-glow, perhaps even to sleep out in the open, but as his cock and his passion shrivelled, Martin became aware of the spiky grass, the cool breeze that dried his sweat and made him shiver, started to think about insects crawling on their bodies, about the house being unlocked, about how exposed they were, about how embarrassing it would be if they dozed off and were discovered in the morning by the milkman or one of their neighbours.

'Clare,' he murmured, 'Clare.' She mumbled against him.

189

He pushed her hair back from her face, kissed her forehead. 'Come on, Clare, let's go inside.'

She sighed, though whether with contentment or disappointment he was not sure. Dreamily she said, 'I love you, and I want to stay here for ever and ever.'

Something over by the shed creaked. Martin twisted his head but saw only blackness.

'I love you too,' he whispered, wriggling his body out from under her as he did so. As he stood up a breeze raised goosebumps on his flesh, making him shiver again. He picked up their scattered clothes and carried them into the house. When he came back for Clare, the grass was rustling around her, and she was smiling as if she understood what it was trying to say.

The rest of the week passed quietly, and by Friday Martin was beginning to wonder whether his initial anxieties had been simply part of the process of getting used to a new house, after all. Since he and Clare had made love in the garden, nothing untoward had happened. She had been a little subdued, and once or twice he had noticed an almost fey expression on her face, but on the whole things seemed pretty much back to normal. They weren't actually spending that much time together, but they weren't bickering either as they had done earlier in the week. Clare had been into her studio twice, albeit grudgingly and only for brief periods, to finish off the card designs for her latest commission. She still spent the majority of her spare time in the garden, stayed out there every evening in fact until it got dark, which at the present time meant ten o'clock at night or even later, after which she generally had a bath and then flopped into bed. Martin had spent the last couple of evenings decorating the sitting room. He found it therapeutic boldly covering over the grubby old paintwork with a fresh colour. It was like stamping their personalities on the house, truly making it theirs. He played music loud as he worked, so that if the house *was* creaking in a manner that suggested more than the settling of timbers he was unable to hear it.

If Martin had been perfectly honest with himself, he would have admitted that there was still something about the garden that bothered him, something to do with Clare, something he

190

couldn't quite put his finger on. However he refused to dwell on the matter, at least consciously, pushed it firmly to the back of his mind, where it niggled now and again but never enough to cause him actively to seek a solution. He kept out of the garden as much as possible, telling himself that he wasn't that interested in it, that it was Clare's domain, and he studiously avoided looking out of windows that overlooked the shed, because ... well, basically it was an eyesore, and he would just be glad when the council finally arrived and took the bloody thing away.

It was Friday evening, and Martin was cricking his neck and wobbling on top of a set of stepladders as he painted the fiddly bit around the coving when he heard Clare calling his name from the back door. He swore and stopped what he was doing, then carefully descended the stepladders, which he had borrowed from their next-door neighbours and which he was convinced were going to collapse at any moment. He switched off the CD player and shouted, 'What?'

'At last! Come here a minute, will you? I need a hand doing something.'

Martin sighed, put down his brush and tramped through to the kitchen, wearing an old shirt and torn jeans, both of which were paint-smeared. Clare was holding onto the frame of the back door, leaning into the kitchen. She was wearing shorts and a T-shirt and, as usual, her green gardening gloves.

'What is it?' Martin asked.

'I'm trying to dig out the roots of the fir trees but they're real buggers. They go down about fifty million miles into the earth. One of us needs to lean on the spade to push up the biggest roots while the other hacks at them with the axe. If we can get the main bit out then all the chopped-off tentacles will hopefully just shrivel up and die.'

Martin pulled a face. 'You make it sound like we're about to dismember a live octopus.' He followed Clare into the garden. She had dug around the stumps of the trees, heaping the soil against the fence. Martin looked down into the first hole and saw a bolus of roots from which thick tendrils snaked out in all directions.

Clare handed him the spade. 'Right, if you can shove it

as far under that big root there as you can and sort of lever it up, I'll give it a whack with the axe.'

Martin did as instructed, his biceps straining. 'Be careful,' he said to Clare as she raised the axe above her head, teeth gritted with determination.

With a grunt of effort she brought the axe swooping down, putting all her momentum into the action. The spade juddered in Martin's hand as the axe blade made contact with the root and cut through it.

And then both he and Clare were jumping back with cries of disgust as thick dark fluid spurted up around the axe blade and splashed over them. The stuff spattered on Martin's shoes and up the legs of his jeans, but it was Clare who came off worse. She'd been bending right over the root she'd tried to sever, and the fluid splashed up over her bare legs, over the hand that was holding the axe, and even flecked her face.

Sap, Martin thought, it's high summer, the thing's full of sap. But the sap was thick and brownish-red, and it smelled rank, like the chili con carne he'd once made as a student, half of which he'd put in the fridge and forgotten about.

'*Ohmygod*!' Clare screamed, dropping the axe and holding up her right hand. The stuff ran down her arm to her elbow.

'Go and wash it off,' Martin said.

'*Whatisit*?'

'I don't know. Just go and wash it off. Here.'

He produced a handkerchief from his pocket which he bunched up and tossed towards her. It opened up and fluttered to the lawn. Clare picked it up and began to wipe the stuff feverishly from her skin, making little whimpering sounds as though it was burning her like acid.

When she had gone inside, Martin bent over the hole and gingerly prodded aside the severed root. The rank smell rose up to meet him and he almost gagged. He swallowed and shuddered, sweat sheening his forehead. When he saw what lay beneath the root, when he saw what Clare had chopped in half with the axe, he murmured, 'Oh my God,' then rose and put a hand to his mouth.

There was an animal down there beneath the root.

Something small and dark and furry that Martin couldn't fully recognise, but which he could only guess was a mole. He didn't think Clare had killed it — from the smell he guessed it had been dead a while. It couldn't have been dead that long though, because it had still been full of blood, and there were no immediate signs of decay or of maggot activity. Quickly Martin shovelled soil over the severed root and what lay beneath it, then he collected up the tools and went inside to see if Clare was all right.

She was sitting in the bath which was still filling up, scrubbing frantically at her arms and legs with a block of lemon-scented soap. Her skin was red beneath the lather she had created. Her hair was dripping and there was water running down her face.

'Hey,' he said gently, 'you okay?'

She looked at him, then shuddered as though shaking herself out of some fugue state. 'Urgh, that was horrible.'

'I know,' he said, and then to stop her scrubbing herself down to the bone, 'I think you're clean now.'

She stopped what she was doing, albeit reluctantly, lowered her knees and slid beneath the water so that only her face was above the surface. Water was still crashing into the bath like a waterfall. The room was filling with steam.

'I've brought all your tools in,' Martin said. 'I thought we could do with a break from all this work. How about wandering down the road to The Malt Shovel, see what the local beer's like?'

'What was that stuff?' Clare said as though she hadn't heard him.

Martin hesitated, then told her what he had found under the root. He expected her to express disgust all over again, but instead she said, 'Oh no, poor thing.'

She was calmer now. She closed her eyes, asked Martin to turn the taps off, which he did. The bath water, lapping just beneath the overflow, was so cloudy with soap that Clare's body looked set in marble.

Martin repeated his suggestion of a night down the pub.

'You go,' Clare said. 'I'm okay just lying here.'

193

'It's all right, take your time, I'll wait for you. It's not eight o'clock yet.'

Clare frowned, opened one eye and looked at him. 'I'll be at least an hour,' she said. 'You're not going to hassle me to hurry up, are you?'

'You're not going to be that long, surely?' said Martin. 'The water'll get cold.'

'I'll put some more hot in. I just want to relax a bit. I've had a horrible shock.'

'You can relax down the pub with me.'

Clare gave an exasperated sigh and her frown deepened. 'I knew this would happen. You're hassling me already. Look, you just go, Mart, okay. I'll join you later.'

'Promise?'

'Yes. Now just piss off.'

He leaned forward and kissed her on the nose. 'Okay, see you in a bit.' He went upstairs and got changed, then went down the road to the pub.

The Malt Shovel was very much a locals' pub, albeit with a relaxed, friendly atmosphere. As he walked in, Martin half-expected everyone to fall silent, to turn to regard him as if he had just blundered into a private meeting, but as far as he was aware he didn't attract even the slightest of curious glances. Although the place was busy, it was not packed like the pubs he was used to back in their old neighbourhood. He bought himself a pint of bitter and went to sit at a table in the corner.

When he was younger he used to hate sitting in pubs on his own — he used to think that people would think he was alone because he didn't have any friends — but now he didn't mind at all. He had had the foresight to bring a paperback with him, which he now took out of his pocket and began to read. Every time the pub door opened with a screech of hinges, he looked up, expecting to see Clare peering through the blur of smoke, trying to locate him. However two hours and four pints later she still hadn't appeared, by which time Martin had resigned himself to the fact that she wasn't going to come. She had probably crawled out of the bath feeling so sleepy and relaxed that the thought of getting changed and leaving the house to sit

194

in a smoky atmosphere drinking alcohol seemed too much like hard work. He fully expected to go home to find her curled up in her dressing gown on the settee, fast asleep in front of the telly.

He finished his pint and looked at his watch; it was almost 10:15. Outside the daylight had finally cracked, unable to halt the darkness rushing in and taking over. Martin felt woolly-headed, a combination of beer, smoke and staring at pages of print for over two hours. He marked his place in his book, stuffed it into his pocket and stood up, which immediately made him feel even more woozy, as if the reactions of his mind were a split second behind the movements of his body.

He waved to the landlady, who called goodnight to him as he left, then stepped outside into air so clear it seemed to sting his sinuses. He walked home, feeling suddenly far drunker than he had in the pub, feeling as though the pavement was swaying like the deck of a ship.

He was mildly surprised to find the front door locked when he got home, but thought that Clare must have decided to go to bed and locked it, assuming he had his key. The keyhole kept dodging out of the way of his key and wouldn't behave until Martin had sworn at it. Finally, however, he pushed the door open and stepped into the porch, wondering whether to call out hello, then deciding against it. He opened the inner door and stepped into the hallway.

At once he was assailed by the smell of smoke.

This wasn't the acrid cigarette smoke that had turned the air of the pub into a blue-grey haze; this was sweeter, more aromatic, the smell of fresh rolling tobacco. There wasn't just a hint of it on the air this time; it was unmistakeable, stronger even than it had been that first night when he had thought he could hear someone moving around downstairs.

Instantly his heart began pumping hard. 'Clare,' he shouted. 'Clare, where are you?'

The door to his left, which led into the sitting room, was ajar. As Martin stood there calling his wife's name, it wafted closed as though pushed by a breeze from the other side, stopping only when it bumped against the frame.

The garden! That was where she would be. He knew at

195

once that the sitting-room door was moving because the back door leading into the garden was standing open.

The smell of Old Holborn, which filled his lungs with every breath he took, imbued him with a sense of urgency, even panic. Without even bothering to switch on lights, he shoved open the sitting-room door, ran through that room, through the dining room, into the kitchen and outside.

'Clare,' he shouted into the secret blacknesses at the end of the garden, 'Clare, are you there?'

There was no reply. Even out here Martin could smell the burning tobacco that his predecessor had smoked. It was making him feel more light-headed than ever and more than a little nauseous.

'Clare,' he shouted again, and his voice sounded brittle this time, etched with hairline cracks, 'Clare, please answer me.'

Over by the shed something creaked. This sound was immediately followed by a different sound, which Martin could only liken to a soft tearing of wood.

'Clare?' he said, but he knew instinctively that it was not his wife who had made the sound, and who was now rustling like bushes in a high wind. This sound was too ... too *big*, too widespread somehow. As Martin began to back away, he suddenly realised what it was about the garden that had been niggling him for the past few days.

What had Clare done with the wood they had carried out of the shed and stacked on the lawn, and more particularly what had she done with all the fir trees she had chopped down? She couldn't have taken them to the tip because she didn't have a car. The only place she could have put them where Martin wouldn't have known would have been behind the shed or even inside it.

But that didn't make sense, did it? What was the point of carrying everything out of the shed only to bung it all back in there again? From the darkness at the end of the garden the creaking and the rustling were growing more agitated. Martin turned and ran inside the house, slamming the back door behind him.

He would have locked it, but the key was not in the door or hanging on the hook in the kitchen. He had his own key

196

on his keyring, which he recalled was still dangling from the lock of the inner porch door. He ran back through the house, reached the hallway and slapped the light on.

For the first time he could see things clearly, and his throat tightened.

There was fresh dark soil scattered all over the floor of the hallway, a trail of it climbing the stairs.

Martin had to gulp a few deep lungfuls of air before he could even croak his wife's name.

There was no reply from upstairs, though faintly from the direction of the kitchen he heard a brief rustling sound. What should he do? Flee the house now or find out what had happened to Clare? In truth, it was really no contest. He couldn't abandon his wife, and even if he did run away, where would he go?

He pounded up the stairs, half-thinking that he could get Clare and drag her out of the house before whatever was rustling and creaking in the kitchen made it into the hallway. Or, if the worst came to the worst, they could climb out of the velux window in the attic onto the roof and call for help from there.

He reached the landing at the top of the main staircase, where soil was scattered in profusion. It continued in a dark, crumbling trail up the twisting stairs that led to the attic bedroom. Martin felt too sick and exhausted with panic to call out his wife's name now, though he was desperate to see her, to hear her voice. He bounded up the last flight of stairs, his heart hammering, using his hands on the walls to propel himself upwards.

The attic bedroom was in darkness, though a bluish light from the clear summer sky above gave the room a hazy definition. The room was so silent that at first Martin thought he was alone, then with a sudden snake-like movement something squirmed beneath the duvet on the futon, making him jump.

'Clare,' he said, recovering, 'Clare, come on, wake up.' He began to stride towards the bed, intending to pull the duvet back, shake her awake.

He was just bending forward when the figure beneath the duvet stretched out a hand and threw the covering aside.

197

Even in the semi-darkness Martin recognised his wife, the paleness of her naked flesh, and yet he paused, feeling fear wriggle like worms in his belly; something was wrong here, something was terribly wrong.

'Clare?' he ventured, his voice a cracked whisper.

She writhed sinuously, rolling her head back on her shoulders, raising her pelvis towards him. She seemed to have far too much pubic hair, seemed to have a mouth that was too wide and black.

'Fuck me,' she murmured. Her voice was muffled, and the words were accompanied by a soft pattering sound. 'Fuck me, Joe.'

Martin reared back, stumbled towards the light switch, slapped it down. The light was too bright; it hurt his eyes, made him screw them up against the white glare.

The few seconds when he seemed blinded were endless, but at last his vision began to acclimatise, his pupils contracting to cope with the influx of brightness. When he saw what was squirming obscenely on the futon, what Clare had become, his body seemed to rush into itself, to compress into a knot of fire just beneath his breastbone. His head swam; he thought he was going to pass out or have a heart attack. He couldn't move or speak, couldn't even breathe properly.

Clare's mouth was open and black soil was tumbling from it, pattering on her breasts, rolling down her too-pale flesh onto the sheet beneath her. Not only her mouth was stuffed with soil, but her eyes and nose and ears. And between her legs ...

Between her legs ...

Martin dropped to his knees, the strength draining rapidly from his body.

'Fuck me, Joe,' Clare moaned, her voice thick and dark and muffled.

Every breath that Martin took was Old Holborn now. The air was hazy with it. With the last of his strength he turned his head and saw it billowing up the stairwell.

Clare lay back, gurgling, convulsing, as though anticipating the arrival of her lover, soil leaking out of her.

Something huge and heavy, creaking and rattling and

198

rustling, put its weight on the bottom step of the twisty stairwell and began to ascend.

Martin watched until its vast misshapen shadow loomed on the wall and creased to climb the sloping ceiling, and then he closed his eyes.

A New Man

He listened.

Silence.

He stared into the darkness, and slowly, little by little, his vision cleared.

It was still dark, he saw, but it was not absolute. There were ... objects. Sharp angles. Definition.

He stirred, tried to groan, but his mouth felt oddly paralysed. There was no sensation in his lips, his tongue, even his teeth. He did, however, have a dull throbbing ache in his limbs. When he cautiously bent an arm the ache intensified to a shooting pain which felt as if his nerves were shattering. Instinctively he tried to scream, but his lips remained clamped shut, refusing to part to release the sound. The scream seemed to bulge, to reverberate inside his head, until finally it dwindled and died.

All right, he thought, all right, no more sudden movements. This time take it nice and easy. With infinite care he bent the arm again, feeling more pain, though not as intense as before. He bent the other arm, and wanted to cry out, but still his facial muscles wouldn't respond.

Rest, he thought as the pain faded, rest a minute, take stock. He stared into the not-quite darkness and tried to work out where he was. Had he had an accident? Was he in hospital? That would account for the pain in his limbs, for the numbness in his jaw, which might have been wired or anaesthetised. But no, this was not a hospital bed beneath him, it was a hard, unyielding floor. Perhaps, then, he had been mugged — robbed and beaten, left to die in an alleyway.

But he was indoors, wasn't he? There were vaguely defined walls around him.

Mentally he sighed. Come on, think. What's the last thing you remember? What's your name? Are you married? Where do you live? How old are you?

Don't know, he replied hopelessly to each question, don't know, don't know, don't know.

Frustrated, he made himself sit up. His back screamed out its agony. He bent one knee and then the other, feeling the pain rip through him. He was almost gleeful at the pain, as though he were torturing himself for his amnesia, as though his physical suffering could tear apart the curtains that concealed his memories.

Who are you? he again demanded of himself. Where are you? How did you get here? He brought his hands up to his face, but there was little feeling in either. The impression he received, though his fingers seemed nerveless, was that he was bald, and perhaps naked. Had he been stripped and drugged, pumped with something that stole his mental faculties and physical sensations? Oh, if only he could remember something. Anything at all ...

But his mind was pure. White. Blank.

He swore under his breath and pushed himself painstakingly to his feet. He felt himself trembling as though balancing on stumps, and shot out an arm to steady himself. His hand closed around a metal rail, set objects jangling softly. He stiffened then realised what the objects were: suits on a mobile rack.

After a few moments of standing and stretching he felt more in control of his limbs. He lifted one of the suits from the rack and quickly put it on. It was a little baggy, but if he was being held captive here, as he suspected, then he had no time to be choosy. He made out a stack of crates in the gloom. And behind the crates − glory be! − a door with a window above it.

A little unsteadily he crossed to the door. Not surprisingly it was locked, further supporting his theory that he was a prisoner here. He looked up at the window, a dim rectangle of diffuse, brownish light. That, too, was fastened from the outside, but if he made steps out of some of those crates, wrapped a jacket round his hand as he punched, he might be able to shatter the glass.

He knew he was taking a risk. If his captors were anywhere in the building, then they'd surely hear him and come running. But the gamble was worthwhile. Sitting tight would achieve nothing at all. The crates were large, made of wood, banded together by steel, but he found them surprisingly light. He was not even aware of his muscles straining. Whoever he was, he was strong as an ox.

When he had built a set of makeshift steps, he slipped a jacket from its hanger and wound it round his hand. It looked strange, a giant boxing glove trailing empty sleeves. He climbed the steps, listening to the wood creak, hoping it wouldn't splinter beneath him. When his head came level with the window he looked out.

Dimly he could make out a large room containing racks of dresses and suits and jumpers, shelves along the walls neatly piled with jeans, shirts, gloves, socks, underwear. He was trapped in a clothing warehouse! Or perhaps even a big store like Debenhams or Marks and Spencer. Shielding his face he lashed out, and was rewarded with the explosive sound of shattering glass, the echoes of which seemed to go on for ever. Working quickly, sure that someone must have heard, he punched out the remaining shards and quickly scrambled through.

He dropped to the floor, feet crunching on a carpet of glass. He unwound the jacket from his hand, threw it aside and began walking. His aim was to make it to ground level and pound on the glass doors that faced onto the main street. Someone was bound to see him and call the police. Then he could find out who he was, where he'd come from, why he was being held captive.

However eagerness made him careless. Sidling around a rack of cardigans, he spotted the silent escalator and broke from cover just as a torch beam snapped on. He threw up his hands as the circle of light blinded him. The uniformed figure behind the light muttered, 'Got you now, you ...' Then his voice changed. He let out a gasp. 'Holy Jesus!' he exclaimed.

Puzzled by the guard's fear, he swung round in the

darkness. Beside him was a glass pillar, and he stared in horror at the reflection that the torchbeam now enabled him to see. A mannequin's face stared back at him — bald, smooth, pink, the features uniformly blank. He felt a scream building inside him. But even now the plaster lips would not part to release it.

The Other One

The television was gone. They must have come in the night and taken it. It was so unfair of them to do that, they must have done it purely out of spite.

He was angry but tried not to show it. The best thing to do was not to give them the satisfaction of knowing that they'd upset him. He would act as if nothing had happened, as if he hadn't even noticed. He sat up in bed, rubbing his eyes and yawning, pretending to be still half-asleep. Then nonchalantly he pushed back his single blanket, set his feet on the floor, stood up and wandered over to the radio.

When he switched it on all he heard was static. He moved his head closer to the speaker, his movements slow and cautious, fearful of receiving another electric shock. Not that he'd had one for a while now, but you could never be too careful. They were cunning as well as spiteful. They hated him far more than he'd ever hated anybody.

Beneath the static he could hear someone speaking. Making sounds at any rate, singing or howling wordlessly. He listened more intently and thought he heard someone say his name. Alarmed, he turned the radio off.

He wondered whether to disable the radio but decided not to. They'd know they'd got to him if he did. Besides, it would probably provoke them, not that they really needed an excuse. The radio couldn't do him much harm when it was silent, not like the microwave, which he'd secretly incapacitated. He wondered how long it would be before they found out what he'd done, and how they'd react. Whatever happened it would have been worth it. He was damned if he was going to allow them to cook him slowly from the inside.

He walked down the corridor to the little bathroom on the right. The corridor was narrow, and the lights set into the ceiling bulbous and blank, like the eyes of fish. It had taken him a long time before he was able to hide the nervousness he felt walking down here. Even now he found the thought that he could reach out with both hands and touch a wall at each side obscurely terrifying. Worse, though, was the certainty that they were watching him at every moment, waiting for the slightest error, the chance to be provoked. They were ghouls feeding on his uncertainties, doubtless crowing with savage glee whenever he let slip the anguish he was surely entitled to feel. That, indeed, was why it was imperative that he mask his true feelings − to starve their sadism, frustrate their joy at his awful predicament. They might be the ones who set the traps but he was not the animal here. Wasn't he the only one who had retained his dignity, after all? Wasn't he the only one who had a reason for his actions?

He washed himself slowly and methodically, paying particular attention to his feet and his genitals. The towels they provided were not much use (although rough, they merely moved the water around on his skin rather than soaking it up) but he never complained. They were probably gawping at his nakedness now, making jokes about his weenie, but he didn't care; let them. He would simply rise above it. He wondered where the cameras were. In the mirror? The taps? The light bulbs? Behind the tiles?

Already the anticipation of his boredom was starting to depress him but he would never let that show in his face. There were things to do yet − get dressed, see if his food had arrived, look out of the window. He tried to make everything he did last a long time. In that way he could convince both himself and them that he was calm and in control. He didn't even mind when they hid his clothes; indeed, rather than disorienting him, it helped to pass the time. Upon returning to the bedsitting room, he discovered that they'd hidden his clothes today. He searched for them with no real sense of urgency, and eventually found them in the fridge.

He'd been naked for a long time and was starting to feel the cold, but putting on his clothes made him feel far colder. For a while, until the heat of his body began to warm them through, his clothes would feel as if they'd been made of ice. He was shivering, but only on the inside; he clamped his teeth together beneath his lips to stop them from chattering. They must have run out of jokes about his weenie; now they would be congratulating each other on hiding his clothes in such a fabulous place. So intent was he on not giving them the satisfaction that he forgot to close the fridge door.

The thing that formed out of the whiteness and tried to speak to him almost emerged, but he managed to slam the door just in time. Now he was shivering on the outside. Damn them! Damn them! Damn them! It might be only a small victory for them but it was a victory nevertheless. He had to subjugate the effects of it as quickly as he could.

Every nerve, every sinew, screamed at him not to, but he opened the fridge door and, what was more, made it look nonchalant. He bent down and peered into the fridge, fear closing up his throat. He felt the cold whiteness shining out and caressing his face, felt the hum change and crack and try to become a voice.

He closed the door again before it could, but this time without revealing his panic. So that they would not see through his show of bravado, he opened every single cupboard and peered inside as if searching for something, though he knew full well that the cupboards were empty. The pristine whiteness of the kitchen units disturbed him, reminded him of the other place. He tried not to squint, though the glare made his eyes ache.

As ever, he could not leave the kitchen without first inspecting the waste disposal unit. The two stainless steel sinks, side by side, looked brand-new, a fact which again disturbed him though he couldn't define why. When he turned on the tap with the blue lid in the first sink (the real sink, for washing things in), water came out more powerfully than he had anticipated. It spattered up off the stainless steel and covered his clothes in droplets that instantly turned to small dark patches, like little shadows. Some droplets speckled his face, sudden and cold and wet as shaving cuts. He closed his eyes and turned the tap off. They would be laughing at his little accident now, and so he smiled to show he didn't care.

The waste disposal unit was in sink number two, which had no taps above it. He opened his eyes and leaned forward a little, aware of the sudden intensity of his heartbeat which made his body feel like nothing more than a living pump. He peered into the metal tube, an exposed throat tapering to darkness. The throat was lined with a tight, prickly spiral of blades like steel teeth which made him anxious and excited at the same time. He was relieved to see that the waste disposal unit was as new-looking as everything else, that there were no ... shreds, clinging to the teeth. What fascinated and appalled him was the fact that the blades were at their most lethal when you couldn't see them. As if to demonstrate the thought to himself, he turned the machine on.

For a fraction of an instant nothing happened; the waste disposal unit remained in stasis. Anyone could have put their finger into the throat in that millisecond and then taken it out again and they would have been fine. But then with a whir the blades began to rotate, and were almost immediately spinning at full speed. Now you could no longer see the blades. They resembled nothing so much as a swirling white mist which looked cool and slow and inviting.

He couldn't help it. He was so entranced by the paradox that he grinned, revealing all his teeth. He knew it was a weakness which they would exploit, and so he folded his lips around the grin and turned off the machine, angry inside.

Abruptly he left the kitchen, hoping to convey the impression that the waste disposal unit had been nothing more than a diversion with which he was now bored. He decided to see whether his food had arrived. Back he went down the narrow corridor, concealing his nervousness, passing the bathroom on the right without so much as a glance.

At the end of the corridor, facing him, was a door. He opened the door onto a gloomy landing, steps leading downwards on his right. Echoing up the stairwell were sounds that worried him. Bumps, slitherings, sometimes even what sounded like voices that broke up into indeterminate echoes before they could form words.

There was no food. He was so eager that he almost saw the box sitting there before realising it was an illusion created by the angles of walls and floor and the strange shadows that formed from these. He shrugged in an attempt to hide his disappointment. Even here he was certain that they were watching him and gloating. Their methods, unlike them, were very sophisticated.

He went back into his flat and rearranged his furniture for the third time in as many days. He tried to look absorbed in his task. He didn't want them to know that he was doing it because there was nothing else to do. He still hadn't looked out of the window, but he felt too dispirited to do so today. Besides, he didn't want to have to fall into a routine. That would be a sure sign of stagnation, which would undoubtedly delight them.

After a while he checked to see whether his food had arrived yet; it hadn't. He hated their petty manipulative methods but he didn't show it, he just shrugged again as if he couldn't care less. He lay on his bed, wondering whether to masturbate, whether to give them something to ogle at. In the end, though, he didn't. He just fell asleep.

Perhaps it was his hunger that enabled him to walk the city in his dreams. He strode with purpose and confidence, and seemed to know exactly where he was going. It was twilight, the outlines of the buildings bold and dark and sure. The sky was like blue marble, venous with darker cloud.

His boot heels trampled the miles underfoot, clicking on paving slabs, crunching on gravel, whispering on asphalt. The city was a vibrant place, full of sights both wondrous and terrible. His eyes feasted on it all – the fire-eaters and snake charmers, the three boys kicking a puppy to death with their bare feet for amusement, the great artists reduced to sketching caricatures of tourists on the quayside. A crone lifted her skirts and flaunted her diseased pudenda; an old man, eyes white with cataracts, offered him a live lobster, its claws snapping. He skirted a crowd who were gathering around a gallows, listened for a while to a lonely black man playing a lonely trumpet on a street corner. He watched fireworks bursting in the sky, a street fight involving young men in immaculately tailored suits. And he embraced it all,

213

for this was his city, his domain, and these people, whether paupers or socialites, were his people.

As usual he failed to reach his destination, wherever it might be. Initially he tried to incorporate the ringing into his dream, but eventually it became too shrill and too insistent and pulled his sleep, and thus the city, apart – for now at least. He awoke with his face half-buried in the pillow, one arm hanging over the edge of the bed, fingers touching the floor. He was desperate to pee and he had a full erection. As ever, he found the incompatibility of this infuriating.

They'd stripped him naked again and, it seemed, hidden his clothes. He was so annoyed he felt like pissing despite his erection, spraying himself and whatever else happened to get in the way. But if he did that he'd be playing right into their hands; they might even start up with the electric shocks again. The ringing was coming from the telephone, which he never used. Trying hard to conceal his nervousness, he picked it up.

He didn't hold the receiver too close to his ear; he wasn't that stupid. Silence rushed at him from the earpiece like gas, filling the room, making him dizzy. He was terrified of speaking in case there was something wrong with the voice that answered him, in case it didn't sound quite human. Far away, behind the silence, he thought he could hear the eerie ringing cry of tortured metal.

How long he stood there holding the receiver inches from his face he wasn't quite sure. It seemed like a long time, long enough certainly to make his arm first ache, and then jump with muscle spasms. At last, however, the silence ended. Crawling from the receiver like an insect came a dry and hideous sound, like bones chuckling. Even now, with the muscle spasms in his arms becoming ever more frequent, he couldn't replace the receiver, couldn't face the consequences of what might happen if he did. Fortunately the decision was taken for him. There was a sound like a heavy dice being rolled and then a flat electric hum.

He replaced the receiver slowly and carefully. It took a great deal of control to prevent it leaping from his hand like a frightened kitten. He was cold, but when he looked down was surprised to see sweat glistening on his chest. His

214

penis was now white and shrivelled as a whelk.

It took him a long time to empty his bladder. The piss, bright yellow and cloudy, gave off a strong-smelling steam when it hit the water. He was almost finished, the piss coming in intermittent spurts, when he heard the clatter of the letterbox. Immediately a trembling started at the back of his legs, travelled up to his buttocks and then pushed through into his stomach.

No matter how much control he tried to assert, this new intrusion could not prevent his body from shaking. The last few drops of his piss hit the toilet seat and speckled the carpet; his stomach lurched, making him gasp, making him lean over the toilet bowl and open his mouth, certain he was about to be sick. It made him realise how little control he actually had. If they decided to really turn the screw they could reduce him to a gibbering wreck in minutes.

The knowledge depressed and infuriated him. Helplessness encompassed his entire body like a wave of black ink. Saliva flowed into his mouth to aid the passage of burning vomit from his stomach. He spat the saliva into the bowl in a long, frothy string and then jammed his hand down on the flush lever. Water roared and seethed in the toilet bowl. He made himself straighten up and breathe deeply and slowly, filling his lungs and then letting it go.

At last the urge to vomit passed, though his stomach and his bladder still ached. He was not sure he would have the strength to walk until he tried it and found that he could. As soon as he stepped into the hall he saw the envelope on the doormat. Trying to convey defiance in his expression and in the way he moved, he walked over and picked it up.

He did not open it until he was sitting on his bed, one leg bent beneath him. The envelope was white and cheap and had nothing written on it. He could tell by feeling it that the object inside was about three inches long and shaped like a pen or a twig or a piece of chalk. There was a dark brown stain on the back of the envelope that reminded him of a tiny butterfly. He tore the envelope jerkily open and tipped out what was inside.

It was a human finger, severed raggedly just above the third knuckle. It was very white, as if whoever had sent it had taken great care to drain as much blood from it as possible before putting it in the envelope. Nevertheless, the splinter of bone that protruded from the stump of stringy pinkish-brown meat was encrusted with dried lumps of blackened blood. It was the finger of a woman, the nail curved and long and painted with dark pink nail varnish, slightly chipped. It still wore a ring, a thin gold band inset with three tiny red stones.

He looked at the finger for a long time before touching it, and wondered whether they would be able to pick it up on their cameras. If so, they would find some way to use it against him, even though it was obvious that he could not possibly be blamed for what had happened. At last, after sitting motionless for perhaps three minutes, he picked up the finger and the envelope and went into the kitchen. The finger was cold in his hand, the linoleum equally cold on his bare feet.

It took some pulling to get the ring off but eventually he managed it. He found the beaker which they'd hidden in the empty bread bin and filled it with water. He popped the ring into his mouth like a pill and gulped water until he'd swallowed it. He placed the finger into the metal throat of the waste disposal unit and turned it on.

There was a reddish-brown tinge to the white blur of the blades and that was all. Next he rolled the envelope into a tight tube and fed that in too. He left the waste disposal unit on longer than was necessary, but even so, when the blades stopped spinning he saw minute clots of matter clinging to some of them. He spent ten minutes picking off the bits of matter, rolling them between his fingers like bogies, and dropping them into the exact centre of the metal throat.

Eventually he was satisfied that he had done all he could. He turned the machine on again briefly to clear the little balls of paper and flesh, and then he walked back into the bedsitting room and lay down on his bed.

At last he felt able to walk back down the corridor to the door to see if his food had arrived. When he opened the door, the first thing he saw were his clothes, folded neatly on the landing. His food, however, still hadn't arrived, which didn't actually bother him as much as it ought to because he

216

was no longer hungry. The sounds drifting up the stairwell sounded unnervingly similar to the ones (of rending metal) that he'd heard on the phone.

He carried his clothes back inside and dressed slowly in the bedsitting room. As he still had no food, he decided to look out of the window. It was a dreary day, rods of grey rain falling almost vertically. From his high vantage point the landscape seemed composed of slabs of polished onyx.

A spark of colour caught his eye. The little girl, pushing a doll's pram between the silent buildings, was wearing a yellow sou'wester with a coat to match. He watched her, craning his neck until she was gone. He was suddenly hungry again.

He pursued someone through the city. His prey wore a dark cloak and a top hat and carried a cane. It resembled a shadow more than a person, forever threatening to merge with the glowing fog and disappear. He was hampered in his pursuit by street vendors and partygoers bedecked with streamers who tried to lure him into their drunken clique with offers of whisky and rum. Something with glowing red eyes whispered to him from an alleyway. Somewhere far away a jazz band was playing.

No matter how quickly he ran, his prey matched him step for step, always maintaining a reasonable lead. The fog shifted and curled seductively, like the sad and silent ghosts of sensuous women.

He found himself beside a canal, warehouses looming blackly over the water. Small waves lapped at the bank, trying to reach his feet. The sound of water dripping beneath the tunnel just ahead was the repetitive sound of a clumsy kiss.

He heard his prey moving in the darkness of the tunnel, saw the vague black flap of its cloak before the fog swallowed it up. He followed, breathing fog into fog, his feet sliding on the slick stone.

In the moving living darkness it was waiting for him. He saw it slumped against the dank wall, its body an inchoate mass, a shadow partly composed of solid matter. Slowly, accompanied by the lap-drip-lap of water, it raised its head.

And he almost saw its face . . .

The telephone woke him before he could. When he opened his eyes he found himself on the floor, reaching for the receiver with his outstretched hand. Before he could prevent it, his hand grasped the receiver and pulled it towards his face.

Immediately a voice asked, 'Is it you?'

'Yes,' he said.

The voice seemed to grin as it asked, 'Did you get it?'

His head was buzzing. He wanted to recall the face in the dream, but the memory of it slipped away from him. 'Yes,' he said again.

'Did you like it?' said the voice.

The question unnerved him. He said, 'I can't trust you. You'll have to come back.'

There was a short silence, and then the voice said, a little pleadingly, 'I can't. Not yet. I'm starting to really like it here.'

'But we promised them −'

'*You* promised them! I didn't promise them anything. I didn't have a choice.'

'It's the same thing. You've got to come back.'

'Come and fetch me.'

The line went dead.

His hand tightened on the receiver until the plastic creaked. At once he was furious and unable to contain it. He hurled the receiver across the room where it was pulled up short by the soft spring of its lead, swung round and sent clattering against an item of furniture. He jumped up, swept a chair from the floor and hurled it against the wall. It split the wallpaper and dented the plaster beneath, but it was not enough to vent his rage. If only he had a knife, he could cut . . . he could cut . . .

Suddenly exhausted, he slumped to the floor.

Later, he walked slowly to the bathroom and washed himself thoroughly, even his hair. He scrubbed himself until his skin hurt but he could not remove the indelible stains of shame and regret that marked him. They would have seen everything, undoubtedly; they would probably have recorded it. It would be something they could use against him for a long, long time. It was not fair that thirty uncontrollable seconds should take so long to erase, but it was the way things worked and he could do nothing about it.

Did he receive an electric shock when he touched the tap? It was so mild, so fleeting, that he was not sure. Bracing himself, he grasped the tap again and felt nothing but metal made hot by the scalding water inside. He was so dejected that he found he didn't much care if he had received a shock. He towelled himself semi-dry and put on his clothes. The coarse material stuck to his damp back and made him itch.

Half-heartedly he checked to see if his food had arrived. It hadn't, or maybe it had and they had taken it away again as a punishment. What could he do now? There seemed so few options open to him. In the end, he lay on the floor of the bathroom and masturbated without issue until his arm grew tired. To avoid weeping, he slept.

The city looked grey, its walls pitted and crumbling. Small dark shapes, rats perhaps, scurried to and fro, keeping to the shadows. He felt aimless now, at odds with this place. He wandered about, trying to remember where he was going, who he was looking for.

It was night, the air murky and cold, the street lamps gauzed by haze. People slipped like blood clots through the arteries of the city. They were subdued, and seemed to shun him, turning their faces away.

There was life somewhere. He could hear it. The sound of calliope music, the good-hearted din of people having fun. And there were flashes of coloured light − blue, green, red, mauve − which appeared at the periphery of his vision and winked out again when he tried to focus on them as if taunting him.

He tried to make for the hubbub, but it remained elusive, always just around the next corner or over the high unscalable wall of a dead-end street. He did not feel welcome here now, he was not the person he had been before. He had come here to avoid weeping, but when he awoke to the clatter of the letterbox, the tears were wet on his face.

There was a parcel on the mat this time, wrapped in brown paper and secured with transparent tape wound round and round and round in the manner of a spider spinning web about its prey. He was still fully dressed. Evidently they had moved on from the minor irritation of taking his clothes and hiding them.

He walked despairingly down the corridor, which seemed to elongate, to recede from him. The parcel, when he eventually reached it, was smaller than he had thought.

Beneath the brown paper, and layers of newspaper whose articles were written in a language he did not identify and whose photographs were so grainy he could not make them out, was a man's left hand, hacked off clumsily at the wrist. The hand, as white as the finger, was covered with a fine layer of coarse black hair. On the third finger was a wedding ring, a plain gold band. The flesh beneath the well-manicured fingernails was a bluish colour.

He picked up the hand. It was colder than marble, but soft and quite pliable. The fingers were curled over slightly. When he straightened one out, it sprang slowly back until it was curled over again. When he pressed his thumb into the soft fleshy area between the bones of the thumb and index finger, the indentation remained and seemed to turn a greyish colour as if his own thumb had been dark with newsprint. The hand was heavier than one might think. He estimated that it came from a man in early middle-age. He turned it over to examine the life line and was a little amused to see that the line curled right around the base of the thumb and became lost in a small forest of spiny black hairs.

Even as he examined the hand, turning it over and over, entwining its fingers with his, he knew that this was a brand-new game and that he was playing it strictly to their rules. There was no way he could win now, or even resist them any more, and the worst part was, it was his own carelessness which had caused this. No doubt they would claim such a circumstance was always going to be inevitable, and maybe they were right. That didn't stop him loathing himself, though; it didn't stop the despair from pounding like nails in his head.

When it came to the crunch, he found that he couldn't even dispose of the hand. He hovered by the waste disposal, agonised by his own reluctance. In the end, he opened the fridge door, tossed the hand inside, and ran sobbing to his bed.

The time before the next phone call passed in a confused blur, like a home movie chopped up and pasted back together in the wrong order. Did he look out of the window? Did he check to see whether his food had arrived? Did he gaze into the whirring teeth of the waste disposal unit? Did he wash himself? Did he sleep and dream of the city?

Yes-No-Don't-Know. Before he was given time to think about it, the phone rang and he was picking it up.

'You liked it, didn't you?' the voice hissed. 'Admit it, admit it.'

This time he went berserk. After destroying most of his furniture, he found himself crouched on his haunches before a metal waste bin in which paper was burning. He scooped up the hand which was lying by his feet and dropped it into the flames.

He watched it for less than ten seconds before plunging his hand into the bin and retrieving the hand. Even in that short time the hand had begun to bubble and char. He dropped it on the carpet, flailed at the flames until they went out. There was a lot of dark smoke, pungent with the stench of rancid fat and burned hair. Skin had begun to peel from the hand and turn black; the fingernails had turned black too. Even now, blisters were forming and bursting on the hand and the heat from it was beginning to singe the carpet.

As if in sympathy, his own hand was hurting like buggery. He jammed it beneath his armpit as if that would help. He staggered to his feet, head swimming with the smoke and his own pain and confusion. Picking up the metal bin, which was hot but not unbearably so, and in which newspaper still flickered with flame, he stumbled ape-like to the kitchen.

He switched on the cold tap full force, drenching himself as it spattered up from the steel sink, and placed the burning waste bin beneath it. The paper sizzled momentarily, then succumbed. Under the onslaught of water it broke up quickly, became a blackish grey pulp which floated on the water's surface like scum. Turning the tap down to half force, he thrust his own singed hand beneath it. The water played over his hand for a long time, dulling the pain of his burns.

221

When he switched off the tap and examined his dripping hand, he saw it was red as sunburn and blistered. Almost immediately, without the cooling water to quell it, the pain began to rage again. Gritting his teeth, he stumbled back into the bedsitting room where smoke greyed everything. His legs felt hollow, his stomach quivery with nausea, his lungs bruised. The hand lay on the carpet like some black crustaceous creature, poised on its curled fingers.

He picked it up gingerly. It was both crisp and greasy to the touch. He stood indecisively in the middle of the room for a few moments, the hand dangling from the index finger and thumb of his good hand, then he carried the hand back into the kitchen and put it in the fridge.

He slept in the bathroom, where the smoke was less dense, his body curled foetally around his injured hand. He shivered with cold and shock, his feet jerked and kicked with involuntary spasms. His breathing was stertorous. The air which he drew down into and up from his lungs tasted of barbecued meat. His head rested on a towel whose dampness stuck his hair to his face.

Before he drifted uneasily into sleep he imagined he could hear the hand scuttling about in the fridge like a large black spider trying to get out. The scuttling followed him into the city, where something large and black was clinging to a wall. Before he could focus on it through the fog and the brownish light, it scampered across the scabrous brickwork and away, losing itself in the shadows.

The city had been devastated, torn apart by riot or war. Buildings lay in ruins, scattering their rubble into the streets. Cars burned, their black skeletons engulfed with flame. Glass crunched underfoot. Items of clothing, washing machines, televisions, furniture, lay strewn and broken, bits of people's lives uncaringly destroyed. Despite the immediacy of the devastation, however, the city seemed deserted. He stumbled from one street to another, sobbing, crying out a name he would forget the instant he awoke. He was lost. One street was identical to the next.

The sound of someone pounding on his door awoke him.

By the time he reached the door, whereupon he dropped

weakly down onto his hands and knees and puked up a mound of dark smoky vomit on the carpet, the pounding had stopped. He felt like shit, both mentally and physically. They would be loving all this, of course, but he felt so bad he had gone beyond the point of caring. He had thought it would take a lot for them to break his dignity and his pride, but in fact it had taken very little.

Outside the door, propped against the wall, was another parcel. He had been hoping it would be his food arriving at last, although he was no longer hungry. It was surprising he had had anything in his stomach to bring up; certainly when he examined what he had produced, he saw nothing in it that he recognised. It looked like a mound of ashes mixed with some sort of colourless gelid material.

The parcel was encased in bits of brown cardboard, cut and bent to the shape of the object inside. The object was long and thin, longer than a snooker cue case but shorter than a paddle. He carried it into the bedsitting room where a haze of smoke still greyed the air and the walls. He listened for a moment but no sounds were coming from the fridge. His burned hand was hot and sore, but the pain was bearable.

Lying amid the debris of cardboard and paper which he tore from the parcel and hurled around the room in a kind of righteous rage, was an arm. It was the arm of a young woman. It had been twisted or gnawed or chopped off at the shoulder. A smooth, rounded knob of bone protruded from the ragged stump like a caravan coupling. This limb, because it was larger, had evidently been difficult to drain of blood. Though for the most part white and waxy, blood had collected beneath the skin in some areas and congealed there. These areas, like terrible bruises, were a purplish blue-black.

The arm had long fingernails, nicely rounded, and painted with pale pink nail varnish, evidently carefully applied and maintained. There were no rings on the fingers, but there was an elegant gold bracelet on the wrist.

'Oh,' he moaned and raised his head to the hazy air, his whole body shuddering, 'oh, oh.' The sound was one of despair or ecstasy; he was not quite certain which.

When the phone rang, he sprang across the room like

223

some predatory beast and snatched it up.

'Do you like it? Isn't it beautiful?' The voice was full of a kind of mocking eagerness.

At first he could not reply and the voice became agitated.

'You do like it, don't you? Please say that you do.'

'It's ...' He struggled to find words and at last he said, ' ... difficult for me.'

The voice seemed satisfied. 'So can I stay here?' it asked.

'I don't know. You have to be careful.'

'I know.'

The line went dead.

In a sort of trance, feeling nothing at all, feeling empty in a way that was almost sublime, he ran a bath half-full of cold water and put the arm in it. The movement of the water made the arm seem to shimmer, to ripple. This illusion of life almost made him weep. However, the instant he left the bathroom and closed the door behind him, the feeling of serenity simply dropped from him like a discarded cloak. He began to snivel, to moan incoherently. He sank into a shivering, twitching heap, listening at the bathroom door, uncertain of what he might hear but terrified all the same.

Finally he could stand it no longer and crawled spastically away. He found he could not make his limbs function properly. He was like a man with a broken back. He slid through the pool of vomit on the doormat, lunged at the handle, perhaps intent on escape (he was not sure), and managed to tug the door open. Creaking, moaning sounds, like metal things dying, were drifting up the stairwell, but he barely heard them. He stared and stared, unable to believe his eyes.

Someone was standing on the landing, looking at him.

It was the little girl he had seen from his window. She still wore her yellow coat and sou'wester, both of which dripped water onto the floor. She looked unreal, like a painting of a beautiful child. Her eyes were very large and dark, and her skin − oh, her skin.

He stretched out a hand and said, 'Did they send you?'

She tried to take a step back but it was too late.

'No.'

The city was gone. There was nothing left but smoking rubble. He awoke to the sound of a woman calling the girl's name, her cries becoming increasingly frantic. He was in bed, naked. The arm was beside him, still damp. This close the arm did not smell so good, but he pulled it to him, hugged it, kissed the pale waxen hand.

Eventually, to his relief, the woman's cries faded.

When he next woke the phone was ringing. He rolled from the bed, sprang to his feet like a panther, swept it up. He felt wonderful. He hoped they were watching. They could not fail to be awed by him.

After a short silence, the voice said flatly, 'I'm sorry. They are coming.'

His confidence fled in an instant. He smashed the receiver into its cradle, wrenched the lead from the wall.

'No,' he screamed, 'no, no.' He screamed the word over and over until it became meaningless, an ululation of rage. He snatched up the arm from the bed, spun with it, battered it against the window again and again until the glass broke.

He tossed the arm through the window, saw it slither and bump across the roof tiles before disappearing.

He ran to the kitchen, tore open the fridge door, took out the charred hand, threw that out of the window too.

The smoke was dissipating, threading its way out through the jagged star of broken glass.

There was a knock on the door and everything stopped.

He stopped. The sounds he was making stopped. His breath stopped.

And then he saw the smoke still filtering out through the window.

He tried to moan but could make no sound.

Out on the landing the voice said, 'It's all right. It's just me.'

He went to the door. 'What do you want?'

'I've come to help you. Let me in.'

'I can't. You know I can't.'

'You can. Just close your eyes.'

He closed his eyes. The door opened and he heard footsteps enter. They moved towards him and then stopped. He heard

225

the bathroom door open, the footsteps enter, the bathroom door close.

There was a pause, then the voice said, 'Okay, you can come in now.'

He opened his eyes, entered the bathroom. It was empty. The voice said, 'I'm here.'

He turned and there was the other one, staring at him from the mirror.

'How – ' he began, but the other one shushed him and said:

'There isn't much time. Listen.'

He listened. They were coming, he could hear them. Coming up the stairs. Making their terrible sounds.

'Join me,' the other one said. 'It's the only way.'

Now he saw what the other one had done, how he had been tricked. 'No,' he said, 'this isn't fair.'

'It's the only way,' said the other one, smirking, his voice full of mockery.

Enraged, he pistoned out his arm, hand balling into a fist. He saw the other one's look of astonishment and horror and then the mirror exploded. Glass fell into the sink, shattering. He saw the blood on his hand and suddenly he felt the old strength surge through him.

They reached the landing, erupted through his front door.

He selected the largest shard of glass he could see and turned to face them.

The Chisellers' Reunion

You know in cartoons when, say, Daffy Duck's terrified and he's been gripping something so hard that he has to peel his hands away with a sound like parting strips of velcro? Well, that was what my hands felt like on the steering wheel when I stopped the car in front of Conrad's house in Warrington.

It was weird and frightening. I hadn't been here in a year, and yet I had been driving almost on automatic pilot, as though I used this route every day, as though it had become second nature to me. It was inevitable, I suppose, that my mind should have been on other things, but it was still scary to think that I had negotiated the M62 without even being aware of it.

The reunion, of course, was an annual black day on all our calendars, but this year was made doubly worse by the shadow of Stuart's suicide. It had been Conrad who had phoned me up and told me the night before last, in a voice of such icy control that as soon as he said, 'Hello, Mark, it's Conrad,' I just knew that something terrible had happened. Apparently Stuart had driven his car at high speed into a brick wall. He hadn't left a note, but nobody seemed to be in any doubt that it was suicide. He hadn't been killed outright, but had died in hospital two days later without regaining consciousness.

As I replaced the receiver, feeling numb as though with cold, all I could think of was his poor wife, Wendy, what she must have been going through. I had been at their wedding five years ago, had seen the joy on her face, her undoubted love for Stuart and his for her. The wedding had come just two weeks after the reunion, and I for one was going through the euphoric stage, having survived the initial week or so of nightmares born from black depression and self-loathing. I never discussed with the others how the reunion made them feel, but I could sense the celebration in the air on this day, and not just because of the wedding. It was like being released from prison, knowing that there were fifty glorious weeks before the dreaded day rolled round again. The euphoria, of course, never lasted for long. The reunion was like the centre of time, sucking us inexorably in towards it year after year. It undermined the foundations of our days, of our lives even, with its dark twisted roots.

Anyway, getting back to Stuart. I wondered whether he had ever told Wendy anything about the reunion, or whether he had hidden his real feelings from her so well that his suicide had come right out of the blue. Knowing what I did, it was awful to think of her shock, her confusion, her frantic grief. Knowing that I could alleviate just a fraction of that grief by providing her with the answers to what must have been desperate, empty questions was unbearable. I dreaded to think what the consequences would be if I *did* tell her. I dreaded to think what might happen now that Stuart wasn't here, now that the balance had been disrupted.

I got out of the car, flexing my hands, the palms of which felt bruised. It was odd, but I couldn't even remember changing gear on the journey, though I knew I must have done. It was a dull day for early August, a granite-coloured bank of cloud dominating the sky, jettisoning the occasional spatter of rain. I looked at Conrad's house for the first time. Its neat suburban angles, low pantiled roof and clipped lawn dismayed me. It wasn't the house itself, of course, but the situation, the fact that we had been sucked into that dark centre once again. The house, like the school and the fields and the viaduct, was a symbol of the reunion.

'Oi, Marky Mark, you chiselling twatter!' The greeting had me spinning round as though startled from a doze. Standing by the open door of his car further down the road was Nick, looking healthy and tanned and relaxed, round-lensed sunglasses hiding his eyes.

I mustered a smile in response to his grin and wandered

over. 'Hi, Nick,' I said. 'How's it going?'

Nick lunged back into his car, grabbed something from the passenger seat, and re-emerged, thrusting whatever he'd grabbed towards me. 'Here,' he said, 'cop hold of this.' I instinctively reached out my hands and a six-pack of Beck's landed in them like a rock.

I looked ruefully at the beer, and thought, it's going to be the same as always, isn't it? Stuart's death's not going to change anything. 'This isn't a fucking party, you know,' I said.

'Then it fucking should be,' said Nick, a second six-pack tucked under his arm. He locked the car door and pressed the button on his keyring which primed the alarm.

'I suppose you heard about Stuart?' I said, as we pushed Conrad's gate open and walked up the path towards the front door.

'Yeah, fucking chiseller. What'd he have to go and do a thing like that for?' To anyone who didn't know Nick, his words would have sounded callous, but I knew his heartiness was a bluff. Beneath it was genuine uncertainty, and a lot of grief. Nick got up a lot of people's noses, but he was all right really. We all knew that the reunion affected him as much as it affected the rest of us, and he knew we knew, but he would never have admitted such a thing.

'I guess he couldn't take any more,' I said, and then I added hesitantly, knowing that I was venturing into a taboo area, 'You can understand how he must have felt.'

'Don't be a twat,' said Nick, with a venom born of what I suspected was fear that Stuart's death might lead to the dissolution of the barriers that we built around ourselves to cope with this day. He hesitated, and then blurted, 'This only takes a few fucking hours a year. It's not worth killing yourself over. I don't fucking let it bother me. The best thing is to treat this day as a bit of a piss-up and a chance to see some old mates. It's not as though we never do anything that we haven't done before, is it?'

'I suppose you're right,' I said, and he was in a way, though that didn't make it any better.

'Course I am,' he said. We reached Conrad's front door.

231

Nick played the 'Match Of The Day' theme tune on the doorbell with his thumb.

When Conrad opened the door, Nick thrust his six-pack of Beck's into his stomach, making Conrad blow out his cheeks, an 'oof' sound escaping his pursed lips. 'You took your time, you chiselling bastard,' said Nick, striding into the house.

Recovering, Conrad said, 'Fuck off, you bald chiselling git. And what are you wearing those fucking sunglasses for? Are you blind as well as bald now, or are you just being a posey bastard?'

The repartee was raucous and crude as usual, though perhaps a little louder than normal, as though we believed volume could conceal the grief and fear we must all have been feeling because of Stuart's death and the hole it had torn in the established pattern of the day's coming events. We were always like this when we got together — lots of swearing, lots of insults. This was because we loved each other like brothers. Stuart's wife, Wendy, called it 'male bonding', and she also used to say that when we got together our conversation exhausted her because it was so competitive. Though these were my best friends, as the years had progressed we had seen each other less and less. In fact, I suppose it's true to say that Stuart's wedding had been a kind of cut-off point for us all. It was the reunion, of course, which had soured our friendship, just as it soured everything else. Seeing each other any time of year apart from on this day brought the reunion too close, made it seem as though it was hovering just beneath the surface of every conversation, even though, like typical men, we never talked about it, never talked about what was really important.

We filed into Conrad's house. Or rather, Nick and I went in — I'm still thinking in terms of us being four, still thinking that Stuart was here, which he wasn't any more and never would be again.

'Fancy a coffee?' Conrad said.

'Don't be a chiselling knob-end. Open the beers. Why drink shite when you can have nectar?' said Nick.

I guess before I go any further I ought to explain this

'chisellers' thing. The phrase was one that had endured from schooldays, though who first gave voice to it I can't really remember. If I had to put money on it, I'd say it was one of Conrad's weird expressions; he was full of them, including his own version of Cockney rhyming slang. It was Nick, I think, though, who coined the phrase, 'chiselling twatter', our most enduring and (we thought) hilarious insult. Of course, it was just one of those silly, cliquey things that cement kids together, that identify them as a gang or club or whatever. I suppose most people relinquish dumb stuff like that when they grow into adulthood, but we never had.

Which just goes to show what a bunch of sad individuals we are.

We sat in Conrad's front room for a bit, swigging beer out of the bottle and keeping up the volume and the insults and the repartee. We talked about everything but what was really on our minds – the reunion – and more particularly how Stuart's death would affect it.

Finally Conrad finished his beer and stood up. 'Anyone fancy another Tyrannosaurus?'

'Tyrannosaurus?' I was a bit slow on the uptake; my mind was on other things.

'Tyrannosaurus Rex – Beck's,' Conrad and Nick chorused, to which Nick added, 'You thick chiselling twatter.'

'Fuck off, you bald bastard,' I said to Nick – sparkling wit or what? 'Shouldn't we be getting over there?' I added.

'It's only six o'clock. We've got hours yet,' said Nick.

'I know, but ... I dunno. I'd like to get there. It'll make me feel as though we're starting to get it over with.'

'We can't get it over with until ...' Nick's voice faltered for the first time since we had entered the house. He glanced at Conrad, who was standing in the doorway, carefully peeling the label off his beer bottle.

'I *know* that,' I said quickly, filling the suddenly uncomfortable silence. 'It's just that I hate sitting around here. I'd rather be over there. I can't explain why. I just would,'

'You're fucking weird,' said Nick. 'Tell him he's fucking weird, Conrad.'

'You're absolutely Patrick,' Conrad said.

This time Nick joined me in giving Conrad a blank look.

'Patrick Swayze – crazy,' Conrad supplied obediently.

'At least I don't look like a cross between Roy Orbison and Kojak,' I said.

Conrad whooped with laughter. Nick said amiably, 'No, you just look like a total cunt.'

The upshot of all this was that we went to Seven Arches a bit earlier than we normally would. My real reason for wanting to break the routine was as a way of ... I don't know, *acknowledging* that Stuart wasn't here, that things were different, that the emphasis had changed. I didn't voice this, of course (I might have done if I'd got either Conrad or Nick on their own, but not when all three of us were together), but Conrad seemed to pick up on how I was feeling, agreeing that we might as well be over there as sitting around here getting stir crazy (his words, not mine). Nick just shrugged and said that he could just as easily get pissed at the viaduct as sitting around here. However he warned me that if it started raining again and he got wet he was going to rip my balls off with his teeth. I told him I'd look forward to it.

We took the beers and went out of Conrad's back door, then climbed over the fence into the playground of the junior school where we had all met over twenty years ago. It was abandoned now, most of its windows either broken or boarded up. Conrad said that developers were going to tear it down and build a new housing complex for old people, but he had been saying that for the past seven years. As we each set foot on the pitted concrete of the playground, still etched with the faint markings of netball courts, memories clustered around us as they always did. I guess officially the reunion didn't begin until Denton turned up, but for me it always started here. This was the equivalent of being a professional footballer and turning up at Wembley two hours before kick-off in the cup final. The nerves started to kick in as the preamble got under way.

Only we weren't here to play football. We were here to relive the worst day of our lives.

Nick and I looked at each other, Nick's eyebrows raising

above his sunglasses as if to say, *here we go*, as Conrad strode to the middle of the playground. We both knew what was coming next. In what used to be the centre circle of the netball court, Conrad halted and turned to face us.

'We all know what happened here, don't we, boys and girls?'

'Yes,' I said as though I was incredibly bored and didn't want to hear it again.

This, however, was tradition. Conrad continued with his story, undeterred. 'It was here that I, at the age of six, removed my purple-headed custard cannon from my undergarments and took a bangers and mash all over this very patch of concrete, watched by a large and adoring crowd. Only someone informed the cling peaches of my nefarious pursuits, didn't they?'

Nick and I were both nodding.

'And who was that, boys and girls?'

'The chiselling twatter himself,' responded Nick.

'Correct,' said Conrad, narrowing his eyes. Tall and thin and pale and dressed in black, he looked like a prophet of doom. 'The chiselling twatter *himself*. And we all know what happened to that cunt, don't we?'

I gaped at him. This wasn't how it was supposed to be. I didn't want to hear this. Even though the memory of it went round and round in my head and always would, I didn't want to hear what we'd done put into words, and especially not by Conrad. If we started talking about it, started admitting to each other that it had happened, then we wouldn't be able to cope with it, we'd fall apart. I really believe this, odd though it sounds. They say a problem shared is a problem halved, but in this instance a problem shared would have been a problem doubled, a problem come to life. Just coming here every year and having to do what we did was bad enough without having to actually bring it out into the open, face up to it. It's hard to explain, and maybe you can't understand my feelings, but if you were in my situation, if you were me, you'd know.

Normally Conrad just told this story straight without putting any accusatory slant on it. I don't know why he told it at all, to be honest. It was just part of the odd, unspoken ritual that we all felt compelled to go through, I suppose, before the reunion proper got underway.

'Leave it, Connie,' I snapped now. 'That isn't fucking funny.'

Conrad glared at me as though I'd done something to make him furious. He looked really weird, as if he was capable of anything, and that scared me. I mean, Conrad could be a weird fucking bastard at the best of times, but he knew the rules as well as we did and he'd never strayed from them before. You could hardly blame him for being a bit weird, having to look at Seven Arches every day when he opened his bedroom curtains. I often wondered how he could bear to go on living here, but maybe he felt he had no choice.

'It's not supposed to be fucking funny,' he snarled. 'It's supposed to be fucking tragic. Stuart's dead, you cunt, and it's because of that fucking chiselling fucking bastard twatting chiseller.' He flapped an arm in the general direction of Seven Arches. 'And I don't fucking care if he *can* hear me, and I don't fucking care what fucking happens any more. Stuart's fucking dead because of him, and that should be the end of it. We should be allowed to get on with our lives. But it's not fucking good enough for that cunt, is it?' He looked up at us, his eyes widening, as though an astounding idea had just entered his head. 'Hey, why don't we tell him to go fuck it this year? Why don't we go down the rub-a-dub instead of over to fucking Seven Arches and drink ourselves into an FC Roma?'

He looked desperate, pleading. I looked at Nick, feeling embarrassed and sick and angry at Conrad for letting the mantle slip, the carapace crack. Nick didn't look at me. His cheeks were flushed and his lips pursed. I couldn't see what his eyes were doing because he was still wearing those stupid fucking sunglasses.

For long, long seconds, none of us said anything. Then in a tight, clipped voice Nick said, 'You know we can't do that. Just tell us the rest of the story, Conrad.'

Conrad's shoulders slumped. He looked a broken man. He'd made his stand, vented his fury, and we hadn't supported him. Now it seemed he had no defiance left.

236

I felt ashamed, but relieved too. In little more than a murmur, he said, 'Denton told Mrs Sykes, who made me stand on a desk in front of the class while she told them what a disgusting like turd I was. All the girls were giggling, and when I looked down I realised that my flies were open and that my shorts were wet where I'd accidentally pissed on them in my fleeting moment of triumph.'

'And what colour underpants were you wearing, Connie?' I asked dutifully.

'They were a Paisley pattern in purple and pink. They fitted me until I was eleven. They were voted the most hideous pair of underpants in the world in the 1977 Chisellers Awards.' He looked up at us. 'That's all.'

'Okay,' said Nick. 'Now let's go over to the Arches and get pissed as fucking stoats.'

His effusiveness had a hollow ring. Nevertheless Conrad and I both nodded. As Conrad trudged towards us, I realised he was muttering something.

'What you fucking rambling on about now, you chiseller?' said Nick with false bonhomie.

'I said, maybe it *is* over. Maybe Denton won't come any more, now that Stuart's dead.'

Nick went barmy. He ran at Conrad and shoved him so hard in the chest that Conrad almost fell over. 'Why don't you just fucking *shut up!*' he shouted. 'He'll come. And while he keeps fucking coming, so will we. That cunt's not going to ruin my life. No fucking way.'

He's already ruined all our lives, I thought, but I didn't say anything.

Conrad, however, like a fool, blundered on. 'How do you know he'll come? Maybe he's happy now. Maybe this was all he wanted.'

'*I said shut up! Nobody wants to fucking hear it!*'

Nick whirled and sprang at Conrad, who made no move to get out of the way. I started to shout, 'Nick, no!' as I saw his arm swing round, but hadn't even completed the first syllable when Nick's clenched fist made contact with Conrad's jaw. It made a sickening noise, like a mallet hitting a thick slab of steak. Conrad just fell without even staggering, poleaxed. Nick stood over him, spitting out the words, 'He'll never let us fucking rest. He's a vindictive little bastard. We stop coming, people start dying. Is that what you want?'

Conrad was conscious, but only just. His eyes were flickering and blood was drooling out of his mouth, and he was making a sound at the back of his throat as though trying to speak through a mouthful of dough. When I reached Nick, he was bent almost double over Conrad, his face bright red. He was muttering now, as though his anger was winding down like an old clock. 'I don't want to hear any more about it,' he was saying. 'Understand? Understand?'

I reached out, hesitated a moment, then put my hand on Nick's back. Even through his jacket it felt hot and damp. 'He can't hear you, Nick,' I said. 'You've knocked him into the middle of next week.'

Nick straightened up and turned on me. For a moment I thought he was going to punch me too. But he didn't, he just said, 'Why did he have to go on like that, Mark? Why couldn't he just shut up? Things are bad enough without ... ah ... fucking hell.'

He pushed past me and staggered across the playground towards the condemned school. He slumped against a brick wall, kind of rolled to face it, his forehead pressed against its rough surface. He looked like a kid playing hide and seek, counting to a hundred while his friends scatter like startled mice. I knelt beside Conrad. He was groaning and spitting blood. He hadn't actually lost consciousness, but he would never have beaten the ten count if this had been a boxing match.

I did all the usual stuff – wiped the blood from his mouth with a handkerchief, asked him if he was okay (stupid question, but what else can you ask?), held up four fingers to make sure he wasn't experiencing double vision. Conrad didn't say much, but eventually he managed to sit up, shedding gravel from his clothes and his hair. I wasn't aware that Nick had moved from his place by the wall until he was squatting beside us, looking shame-faced.

'Hey, sorry, Connie. Sorry, mate. You okay?' he mumbled, reaching out tentatively to help me help Conrad sit up straight.

'Yeah,' Conrad replied mushily, then abruptly twisted his

head and puked up the beer he'd drunk. If that had been me, I thought, I'd have puked all over Nick's bald head.

Nick and I pulled him to his feet and walked him around a bit. Nick kept apologising and telling him to take deep breaths. Eventually Conrad was able to walk around himself, though we stayed close by in case he should stumble and fall. With his fingers he probed tenderly at the left side of his jaw, which was already discoloured and starting to swell.

'Ow,' he said, 'that hurts.'

Nick grimaced. 'Sorry,' he said again. 'Things just got out of hand, you know.'

'I think you've broken one of my Hampsteads,' Conrad said, poking about inside his mouth with his tongue. Suddenly he flinched. 'Fuck me, you have, you chiselling twatter. There's something dangling around in here. I'm sure it's an exposed nerve.'

'Sorry, sorry, sorry, sorry, sorry,' said Nick. 'What can I say? I'll pay all your dental bills. I'll prostrate myself in your presence.' He strode across to where we had dumped the beer prior to Conrad telling us his pissing on the playground story. He extracted the remaining three bottles from the first six pack and ripped off their caps with the bottle opener he kept in his pocket.

'Here,' he said, 'have a beer on me. I'm really sorry, Connie. No hard feelings, eh?'

We took the beer and drank, Conrad tentatively. He swilled his first mouthful around and then spat it out. It emerged pink and frothy.

'You disgusting chiseller,' I said.

'Better out than in.'

'I thought that was farts,' said Nick.

'Whatever.'

We stood around in the playground and drank beer for a couple of minutes like teenagers whose exams had just finished. Desperate stuff, but like I said earlier we're a sad bunch of bastards. We were all twenty-six and had made little of our lives. Nick had already been married and divorced twice, unable to sustain a relationship, whereas Conrad and I hadn't even got off the starting blocks in that particular race. Career-wise we hadn't fared much

239

better. Nick was one of those guys who are full of big schemes that, through a combination of bad luck and bad planning, never quite come off. Conrad worked as a clerk for North West Water. And I was currently unemployed, having drifted through a variety of jobs since leaving school: night-watchman, 'Pizzaland' waiter, book shop assistant. I even had a job in a sausage factory once, as a result of which I will never eat sausages again.

His beer two-thirds gone, Nick wandered across and picked up the remaining six-pack. 'Only six bottles left,' he said. 'We'll never get pissed on that. Why didn't you stingy bastards provide any alcohol?'

'You can have mine,' said Conrad. 'Drinking makes my North and South hurt anyway.'

'And I'm not that bothered,' I added. 'Like I said before, this isn't a Russell.'

'Russell?' Nick raised his eyebrows.

'Russell Harty, you chiseller,' said Conrad.

'Oh yeah, right.' For a man who'd just been given a sizeable beer donation, Nick looked pretty put out. 'Have you two signed the pledge or what?'

'Nah, we're just not in the mood,' I said.

Nick looked at us in disgust but didn't ask why. He already knew the answer, and didn't want it spoken aloud.

He contented himself with muttering, 'Chisellers,' then the three of us made our way across the playground and behind the school onto the playing fields beyond which lay Seven Arches. The fields covered such a vast area that a kid playing golf was just a speck in the distance. Nobody said anything when the viaduct came into view. I shuddered, unable to decide whether the arches themselves were like eyes watching our arrival or black mouths sucking us in.

I was scared. Really scared. Things were different this year, things were unravelling badly. As we passed beneath a set of sagging goalposts, the ground in front of them churned to mud by Grobelaar wannabes, Conrad muttered, 'Remember when I wrote a note asking Jackie Prentice out? We were all playing football here when she walked up with her mates and ripped the note into tiny little pieces. Chucked it all over me like confetti. I felt a right James Hunt.'

Nobody responded and Conrad fell silent. As we got nearer to Seven Arches, it seemed to rise above the green horizon, like a great stone spider pushing itself from its lair.

And then, inevitably, we were there, at the centre of all things, scrambling down the weed-choked bank. A stream moved sluggishly through one of the arches, beyond which an incline led up to a secluded corner of a park that used to be wasteland when we were kids. All we could see from here was a bit of landscaping and a screen of trees beneath which nestled an empty bench. There were no people around, and no sounds except for the gurgle of water and the stealthy whisper of wind in long grass.

We passed beneath the viaduct, beneath stone walls that breathed out cold. Despite the vast openings at either end, the through draft of air, it always smelled under here, a damp, stale, sweaty smell, like a small room after a wild party. And yet it was freezing; it was *always* freezing. I hugged myself, feeling not only my skin but the muscles beneath tightening up. Used condoms lay among the rubble on the ground like bleached slugs; ancient beer cans rusted among the weeds. Scraps of paper clung to stalks of long grass, occasionally fluttering like ensnared moths. And on black walls thickly beslimed with some milky substance, graffiti swarmed, mementoes of clandestine meetings, first fucks, teenage summers.

Nick crouched down, parting weeds. 'Still here,' he said.

I stood behind him and looked down. On the section of wall he had uncovered, beneath a crude sketch of a woman performing fellatio, were our names in yellow paint: MARK, CON, STUART, NICK.

'Hey!' shouted Conrad, waving something in the air. 'Look what I've found! A wank mag!'

We crowded round to look at the pulpy pages, at the bodies of over-developed teenagers, oiled breasts speckled with mould. One girl was a circus freak, tits big as coal sacks, hanging to her knees.

'Reminds me of my first wife,' said Nick wistfully.

The three of us scrambled up the embankment towards the railway tracks. It was steep and fairly treacherous, layered with smooth white stones. Because Nick was carrying the beer and couldn't keep his balance properly, he nearly slipped back down a couple of times, ending up on all fours as stones rattled around him. By the time he joined Conrad and I, who were sitting at the top with our backs to the track, looking out over the valley, he was red and dusty and swearing a lot. He plonked himself down beside us and grabbed himself a beer.

'Actually I think I *will* have one,' Conrad said brightly.

'Yeah, me too,' I added.

'You can both fuck off,' growled Nick.

We sat there for a while, chewing the fat, trading insults, trying to hide our increasing nervousness from each other. I was feeling Stuart's absence keenly, and not just because of what the implications might be for the reunion. It felt bad to be all together without Stuart. This might sound odd, but it felt as though we were excluding him somehow, as though we'd gone behind his back, met without telling him we were doing so. As we sat there it got chillier and the sun started to go down. The approaching Liverpool-Manchester train made the rails whine like an injured dog.

As the train roared by, just a few feet behind us, Conrad did his usual thing of moving his lips without sound, pretending he was holding a conversation. The train sound began to fade and Conrad said, as though it were the end of a story, ' . . . licked off all the clotted cream.'

Nick and I both laughed.

'How's your face?' I asked him.

'Fucking hurts.'

'Fucking hurts me too,' said Nick.

Below us was a sort of gully choked with weeds and rubbish. Beyond that the ground sloped back up to the edge of the playing fields. I picked up one of the smooth white stones and lobbed it into the gully, aiming at a discarded Tizer bottle. I missed by about three feet, hitting the edge of a rusting bed-frame.

There was a deep clang and the stone bounced into the air like a white mouse hitting a trampoline. Conrad snatched up a stone and followed suit.

242

'Person who manages to smash the bottle gets a blow job,' he said.

'From who?' Nick wanted to know, looking at Conrad suspiciously.

'Er ... Michelle Pfeiffer. I'll give her a bell when we get back.'

As if believing by some miraculous quirk of fate that the prize could become a genuine one, the three of us snatched up stones and hurled them frantically at our target. Perhaps because we were all so eager to win, perhaps simply because we're a bunch of losers, it took a ridiculously long time to hit the bottle. Stones lay scattered about like petals, in the midst of which the bottle lay, intact. Nick's aim got steadily worse the more beer he drunk, and my arm started to ache like a bastard after a bit. I'm your typical Mr Average – average height, average build, average looks – but for some reason I've always had incredibly weak arms. I can never hold anything in the air for very long, and I sprain my wrists quite easily. However, weak arms or not, I eventually threw a stone that I knew, the instant it left my hand, was a winner.

The stone hit the bottle dead centre, and we were all treated to the incredibly satisfying sound of breaking glass.

'Champeo-nee, champeo-nee, oh way-oh-way-oh-way,' I chanted.

'Nice one,' said Conrad. 'The only thing I forgot to mention, though, is that I wasn't talking about Michelle Pfeiffer the actress, but Michelle Pfeiffer who works in the local fish-gutting factory. She's sixty-two, weighs twenty-three stone, has nostril-stinging BO and a face like a Yak's sphincter.'

'Sounds like my kind of girl,' I said.

'Oh, and she's only got one eye.'

'Gorgeous!'

'And two noses.'

'Pass me a Kleenex, I'm drooling.'

'Hey, I know her,' said Nick. 'She once ate our next-door neighbour's Doberman.'

And so it went on. We all felt like shit and yet we kept the jokes coming. This is probably what it was like in the trenches, or the jungles of Vietnam. A laugh a minute.

It was getting quite dark now. Was it really four hours since we had arrived? As usual the time had just gone, disappeared, as though great chunks of it had been gobbled up. Nick only had two bottles of Beck's left, plus the one he was drinking. It didn't seem to be affecting him much, though, except in his throwing arm. Eventually the banter tailed off and we fell silent. Nobody was looking at their watches, but we knew the beginning of the reunion − the real beginning − could not be too far away now.

I closed my eyes, rubbed my hands over my face. My stomach was trembling.

And then I heard Conrad whisper, 'Here we go.'

I opened my eyes.

And saw the fire.

It was licking at the grass beside the railway track as it always did, startlingly white in the dusk. At first the fire was small, but it was already spreading, darting tongues of flame sprouting into new life in the undergrowth.

'We've got to put it out,' said Conrad, and already his voice sounded different − younger, clearer, cocksure without him having to force it.

The change was upon us without us even realising it. We had stepped back onto the treadmill of time, and now nothing could stop the events that were about to unfold.

It's hard to explain how it feels. A friend of mine once went to a show given by a hypnotist, and was dragged up on stage and made to behave like a chicken laying an egg and all that kind of stuff. When I asked him what it felt like, he said that he knew what he was doing but that he couldn't stop himself. I guess that's how the reunion feels in a way, as if we're trapped inside bodies that we know are our own but which we have no control over. And yet it's not *quite* like that, not quite so clear cut − it's also a little bit like dreaming while awake. When you dream, you can be a child again without realising it until you wake up; you can see people who've died, can talk to them, and impossible though it seems later, you forget they're dead.

So it was with the reunion. Just for a little while, our minds slip back to that corresponding day twelve years ago when we were all fourteen. We don't actually fall asleep, and we don't wake up afterwards. When the reunion's over, we just kind of click into gear again, remember who we are, and worst of all, what we've done. And we don't remember it as a fading memory, as something long past, but as a fresh wound, a new trauma. The reunion is not only a nightmare, but a nightmare relived. Again and again and again.

So why do you come here year after year? I hear you asking. If it's so terrible, why not just stay away?

The simple answer is, if we didn't come here then people we loved would die. It happened on the eve of the first reunion. For maybe three or four weeks leading up to that day, I couldn't get the thought of going back there on the anniversary of what had happened out of my mind. It was more than an idea, it was an obsession, and at first I thought it was just me being morbid. At night I dreamt about going back; during the day I thought about it constantly. It was as though the place was tugging me towards it, as though it had me on the end of a long line and was reeling me in.

Anyway, eventually it got so bad I mentioned it to Conrad, and of course he too had been plagued by the same obsessive thoughts. And so, we quickly found out, had both Nick and Stuart. It was only now that we concluded that Denton was somehow doing this to us, and we decided there and then that no matter how bad the urge to return became, there was no way we'd go back to Seven Arches – we'd see each other through this.

But Denton, being the vicious bastard that he was, had other ideas. The day before the first reunion, each one of us had someone in their family die. For me, it was my granddad's brother who committed suicide by hanging himself because, so everyone said, he was terrified of retiring; for Nick it was his cousin's nine-month-old daughter who died of Cot Death Syndrome; for Con it was some old aunty or somebody who fell downstairs, and for Stuart it was his mother's cousin, who got killed in a motorway pile-up.

Ridiculous as this sounds, we might even have put these four totally unconnected deaths down to coincidence if it hadn't been for the fact that that night, the night before the first anniversary, we each of us had an intensely vivid dream where we were at the funeral of someone we *really* loved, not

245

just some distant relative whose death was a quickly forgotten shock. I was at my mum's funeral. I was looking down into her open coffin. She was dressed in this blue sort of surplice with a ruffled collar and she had her hands crossed over her chest. She looked sunken by the disease which had ravaged her. And yet, despite knowing about the disease, I had this awful unshakeable feeling that *I'd* done this to her by not going back, that she'd been punished for my mistake.

I woke up crying and sweating and thrashing about, and instantly I knew that if I didn't want my dream to come true, if I didn't want people to suffer because of me, I had to go back.

And so it has been every year. No doubt this is one of the reasons why none of us has ever managed to forge lasting relationships (except Stuart, of course, and look at what the strain of that did to him). To put it bluntly, the ever-looming shadow of the reunion has ensured that our lives are barely worth living. We just about cope, I suppose, by outwardly denying to each other that the reunion − the *real* reunion, the one that starts with the fire − exists until it happens. We endure our lives by bottling it all up, keeping it inside ourselves, where it buzzes and flutters like a trapped wasp.

But I'm getting ahead of myself here, becoming bogged down in explanations. The thing is, it always starts with the fire, and with Conrad saying, 'We've got to put it out.'

We all hauled ourselves to our feet and ran over to the burning grass and started stamping on it. It wasn't a big fire, but it was a stubborn bastard, and as soon as we stamped on one bit and reduced it to a frazzled, smoking patch of what used to be grass, new flames would pop up elsewhere, like fucking moles sticking their heads out of the ground. To this day, I don't know for certain who started the fire, though obviously I have my suspicions. We just happened along, mooched around a bit, climbed up the embankment and there it was.

Anyway, we were all stamping, and just about getting on top of the thing, when there was this blue-white flash of light that virtually blinded me, and no doubt the others too, and I heard someone shout, 'Gotcha!'

246

My very first thought, which only lasted about a second, was that one of us had inadvertently stamped on a bomb or something that had gone off in our faces. For a few seconds I couldn't see a fucking thing because of the after-image of the flash, hovering in front of my face like a neon butterfly. However Nick, who was standing to my right, couldn't have been as badly affected as I was. I heard him say, 'What the fuck d'you think you're playing at, *Denton*?'

He spat out the kid's name like an insult, and if Denton had been in your class at school you would have done too. The kid was — how shall I put this? — a total cunt. He had no redeeming features whatsoever. He stirred up trouble for everyone. He was manipulative, two-faced, snide, a bully to the little kids, a cheat, a liar and a tell-tale. And believe me, those were just his good points. He was the original 24-carat chiselling twatter.

He looked the part too. I'd be insulting rodents if I said he had a face like a sewer rat. As the glare from what I now realised was a camera flash faded from my eyes, I saw him standing there, halfway up the embankment. Only Denton could have scuttled up that pile of loose stones without anybody hearing him. 'Getting evidence, what's it fucking look like?' he sneered in answer to Nick's question.

God, that fucking voice! I heard it every day at school, but it never failed to set my teeth on edge. The voice alone was enough to make you want to punch the wanker's lights out.

'Evidence?' Conrad said in disgust. 'Evidence for what, Rat-boy?'

Nick and I laughed, but to Denton the insult was sewage off a rat's back. He must have had so many in his life that he had developed an immunity.

'You'll be laughing on the other side of your faces when I develop this film,' he whined. 'Setting fire to railway tracks is a serious offence. You're endangering lives.'

'Since when did you join the Sweeney?' I said.

Denton fixed his ratty little eyes on me, and just for an instant I swear they flashed yellow.

'Shouldn't you be at your mother's funeral?' he said.

A few seconds of shocked silence followed this remark.

All the lads knew that my mum had cancer and had been in and out of hospital having chemotherapy for the last nine months. The doctors currently rated her chances at 50–50. It had been a very tough time for all of us.

It shouldn't really have surprised me that Denton would come out with a remark like that, but it did all the same. However much you guarded against Denton, however much you convinced yourself that he was a shit and that what he said didn't matter, he still had this knack of getting under your defences, sticking his knife into the places where you were most vulnerable.

I composed myself pretty quickly, but I could see by the way he smirked that he knew his remark had hit home.

'Why don't you come up here and say that, Reptile-breath?' I said calmly.

'What, and have all three of you onto me? I'm not stupid.'

'*Really*?' said Conrad in apparent astonishment. 'I always thought you were. Stupid and ugly and a snivelling little shit who hasn't got any friends.'

Denton just snorted and shook his head as if to say: *is that the best you can do*? Then suddenly his face adopted a sly look and he said, almost mockingly, 'Where's your other little bum chum, Stuart, tonight?'

I felt something lurch in my stomach, as though I had only just remembered something vital that I was supposed to have done. The feeling settled into a wriggle of unease and a sense of astonishment. Fuck, where *was* Stuart? Why wasn't he here? For the life of me, I couldn't think why he wasn't with us, or, more importantly, why I hadn't noticed until Denton had just pointed it out. I looked round at Conrad and saw that he was just as bewildered as I was. I had this feeling – no, more than a feeling, a *certainty* – that Stuart *should* be here. And following hot on the heels of that was the conviction that the fact that he wasn't here meant that something was badly wrong.

Then the moment, like a glitch in time, passed, and Nick said aggressively, 'Who you gonna show that fucking photograph to anyway?' It was obvious that the matter was preying on his mind.

248

'The police. I'm sure they'd be interested. And I might send a copy to your dad.'

Nick's dad was an evil bastard. If he wasn't off with some tart, he was at home knocking his family around. If someone sent him what appeared to be photographic evidence of his son setting fire to railway tracks, there was no telling what he might do. He'd broken Nick's mum's arm once, and quite often Nick had bruises on his back when he got changed for games. Once he came to school with a black eye and his body covered in bright purple marks in the shape of a belt buckle. I tried to persuade him to tell a teacher what was going on, but he wouldn't.

'The police wouldn't be fucking bothered,' Nick blustered.

'Maybe not, but I'm sure your dad would,' sneered Denton.

'Would he fuck. Anyway, we were putting the fire out, not starting it. Any cunt can see that.'

Denton shook his head. 'I don't think so. Anyway, why don't we let your dad decide?' He turned and started to pick his way back down the slope.

Nick started to go after him, but Conrad grabbed his arm. 'Leave it, Nick,' he said, 'he's just a fucking chiseller. He won't do anything. He's just stirring it.'

But Nick had that look in his eyes. He wasn't going to let this one go. He shook his arm free of Conrad's grip and began to lope down the embankment, stones scuttling in front of him as though trying to get out of his way.

'Give me that camera, you chiselling turd,' he shouted. Denton had reached the bottom of the embankment now and was halfway up the slope that led to the playing fields. There was no way that Nick was going to catch him.

'Make me,' said Denton, turning and flicking us a V. It was at this point that it occurred to me to wonder just why Denton had been carrying a camera around with him. I'd never seen him with one before. Had he set this up, maybe started the fire himself? I never found out the answer to these questions, and I guess I never will.

Conrad went and stamped out the last of the fire while Nick continued to scramble down the slope of the embankment in the vain hope of catching Denton. I stood on the top of the embankment and watched, and that was when the idea came to me. I stooped and picked up a stone and threw it at Denton's ratty little body. It missed, but only just. Denton paused in his retreat and turned round.

'Fuck off!' he shouted in that whiny voice of his. 'If one of those hits me, I'll have the police on you for assault.'

That was enough to make me pause, but not so Nick. In fact, Denton's threat only seemed to goad him further. He started picking up stones and hurling them with savage force at Denton, who was clinging to the grassy slope like a spider, screeching, 'Fuck off! Fuck off! Fuck off!'

The first half-dozen stones that Nick threw missed his target, a couple of them wildly. Then a stone about the size of a cricket ball struck Denton in the small of the back. He squealed, and almost immediately started crying.

'Bastards!' he sobbed, dragging himself up the slope with renewed panic. 'Bastards, I'll fucking get you. Bastards. Bastards.'

Nick's next couple of rocks missed Denton, then he threw one that hit him on the leg. Denton squealed again, but he was almost at the top of the slope now.

I have to admit that at this point ten per cent of me was scared that we were going to hurt Denton badly and get into real trouble, but the other ninety per cent was viewing what was happening with a kind of savage glee.

Conrad must have felt the same because I heard him shout, 'Don't let him get away!'

Then suddenly all three of us were picking up rocks and hurling them as hard as we could.

I don't know which one of us threw the rock that hit Denton on the head, but all at once he screamed – not just squealed, but really screamed this time – and sort of slumped to the ground. Immediately I flinched, feeling like an animal that has ventured too far and touched the electric fence.

'Fuck,' Conrad said and dropped the rock he was holding. In a kind of wonderment he said, 'Do you think we knocked him out?'

250

'Nah, he's moving, look,' I said with a bravado I didn't feel.

And he was, though in a sluggish, uncoordinated way, like a fish left on a beach when the tide goes out.

Nick reached him in about another ten seconds and dragged him round onto his back.

'Is he bleeding?' I shouted.

'Only a bit,' said Nick disdainfully. 'He's just being a fucking puff.' He picked Denton up by the lapels of his jacket and dropped him again. I winced.

I heard Nick say, 'I'll take that, thank you very much,' and next moment he was coming back towards us, waving Denton's camera above his head.

He was halfway up the embankment when Denton stirred and sat up, holding his head. All at once he seemed to come to and realise he no longer had possession of his camera. *'Give me that back, you bastard!'* he screeched, in a voice that was raw and wild and hysterical. He sounded really, really crazy, as if he was capable of anything. Then he jumped up, ran down the slope and started climbing the embankment towards us.

We watched him coming, and I have to admit I felt a bit nervous because he really did look just like a loony from a horror film. Nick, though, didn't seem to care. He was still laughing and waving the camera about like an athlete with an Olympic medal.

'Come and get it, little Rat-boy,' he crooned. 'Ah, has diddums lost his toysy-woysy den?'

'You're dead, you cunt!' Denton screeched.

'Am I?' said Nick. 'I wasn't the last time I looked.'

Denton reached the top of the embankment. Now he was just a few feet away from Nick ...

At which point Nick lobbed Denton's camera, like a grenade, towards the stream below. It landed in the scummy water with a loud 'splosh' and disappeared.

'Fucking hell,' I said with a mixture of horror and gleeful disbelief, and put a hand to my mouth.

'Hole in one!' shouted Conrad. 'And Nicky-boy takes the title.'

Denton just turned and stared at the stream, unable to

251

believe what Nick had just done. When he turned back, he looked momentarily shell-shocked, eyes wide, mouth hanging open. I heard the distant but approaching whistle of a train, and thought for a moment that it was Denton's escalating rage; I half-expected to see steam start blowing out of his ears.

Then, without a word, he launched himself at Nick, both fists pistoning out like Superman taking off. Denton was a weed, and he couldn't fight for toffee, but the attack was so sudden that Nick sprawled back in the dust and stones by the side of the rail track, taken by surprise.

Denton leaped on him and began to scratch and bite and pummel, making me think that this was how a rat must fight when confronted with a larger opponent. If this had been happening in the school playground a large and excited crowd would have gathered around the combatants instantly chanting, 'Scrap, scrap, scrap, scrap.' However there was only Conrad and me to watch the contest here (again, with a feeling almost of doom I wondered where the fuck Stuart had got to). I looked up the track and saw the lights of an approaching train, heard the rails begin to whine.

'Hey, pack it in!' I shouted. 'There's a train coming! Pack it in!'

It was at this point, at this year's reunion, where the paths really divided, where Stuart's absence was really felt. To tell you what happened, I have to tell you first what *should* have happened. I have to tell you what happened on that fateful day, August 5th 1981, and what, until this year, had happened on every anniversary since.

What happened was that the three of us − me, Conrad and Stuart − dragged Denton, kicking and screaming, off the top of Nick. Nick had a scratch on his face but was otherwise unhurt. He looked more embarrassed than anything.

'Let me go, you bastards!' Denton was half-sobbing. 'Let me fucking go!'

'Don't be a twat,' Stuart shouted at him. 'There's a fucking train coming.'

Nick was climbing to his feet. We could hear the thunder of the approaching train now, see its headlights growing larger and larger. Denton went suddenly limp, as though responding to Stuart's words or realising he was defeated. As a result we relaxed our grip on his arm just slightly, and next instant Denton had torn himself free from all three of us and was lunging towards Nick with his hands outstretched, evidently intending to shove him into the path of the train.

It was Stuart who reacted first and saved Nick's life, Stuart who kicked out at Denton's lunging body. I know that Stuart only meant to trip Denton up, make him land flat on his face by the side of the track. But Denton had put everything, all his rage, all his strength, into his attack, and somehow he lost his balance and Nick dodged out of his way, and Denton's forward momentum made him stumble right into the path of the oncoming train.

It hit him with a bang like an explosion. It all happened so fast that I didn't see any blood or any limbs fly off or anything like that. There was just this bang, then this impression of something large flying through the air and landing with a crash in the gully below.

The air became filled with the stink of fumes and hot metal and the blistering squeal of the train's brakes. I felt like I'd turned to water. I remember looking down into the gully in the gathering darkness and seeing a dark bundle there. I couldn't believe it was Denton. There was nothing about it that seemed even vaguely human. I'm not saying there were guts all over the place or anything like that. It was just ... a heap, that was all, could just as easily have been a mound of earth or a big bundle of rags.

Anyway, that was when we ran, and of course Denton's body was found and the whole thing was seen as a tragic accident, another kid playing silly buggers by the side of the railway track with friends who were never identified. And then, for us, the nightmares started, the odd thoughts and compulsions, the panic attacks, feelings of paranoia. All of which culminated, as you know, in the reunion, but I've already explained all that. Let me tell you what you may by now already have guessed.

This year, because Stuart wasn't there, there was no one to trip Denton up as he lunged towards Nick. Conrad and

253

I grabbed at Denton as we had always done, but our hands encountered empty air. Nick, still a bit shaky and bemused from Denton's earlier assault, only half-raised his arms in token resistance. There was a thump as Denton's hands slammed into Nick's chest, and then Nick was falling backwards, right into the path of the train.

'*Nooooo*!' I screamed, hands flying to my face. I was still screaming when the train thundered over him, still screaming when my own horror was eclipsed by the screaming of the train as the driver applied the brakes. The train didn't just run over Nick, but picked him up like a swooping predator and dragged him halfway down the track. I saw something rip away from his body, something large, probably a leg, and tumble down into the gully. Something passed over me then too, not a train but a buzzing black cloud of nausea, and I passed out. The last thing I recall was the screaming of the world spiralling away from me before everything went silent.

When I came to I was shivering, despite the blanket that had been placed over me. My head was propped on something. I realised when I opened my eyes that it was the lap of a young policewoman whose face was looming over mine.

'Back with us, are you?' she said, not unpleasantly. I was peripherally aware of lights flashing, people shouting, lots of activity.

I groaned and tried to sit up. 'Hey,' she said, 'take it easy.'

I looked around. The train was stationary on the track behind me, curious faces peering out. I felt sick. 'What happened?' I said.

'I was rather hoping you'd tell me that,' said the policewoman.

'Nick's dead, isn't he? He fell in front of the train.'

'What were you doing?'

'Nothing. Just mucking about. We're old school friends. We come back here every year. A sort of reunion.'

'Had he been drinking?'

I nodded.

'A lot?'

254

'About six or seven bottles of Beck's.'

She sighed and said, 'Can you stand? I think we ought to continue this conversation down at the station.'

My legs felt very wobbly, but with her help I got to my feet. She led me carefully down the embankment and across to where a police car was waiting. At her behest, I got into the back and she shut the door on me then got into the front passenger seat. A policeman who looked younger than me sat in the driver's seat, tapping his fingers on the steering wheel. By my side sat Conrad, motionless, staring down at his hands.

The policeman started the engine and backed slowly along the track, away from Seven Arches. Once we were on the road, and putting miles between ourselves and the viaduct, I reached out and touched Conrad's sleeve. He turned to me, his eyes red from crying. He looked ... weird, as though he'd shut himself off, as though there was a screen behind his eyes.

He took my hand and whispered, 'Nick's dead, Mark. Denton killed him.'

I saw the policewoman's eyes framed in the rear-view mirror. She was frowning. I wondered if she had heard.

'I know,' I said. 'I know.'

'So what happens now? Do we still carry on with the reunion or what?'

I looked out of the window at the uninspiring streets of Warrington. The world looked so fucking normal. I turned back to Conrad and squeezed his hand.

'Do we have a choice?' I said.